WHISPER

By Christopher Bailey
Published by Phase Publishing, LLC

Without Chance

Starjumper Legacy:

The Crystal Key
The Vanishing Sun
The Plague of Dawn

Coming Soon:

Sub-Heroes: Tales of a Fourth Grade
Superhero

and

The Never

WHISPER

by

Christopher Bailey

Phase Publishing, LLC
Seattle

Phase Publishing, LLC first paperback edition
November 2016

ISBN 978-1-943048-94-6
Library of Congress Control Number 2016954278
Cataloging-in-Publication Data on file.

Acknowledgments

For all those whose hope has been lost. You're never alone. Keep fighting.

And for my Angel, my very own light in the darkness.

Prologue
The Whisper

I don't remember the day I was born, but I remember the day I died. People talk about your life flashing before your eyes in that instant before death. I can't speak for anyone else, but in my case that was only partially true.

The events that led to my death didn't start off as much of anything. They started with the just faintest of whispers in a noisy room.

The locker room was loud, as it always was right after we'd won a game. The boys were bustling about as usual, showering, getting dressed, packing up their football gear to go home, only it was all punctuated with the excited, adrenaline-filled undercurrent of a recent victory.

The team we'd beaten wasn't our biggest rival, we didn't play them for another two weeks, but we were still early in the season and were starting off strong. Thomas clapped me on the back as I sat down on the bench to pull on my shoes.

"Awesome play, Jacks!" he said. It hadn't been a game-winning play, and we'd have won even without it, but I was pretty proud.

"Thanks, man," I said with a grin.

Thomas was the other halfback on the team, so we were two of the fastest guys in school. I was faster, but only barely, and I had to work hard to stay that way. Thomas and I had a friendly competition going, and it really helped build up each other's game.

He was also my best friend, and had been since the fourth grade when we got into a fight over a girl. I couldn't even remember her name, now. It was funny how life was like that sometimes.

"Hey, you coming by my place later?" he asked.

"Like I don't have anything better to do than sit around at your house and check out your sister," I replied.

"Dude, you've got to quit saying that," Thomas said with a shudder, "it's creepy."

"I can't help it if she's hot," I argued. This had been a running bit between the two of us for several years. I wasn't really into her, she was way too stuck-up and seemed to think that makeup should be applied with a paint brush, but she definitely had a spectacular body.

"Yeah but… she's my sister."

"You don't have to check her out, you know, speaking of creepy," I said with a look of disgust. Thomas laughed and shoved me, hard enough that I almost fell off the bench. I laughed with him.

"Okay, okay. I'll be over later," I told him.

He nodded and picked up his bag, heading for the door. I finished tying my shoes and stood, pulling on my shirt.

"Jackson!" I looked toward the door. Hayden Byers gave me a wave. "Good game, bro!"

I smiled and waved back, surprised. Hayden was our star quarterback and was top of the popularity A-list, and while I wasn't the bottom of the food chain, I was definitely B-list material. Hayden never more than nodded my way unless it was in the line of football business, even though we were on the same team.

I'd been working for nearly a year and a half to try to impress him, and maybe edge my way into his crowd. Maybe I'd finally managed it. He turned and walked out, and my casual smile split into a grin.

Two months into the school year, and it was already looking like it was going to be the best year ever.

I heard a voice behind me whisper something, but I couldn't make it out. I glanced around. There were still quite a few guys finishing up, but none were looking my way. Whatever, I thought.

Leaving the locker room, I was immediately greeted by an enthusiastic pounce.

"Jacks!" Amber shouted as she jumped up from her perch on the low concrete wall and hopped up to put her arms around me. I wrapped my one free arm around her before dropping my bag and gave her my full attention.

"Hey," I managed to get out before she kissed me. Happily, I shut up and returned the favor. It was just intense enough to leave me wanting more when she pulled away. I grinned at her. She buried her head in my shoulder and squeezed me tightly. Her chocolate brown hair was in my face, but I didn't care.

"Did you know that you look amazing on the field?" she asked, like she did after every single game. I didn't mind. In fact, I looked forward to it.

"Nah," I replied, "it's the pads. Everyone looks ripped in those pads."

"I don't know," she said, pulling back to eye my

body critically, "you look pretty good without the pads, too." I wasn't ripped, not like some guys on the team were, but I liked to think of myself as 'sleek'. It worked well for my position, anyway.

"Don't get me started," I warned her playfully, "we're in public." As if to punctuate my warning, two of my teammates came out of the lockers behind me. One whistled, and the other nudged my arm as they passed, causing Amber to blush slightly.

I laughed and moved her around to my side, leaving one arm around her and we started walking.

"Come on, Mom will give you a lift home."

"Don't take this wrong, Jacks, but I'd rather walk. If your mother gives me one more of those 'don't you dare molest my baby' looks, I might scream." I couldn't help but laugh.

"She's a bit over-protective, yeah. She really does like you. Funny that she thinks you're the one going to take advantage of me, though."

Amber looked up at me, and I leaned down with a playful growl. She giggled and shoved me back. As I took a side-step away from her, she grabbed my shirt and pulled me back over to cuddle up against my side.

"Besides," I added, "in four months I'll have my license and I can drive you anywhere you want to go."

Someone whispered behind me again, but like last time I couldn't quite make it out. I looked back over my shoulder, and an older couple passed behind us, walking to the side parking lot. Neither was speaking, or looking our way. I frowned slightly.

"What?" Amber asked, and looked back over her shoulder as well. I shook my head.

"Nothing. Hey, maybe we can get Mom to take us

by the arcade for a bit before we go home."

"Can't, I have dance," she said. "Besides, the last thing I want to do is spend the rest of my Saturday afternoon watching you get schooled at whatever that game was by a sixth grader again." I gave her a look of mock offense.

"That was one time. One time!"

"Yeah, and she was really good," Amber said with a teasing wink. Amber was right though, that little girl was an absolute shark.

"For all you know, her dad invented the game," I retorted, to try and save what was left of my pride. I wasn't too offended though, and Amber knew that or she wouldn't have been teasing me about it. She was gorgeous, but that wasn't why I loved her.

"Maybe so. Your dad clearly didn't."

"My dad couldn't invent solitaire," I said. I waved at my mom, who was waiting by our blue BMW. She waved back with a smile.

Cold… the whisper said behind me, before it became too faint to make out again.

I whipped my head around, but this time nobody was behind us. Nobody was anywhere near enough to have whispered. Amber paused and looked at me, concern in her eyes.

"Hey," she said, drawing my attention back down to her clear, blue eyes, "you okay?" I forced a smile and nodded.

"Yeah, I'm fine. I'll text you later, okay?" I told her as I leaned down to give her a quick kiss. My mother would give me a hard time about that, but she always did.

"Okay," Amber said, her focused gaze making it

clear she didn't believe I was fine at all.

I turned and jogged to the car, glancing over my shoulder again. There was nobody there.

Chapter One
No Talking in Class

"Mom!" I called out. She was upstairs, but I knew she could hear me from the kitchen. I didn't hear a response though, so I tried again, a little louder.

"Jackson!" she called back. "Don't holler at me from across the house!" I waited a moment, but she didn't continue.

"Mom!" I shouted, unable to suppress my grin.

"Jackson!" she shouted back, coming down the stairs. She gave me a stern look, but I laughed. She smiled and shook her head.

"You're incorrigible," she told me, reaching up to tousle my hair.

"Mom, stop!" I said, protecting my hair. It was blonde and a little long, with the perfect wave at the ends, if I styled it right. She shook her head.

"You spend more time on that hair every morning than I ever did when I was your age," she told me, not for the first time.

"That's because I got Dad's hair," I told her. She looked at me, love for both me and for my father in her eyes.

"Yeah, you did. I always loved his hair."

"I know, you've said that like a million times," I

told her. I didn't mind hearing it, though. I knew too many guys whose parents had split, or were still together and hated each other. My parents loved each other, and both made it pretty obvious. It could get a little nauseating at times, but I couldn't deny how much happier it made all of us.

"At least two million by now, wouldn't you say?" she said, fussing with an earring as she tried to get it properly placed. She was wearing her blue business suit, which she only wore when she was meeting with the board, so I knew today was serious.

"Here, let me help," I said, moving forward to take over the earring installation project. They were her pearls. This really was a serious one.

"Big one today, huh?" I asked. She nodded, drawing an irritated grunt from me as her ear moved away from where I was just about to put the earring.

"Sorry. Yes, the board is discussing the second quarter financials, and Mr. Edmond says he found some discrepancies. I have to go defend the entire accounting department, or someone is going to get fired. Maybe me."

"They'd never fire you," I told her as I put the back of the earring on, securing it in place. "They'd never be able to replace you, and they know it. You're too awesome." She smiled warmly at me and kissed my cheek.

"Thanks," she said, then pointed at the earring, "and thanks." I rubbed at my cheek in annoyance.

"Come on, Mom, you're going to get lipstick on my face."

"Oh, stop. Your cheek is fine," she said, but I noticed she reached up and rubbed at it anyway. "So what were you hollering at me about?" she asked.

"Oh, right," I said, getting back to the important task at hand. "Where are the bagels?"

"Can't you eat cereal like a normal kid?" she asked, moving to a cupboard.

"I hate cereal," I told her.

"I know, I know," she said as she pulled a bag of bagels from some mysterious hidden corner of the pantry. I swore I'd just looked there.

"Thanks, Mom," I said, opening the bag.

"All right, I have to go. Your father will pick you up from school today, he said he'd be finished with his project by three."

"Okay, Mom. Good luck, you'll do great!"

"Thanks, hun," she said, leaning in to kiss my cheek again.

"Mom!" I protested, and she rubbed once more at my cheek.

"Sorry," she said, but we both knew she didn't mean it.

Turning, she left the kitchen. I heard the front door open and close as I dropped the bagel into the toaster. Picking up my phone, I texted Amber.

"You up?" I texted.

"No," came the response only a moment later. I grinned.

"Biology today," I sent back.

"Duh," came her response.

Forty-two... I heard the whisper behind me.

I spun around, dropping my phone. The phone hit the ground and I heard the screen crack. I was frozen in place, my gaze whipping frantically around the kitchen. It was empty. I hadn't heard the whisper since just before coming home from the game six days ago.

"Who's there?" I shouted, trying to sound tough.

Silence was my only response. I stood still for several long seconds before turning and bending down to pick up my phone. The screen was cracked, and black. I cursed and slammed the broken phone down on the counter angrily.

Thursday… came the whisper, before becoming faint once more. I listened intently, eyes wide as I scanned the kitchen again. *…not coming today…* the whisper trailed off once more.

"Who is that!" I shouted.

I knew I was scared, but I also knew if I got angry enough I wouldn't be scared anymore. I listened for a long time.

"This isn't funny!" I yelled. Silence again. "Thomas?" I called, for a brief moment desperately hoping this was my jerk friend playing a stupid prank on me. I listened intently.

POP! The toaster popped up behind me, causing me to jump and spin around. I took a moment to try and get my heart rate back under control. I grabbed my bagel and cursed again as it burned my fingers.

I looked around the kitchen again, but as usual, nobody was there. The house was empty. It felt empty too, but I also didn't feel entirely alone. It was weird, and very creepy.

I ate my breakfast quietly, listening closely for the sounds of anyone moving around, or the sounds of some electronic device or speaker that might be transmitting the whispers.

I heard the front door open. Nobody should be here, I thought as I stood, clenching my fists and ready to defend myself. Thomas came around the corner. He paused as he saw me, looking puzzled.

"Jacks, I've been texting you for like ten minutes. You good?" he said. He glanced down at my clenched fists, but didn't react beyond a slight lowering of his brows. I then remembered he was giving me a lift to school today. I pointed at the broken phone on the counter.

"Aw man, that sucks," he said. "What are you going to do without your phone?"

"I don't know. Amber probably thinks I'm mad at her or something. Or she's mad at me for not answering her. I started texting her this morning and dropped my phone."

"I hope you can get it replaced today. No phone, I mean that's like… caveman time."

"Can we just go?"

"Sure, whatever you say, caveman."

"Knock it off," I told him.

"What's up with you today, man?" he asked. I shook my head.

"I just don't feel so hot this morning, sorry."

"It's cool," he replied with a dismissive shrug. He didn't stop looking at me with concern evident in his eyes, though. "You going to stay home sick?"

"No, I need to get out of here," I told him. He nodded.

I grabbed my backpack and my broken phone, and followed him out the door.

As I locked the door, the whisper came again, though I couldn't make any of it out.

"Shut up," I muttered under my breath.

"What?" Thomas asked.

"Nothing, never mind," I said.

"Dude, you okay? You sure you don't want to stay home?" Thomas asked.

"I'm fine, really. Let's go."

"Okay, if you say so," Thomas replied.

I finished locking the door and we climbed into his dad's truck.

"Hi, Jackson," Mr. Everett said.

"Hey," I replied as I buckled my seatbelt.

The drive to school was quiet. Oddly, I found that both relieving, and a little scary. I knew whatever was causing that whisper wasn't gone. I could almost feel it around me, though I didn't know what it was.

It wasn't until second period that the whisper spoke again. As if listening to my math teacher droning on wasn't hard enough.

"Now, using the interior alternate angles…" Mr. Solomon was saying.

No rain… the whisper said.

I looked around as carefully as I could. Everyone looked just as zoned out as I was a minute before. I focused hard on the whisper.

…the water running in. Not as… the whisper faded out again.

"Mr. Holt?" Mr. Solomon asked me. I spun back forward.

"Sorry, sir." I replied. He nodded, and turned back to the whiteboard.

"Now, if you multiply the two ratios by…" he continued.

…hear the river… the whisper said. I put my hands up and covered my ears.

…forty-four seconds this time… I heard, despite my ears

having been covered. It didn't even sound muffled, just distant and faint, like always.

"No," I whispered myself. The voice was in my head. It couldn't be in my head. No, please don't let me be crazy.

...if he'll replace...

"Stop," I said, a little louder.

I pulled my hands away from my ears and glanced around as I realized I'd just spoken aloud. Some of the kids closest to me were watching me. One or two looked concerned, but true to style, most looked like they were about to laugh. I looked back up at Mr. Solomon. He was still talking and facing the board. A faint crunching sound reached my ears, or maybe my head, like boots on gravel.

...not supposed to be here! It's Thursday! The whisper came, much louder, and sounding frantic. The edges of my vision dimmed slightly this time.

"No!" I exclaimed, much louder than intended. Several kids snickered around me.

"Is there a problem, Mr. Holt?" the teacher asked, turning around with an angry expression.

"No, sir. Well, yes, sir. I have a really bad headache. May I go to the nurse's office?"

Mr. Solomon looked at me hard. He must have seen the distress in my face, because he finally nodded and sighed.

"Grab the hall pass on your way out," he said. I nodded and stood, heading for the door.

"Jackson," came a voice. I fiercely ignored it for a full two seconds before I realized this voice was real. Jon, the kid who sat beside me, was holding up my backpack. I stepped forward and took it.

"Thanks," I said quietly. The whole class was watching me. I hated that. Turning, I quickly left the room.

Once in the hallway, I slowed down. I couldn't go to the nurse with this. I wandered aimlessly, holding the hall pass, which was just a wooden ruler with "Hall Pass 12C" written in black marker along the back.

I hadn't realized I'd been wandering so long until the bell rang and kids started pouring out of the doors on either side of the hallway. I ignored them, and kept walking. The whispers were blessedly silent.

"Hey, Jacks!" I heard Amber call behind me. I stopped and waited for her to catch up. "What's the deal?" she asked. She definitely sounded annoyed. I started walking again and she fell into step beside me.

"Sorry, Amber. I dropped my phone this morning, broke the stupid thing."

"Oh," she replied, considering this. "All right, no big deal. We have bio next. Walk with me?" she asked. I nodded.

"Of course," I said, trying to smile at her.

"Jacks, you look pale. You okay?"

"Yeah, I'm…"

"Don't lie to me. I hate that."

"I'm sorry. I really don't feel great." I told her honestly. I decided it wouldn't be a great idea to tell her I was nauseated because the voice in my head was freaking me out.

"Okay, that's fine. Sucks, but thanks for not giving me that 'I'm fine' tough guy crap again."

…over soon. It'll be over soon. Over soon. Over soon…

I hadn't realized I'd stopped walking until Amber spoke again.

"Jacks. Jackson!" I looked at her.

"What?"

"What the hell is going on with you?" she asked.

"Do you hear that?" I asked, unable to stop myself. I had to know. I already knew, but I needed to hear her say it.

"Hear what?" she asked. "I don't hear anything." Her expression was an odd blend of concern, irritation, and confusion.

...over soon. Over soon. Over soon... The mantra sounded desperate, and the voice was clearly in pain.

I looked around. The halls were thinning, as kids went into the rooms around us. She looked around too, then back at me.

"Jackson, you're scaring me," she told me softly.

"Me too," I whispered. "Listen," I said, more loudly this time, "I'm going to see the nurse. Go ahead to biology, okay? Tell Miss Colby where I am, please."

Amber watched me for several seconds, considering, then nodded and leaned up for a quick kiss. I kissed her briefly, but neither my mind nor my heart was in it. She noticed, of course. Her expression didn't change. Turning, she walked off down the hall.

The whispering voice was still.

<h1>Chapter Two</h1>

Concern

"No Dad, I'm fine!" I insisted.

"Then why did you call me to come get you early? I left my project almost finished to come pick you up, you know." He had a point, but he was taking this too far.

"Dad, I don't need to see a doctor. Do I look sick to you?" he glanced at me for a moment, then back to the road as he drove toward the hospital. My father was the king of over-reactions. I never should have called him. I knew better than that.

"I think if it's serious enough for you to leave in the middle of a school day, it's serious enough to get checked out. What are your symptoms?"

"Come on, Dad. It's just a headache, I'm fine." I'd discovered that the harder I listened to the whisper, the more my head really did start to hurt. The whisper had been completely silent for almost two hours. I'd tried to muscle my way through history class, but even though the voice had gone still, I couldn't focus.

"Headaches can be a symptom for all sorts of terrible things," he said.

"I know, Dad, but they can also be a symptom of just a good old-fashioned headache. People get them all the time, you know."

"You don't," he replied.

Another good point. I couldn't recall the last time I'd had a headache. Well, that wasn't true, I had to admit to myself. My head had hurt for a while after I'd been tackled while in mid-air going for the ball at a game last year. The doctor, which of course my father had brought me to, said I didn't have a concussion, but my father had watched me like a hawk for three days.

"Yeah, well, I have one now, and it's just a headache. I just want to go home and lie down."

"You can lie down at the doctor's office."

"How is that restful?" I asked in irritation.

"It's not meant to be restful, it's meant to be helpful."

"Making a sentence symmetrical doesn't make it words of wisdom or anything, Dad."

"What does that mean?"

"Something my English teacher said. She was going off about memes or something."

"Using a saying you don't understand the meaning of doesn't make you smart, Jackson."

"Touché," I replied with a smile. He glanced at me again, and smiled a little himself.

"So we pass on the doctor. What then? What if it doesn't go away?"

"Dad, I'll take some aspirin. If it doesn't go away by tomorrow, then I'll go willingly to the doctor. Okay?"

"Tonight."

"What?"

"It has to be gone by the time we finish dinner, or we're going to the doctor," my dad said. I sighed. That was the best I was going to get. I could hear it in his tone.

"Deal."

He turned left instead of right, and I knew he was heading back home.

"I'm sorry I pulled you away from your project," I told him.

"That's okay. I'll have to go back after I drop you off, though. It's important that we finish these schematics as soon as possible, we're already behind deadline."

"I understand. I'm just going to go lie down, I don't need you to stick around or anything. Hey, my phone broke this morning. Can you maybe stop and see if you can replace it on the way home?" I pulled out my phone and held it up. He glanced at it and frowned.

"Jackson, we've told you to be careful with that thing. Those aren't cheap."

"I know, Dad. I'm sorry."

"All right, just leave it in the console there."

"Thanks."

We pulled into the driveway and I got out, dragging my backpack out of the back seat as I went. My dad started to get out, but I stopped him.

"I got it, thanks Dad." He nodded and closed his door. He waited until I was inside before he pulled away though.

I reached for my phone by habit, then sighed when I remembered I'd broken it and didn't have a new one.

"Great," I muttered, as I turned my key in the lock.

It was only early afternoon, but I was already tired. Maybe I really would go lie down. I'd planned to eat some lunch and get some video game time in, but right now sleep actually sounded better.

I had barely touched the pillow on my bed when sleep overtook me.

It was dark. Cold, dark, and wet. It took a long time for my eyes to focus on anything, like they were slowly adjusting. There was a little bit of light off in the distance at what looked like the end of a curving tunnel.

The tunnel was damp, and I could hear water dripping in the distance, and a gentle trickling not far from my head. The walls of the tunnel were rough, rocky and jagged. I was sitting on a patch of floor that was surprisingly smooth. I tried to look down, but realized I couldn't move at all.

In a panic, I tried to move my hands, but they didn't respond either. A scream hung in my mind, but never made it to my lips. I had no control over my body.

Suddenly, my body shifted without my command. It was a simple movement, meant only to adjust position slightly. My gaze moved down, again all by itself, and I saw my hands. They were covered in dirt and grime, and were… they were not my hands.

Cast iron bands were around both of my… of these wrists. It took a moment for me to realize they were shackles. A heavy chain ran from each wrist back behind my line of sight. I tried instinctively to follow the chains, but I couldn't make this body respond.

The sound of an engine firing up and car tires moving on gravel echoed down the hallway, and my gaze unwillingly moved up to look down the hallway. A single, relieved thought came from inside my mind, but it was not mine.

He's gone…

I woke up with a violent start, and promptly threw up all over my bed. My head was filled with a foggy haze, and I was having trouble getting my eyes to focus. I sat up, and immediately wished I hadn't. My head swam, and colors flashed across my vision.

Groaning, I steadied myself and eased myself to a sitting position at the side of the bed, planting my feet on solid ground. The stability of the position helped, and with long, slow breaths I was able to calm both my swirling mind and my churning stomach.

The stink of my own vomit hit me and I gagged. Immediately, I knew with every fiber of my being that I'd never be able to eat sloppy joes again. I grabbed a corner of my blanket and wiped my mouth before pulling all the blankets, sheets, and pillows into a big pile, which I carried to the laundry room.

It only took a few steps before my equilibrium came back and I felt steady again. Dumping the soiled linens in the washing machine, I poured in some soap and turned it on.

Moving into the bathroom next, I washed out my mouth, brushed my teeth, and washed out my mouth again. I didn't hear my parents around, so it was probably still pretty early.

Putting new sheets and blankets on my bed felt like a lot more work than usual, but I pushed through and promptly lay back down on top of the blankets. My body ached in strange places, from my wrists to my groin, and I couldn't figure out why. Taking a deep breath, I tried to steady my nerves. It took only moments and I was asleep again. This time, the sleep was thankfully empty of dreams and whispers.

When I awoke the second time, it was a much more

comfortable experience. I felt better, the nausea was gone, as was the achiness. Even my headache had disappeared. I took a deep breath and sat up. No dizziness or swirl of colors. That was good, I told myself.

I could hear my parents talking downstairs. I got up, and moved to the railing. I was about to call out when I realized they were talking about me.

"His math teacher said he was acting strangely. I called Thomas's parents as well, and they said he was fine, but he'd told them that Jackson seemed sick this morning," my father said.

"I'm sure he's fine, he's a teenage boy. Maybe it's a growing phase," Mom replied.

"I don't remember a phase like that. Did you notice he washed his sheets? I thought he might have wet them, but when I stepped into his room to ask, he was sleeping and the room smelled of vomit."

"Honey, I'm sure he's fine. I'll give him some medicine when he wakes up. If he's still sick tomorrow, we can take him to the doctor."

"I told him I'd take him tonight if he didn't feel better," he said.

Great, I thought. Dad's still trying to push his doctor agenda. Time to make an appearance. I walked down the stairs with as much pep as I could muster.

"Hi, Mom. Hi, Dad. What's for dinner?" I actually didn't know what time it was, and wasn't particularly hungry, though the idea of food surprisingly wasn't bad.

"Hi, hun. How are you feeling?" Mom asked.

"Much better, thanks," I replied with a smile. Mom turned and threw Dad an 'I told you so' look. He shrugged, but eyed me suspiciously.

"Sometimes a little stomach bug can be like that. Hits you hard and fast, but once you throw up you feel better," Mom told me. I nodded my agreement.

"Seems that way," I said. I noticed nothing had been cooked and wondered what time it was.

"It's a bit late for dinner," Dad told me. I leaned forward so I could see the clock on the oven timer. It read just past seven.

"Sorry," I said. "I must have slept right through. You guys ate though, right? I'll just grab a snack or something then."

"No, let me make you something," Mom said.

"It's cool, we've got plenty in the fridge I could just microwave up."

"Okay, if you're sure…" she said, reluctantly.

"It's cool, Mom. I've got it."

My parents went and sat down at the table, obviously planning to sit with me while I ate. *It just keeps getting better,* I thought.

It's not that I didn't like my parents. I loved them and they were both pretty cool, except for my dad's medical paranoia. I must have been to the doctor more times in my first five years of life than most people go their whole lives. Every bump, every scrape, every cough or runny nose was enough to warrant a doctor visit. My medical bills must have been astronomical, though I'd actually never been seriously ill or injured.

"Maybe you should stay home from school tomorrow, just in case," Mom said.

"I'll take you to the doctor in the morning," my Dad said. I tossed a pizza pocket in the microwave and turned it on.

"Come on, Dad. I told you I feel better. Can we hold off on the emergency room visits at least until I'm sick for longer than a few hours? You know, most people don't actually go to the doctor for colds and flus at all, and almost never for headaches. And they don't die! Amazing, right?"

"Watch your tone," my father said.

"Sorry," I muttered, turning back to the microwave.

"All right, we'll hold off on the doctor," my mom said, giving my dad a pointed look, "but you tell us if you start feeling sick again."

"I promise," I told her with a grateful smile. My dad didn't look happy about that, but he didn't say anything.

As I pulled the pizza pocket out of the microwave and sat down, I promised myself I would completely ignore the whisper if it came again. Taking a bite of the pizza pocket, I yelped at the scalding hot filling.

"Geez, these things are like lava!" I protested.

"Careful, hun," my mom said, a little late.

Sunset… came the whisper.

I almost choked on my second, much more cautious, bite. Glancing at the window, it looked like there was still a bit of time until sunset. I frowned.

"What?" my father asked, leaning forward intently. The man was practically begging for me to give him an excuse to take me to the doctor. I rolled my eyes.

"Nothing, Dad. Just thought I heard something."

Chapter Three
Seizures

I loved that moment, when I was running across the field. It didn't matter if I was chasing a ball, prepping for a catch, or running the field, I just loved the way my body felt when it was moving like that. It was freedom. Freedom in every way, for me at least.

It had been four days since I'd last heard the voice, and I was happily running down the field. Practice was nearly over, and we'd been working hard. Thomas was running beside me as we did a few laps, his own speed urging me to push just that much harder. He glanced at me and grinned.

I leaned a little harder into the run and laughed. I could see Amber sitting in the bleachers to the side. She smiled and waved when she saw me glance her way. Too busy running, I didn't wave back, but she saw my grin. That was enough. The coach's whistle blew.

Thomas and I both slowed and turned, working on a light cooldown jog on the way back as the players all headed back in.

Thomas glanced at me, and frowned. I don't know what he saw in my face in that moment, but it obviously worried him.

The voice hit me then. It wasn't a whisper this time, it was a scream. No words, no meaning, just a raw expression of pain. It slammed into the back of my mind like a hammer. I stumbled, and Thomas reached out to stabilize me.

"Woah, okay. Sit down, bro," Thomas told me. "Coach!" he yelled back over his shoulder. He eased me down to the grass. I barely noticed.

Darkness swam in from the edges of my vision, and suddenly I wasn't in the grass anymore. For a moment all I could hear was the scream.

Then I heard a grunt of effort and pain exploded across my leg. It took a moment to realize the scream was coming from me. Another grunting sound and the pain erupted on my side, just below the ribs.

My vision was totally black, but with the odd swirling colors that you see when you squeeze your eyes tightly shut. I tried to open them, but they wouldn't move. Another grunt and another burning pain tore across my leg.

Light blinded me, and the pain vanished. I opened my eyes, and had just enough time to focus on the coach's face leaning over me looking frightened, before my vision blacked again. Another grunt, another explosion of pain, this time in my arm. The arm I still couldn't move. I felt something break and the screaming renewed in full. Then a blow struck my head and everything went still and quiet.

———

When I opened my eyes what felt an eternity later, I was almost blinded by the light. It was a cold, sterile light, not the warm sunlight I'd seen before when I'd tried to open my eyes.

"He's awake," I heard my mother say with a sob.

Next thing I knew, her face appeared in my vision. Perspective threw me off for a moment, until I realized I was lying flat on my back and she was leaning over me, like Coach had been.

With that realization, everything sort of clicked into place and I realized the cold white light was coming from the fluorescent lights in the white ceiling. I shifted my gaze around and realized I was lying in a bed, attached to a couple of tubes, and alone in the room with my mother and father.

"Mom?" I asked, confused. She choked back another sob.

"My baby," she said, arms around me and head plunging down to bury in the pillow beside mine.

Her sobs were intense, and the relief in them was evident. My father stood still on the other side of the bed, but I could see the intensity of his own worry. His expression wasn't tinged with relief like my mother's voice was, though.

"Dad?" I asked. "What happened?"

"You had a seizure, Jackson," he replied, tone carefully controlled.

"A what?"

"A seizure. You've been unconscious for several hours. The doctors have run a number of tests, and we're waiting for results."

"Mom, you're kind of choking me," I told her, as her grip tightened.

She let go and stood up, reluctantly. Her hand still gripped mine tightly, though. I was glad she wasn't holding the one with the IV in it.

"Sorry, honey," she said, wiping at the tears in her eyes with her other hand.

"I knew we should have taken you in when you first had that headache," Dad said.

"Stop," she said sternly to him, "now is not the time, and you know it." He clenched his jaw, but kept his mouth shut.

The doctor came in at that moment, which was good because my father had that look in his eyes that told me he was considering whether he should say something anyway.

"Mr. and Mrs. Holt? Oh hello, Jackson. Glad to see you awake and alert."

The doctor smiled, but something about the way he said that last part made me wonder if they didn't expect me to wake up at all, let alone in full control of my faculties. I didn't respond to him, so he turned to my parents.

"Mr. and Mrs. Holt, the MRI came back clear. The good news is that means he doesn't have a tumor."

My heart leapt into my chest. That hadn't even occurred to me. The doctor continued on calmly, however.

"The bad news is that means we don't yet know what is causing the headaches and seizures. Epilepsy is still a possibility, though we'll have to run a few more tests to determine if that's the case. Or," he paused and looked at me, though he spoke to my parents, "actually can I speak to you outside?"

"What is it?" I asked. I didn't like the idea at all that the doctor wanted to talk to my parents without me hearing. He was okay with me hearing 'tumor' and 'epilepsy', what would he be afraid to say with me present?

"We'll be just a moment, hun," Mom said, and she and Dad stepped out into the hallway and closed the door. I lay there still and quiet for a moment, trying to hear, until I heard my father suddenly shout.

"Absolutely not! My son is not a drug addict!"

I suddenly understood why the doctor didn't want to bring that up in front of me. He was out there busily accusing me of being chronic. He probably thought I had gotten tuned up on some drug and had a bad reaction to it. I suddenly felt very proud that my father immediately rejected that as a possibility. It said a lot for his faith in me that he would instantly come to my defense like that.

They chattered for a while, but I couldn't make out anything else. After a few minutes, they came back in, without the doctor.

"All right, honey. They're going to keep you here overnight while they wait for all the test results to come back in. Don't worry though, I'm going to stay right here with you. I've already called the office."

"Mom, I don't need to stay here. I don't want to stay here, I feel fine!" I said, but honestly I knew I wasn't fine. I felt okay at the moment, but whatever had happened on the field was definitely not fine.

"It's all right, champ," Dad said. He hadn't called me that since I was five. I knew he was scared, too. "The doctors will figure it out and we'll get you back up and running in no time."

"And if they don't?" I asked, quietly.

"Of course they will," my dad replied. "We have the best medical staff in the state in this hospital. As soon as they get the rest of those test results back, they'll know what's wrong and can get you fixed right up."

It was odd having my father being the one to reassure me when it came to a potential health concern. He was always the one in his oddly calm panic, rushing about efficiently to get me to the doctor the moment I had the slightest symptom. He had even taken me to the emergency room once for a splinter when I was a kid. He'd thought it might have been infected.

I relaxed back against the pillow and took a deep breath.

"Okay, Dad. I'll stay."

"Good boy," he said. I resisted the urge to bark at him. Barely.

He bustled about making a list of things he needed to go pick up at home to bring back for Mom and me, while Mom rambled on about how much fun it was going to be, and how it'd be just like a sleepover. I didn't mention that I wasn't nine years old anymore, and a hospital hardly resembled a friend's house. She needed the reassurance even more than I did, at that point, so I let her go on.

"Can I have my phone?" I asked. Mom paused and looked at me. "I need to text Thomas and Amber. I need to tell them I'm okay."

She looked at my dad, who nodded. She dug into her purse and pulled out my phone. I took it and immediately started typing, recognizing only a few seconds later that the phone was new. My dad hadn't wasted any time getting it replaced.

"In the hospital. Won't be at school tomorrow," I texted to Thomas. I was halfway through writing a message to my girlfriend when Thomas replied.

"You're not dead!" I shook my head with a smile and started typing again.

"Not yet, dude. Hospital food might kill me, though." I hadn't eaten anything yet, but hospital food was supposed to suck, and Thomas would appreciate the joke.

"What's wrong?" he replied almost immediately.

"Don't know yet. Need more tests. Not a tumor, though," I sent back.

"No lovin' from Amber for you tonight, then," he sent.

"No lovin' from anyone for you tonight. Or tomorrow night, or... At least I might get a sponge bath from a hot nurse." I sent back to him.

"Lol. Shut up," came his response. I turned back to my message to Amber.

"Stuck at the hospital tonight. I'm okay, but they want to do more tests. You okay?" I sent. And then waited for a long time without a reply.

Mom had finished bustling about and had pulled a deck of cards out of her purse. I swear that bag was like Mary frickin' Poppins' bag. It was incredible what my mother could randomly pull out of that thing. It had to break at least two laws of physics. She was dealing out a hand of rummy when Amber messaged back.

"OMG, Jacks! I'm freaking out here! What's wrong?"

"Don't know yet. Need more tests," I repeated.

"Can I come see you?" she sent.

"Not until tomorrow," I typed back. I wasn't actually sure, but Mom was so high-strung right then that I didn't want to add Amber, who also seemed pretty high-strung, to the mix. I was tired and didn't think I could handle that much freaking out.

"Can I come tomorrow, then?"

"I hope you do," I sent. I wasn't certain that I did, though. I was always her tough guy. Her big, strong football player boyfriend. Her seeing me lying in a hospital bed tied to an IV because I'd fainted on the football field? That wouldn't do great things for her image of me.

I did want to see her, though. She might actually be able to calm down the anxiety I was trying to keep hidden myself. I played a few hands of rummy with my mom before she replied back again.

"See you after school tomorrow then. Text me in the morning, and all day so I know you're still okay," was her message. I sighed. A bit over the top, but it was sweet that she cared that much.

"K," I sent back.

I turned back to the game with my mom. She was chattering on about something, but I was only half-able to pay any real attention. She beat me nine games out of ten. We played cards for hours until I couldn't stay awake anymore. Thankfully, there were no dreams.

Chapter Four
Home Again

Help… the whisper called. Over and over, and without much enthusiasm, but with a steady, persistent rhythm.

It was so faint I could barely hear it, but it was there. I had been lying awake for hours, unable to sleep. It was late morning anyway, but that didn't seem to matter. I'd been awake since long before the sun had come up.

Mom had gone down to the cafeteria to get herself some breakfast I'd picked at mine, the food they'd delivered me having looked about as appetizing as week old fish. She'd just woken up, having been up late worrying about me. I felt bad about it, and told her to stop worrying, but moms are like that. The doctor came in.

"Oh, hello, Jackson. Where are your parents?"

"Mom's getting food from the cafeteria. Dad's at work."

"I was hoping I'd find them both here, but that's all right. I can speak with your mother when she returns. Until then, would you mind doing a quick experiment with me?"

"As long as you're not going to stab me with

another needle, sure," I replied. He smiled, though he obviously didn't think it was funny.

"I would just like to do a quick neurological test. It's nothing invasive, I'll just ask you to do a few things, and we will just see if you can do them. All right?"

"I don't know ballet," I replied. Again the un-funny smile. I had to admit it wasn't as funny as it sounded in my head. Exhaustion and worry were killing my edge.

"Nothing that complex, Jackson. Can I ask a few questions first?" He pulled over a chair and sat.

"Shoot."

"What's my name?"

"Dr. Rasmussen. It's on your ID badge." He at least had the decency to look embarrassed about that one. He moved on.

"How about the name of the elementary school you went to?"

"Carter Primary," I replied. He was taking notes. For some reason, that irritated me.

"What was the name of your kindergarten teacher?"

"Lee."

"And your best friend in fourth grade?"

"Thomas. We're still best friends," I answered.

"That's good," he said, but moved right along.

"Can you look at the clock on the wall and tell me what time it says?" he asked. I glanced up.

"Ten twenty-four," I answered.

"Good, good. Can you stand up for me?"

I shifted over to swing my legs over the side of the bed. Planting my feet on the cold laminate floor, I got sudden goosebumps. Standing, I was mostly steady. After a second or two I felt more stable.

"Can you balance on one foot?" he asked. I leaned onto my left foot and raised my right slightly off the floor.

"And the other?" I did so. "How about holding both arms straight out to either side, like this?" He demonstrated. I imitated him, and held my arms out.

"Now what?" I asked, when he didn't say anything a moment.

"Just keep holding them," he replied. He was watching my arms, his glance switching from one to the other. "They getting tired yet?"

"You kidding?" I asked. "I could do this all day."

"That won't be necessary," he replied. It's official, I thought to myself, my sense of humor was not the problem. Dr. Rasmussen's sense of humor was DOA. This guy was about as dry as they came. My mother walked in then.

"Hello, doctor." She paused and took in the situation. "What exactly is going on?" she asked. Dr. Rasmussen stood.

"Just conducting a quick neurological check. Just one more thing on my checklist."

"And?" I asked, arms still outstretched.

"Oh, you can put your arms down," the doctor said. I lowered my arms. "Mrs. Holt, we've gotten back the results from the blood panel, and everything came back normal. No trace of unusual substances," I knew he meant drugs, "all his counts are good, no anomalies. By all reports, your son is perfectly healthy."

"Well that's good, right?" my mom asked him. He nodded.

"Oh, certainly, but it means we still don't know why he had his seizure. Epilepsy is still our number one theory, but I'd like you to take him to a specialist I'll recommend. You're free to take him home, but I strongly urge that he not participate in any strenuous or dangerous activities, and that you keep a close eye on him for a while."

"I have football," I replied.

"Absolutely no football," the doctor replied firmly. I looked at my mom in shock, but she just nodded. I could see her regret, but it was clear that she wasn't going to back me on this one.

"But Mom!" I protested. She shook her head.

"Not until we can find out what's wrong."

"We play the Vikings next weekend!" I argued. She shook her head. I couldn't believe this. They were going to take away the one thing I really loved.

"Take him to see Dr. Garner at this address," the doctor said, handing Mom a card. "It may take a week or two to get an appointment, but I urge you to call right away. The nurse will be in momentarily, and once she's finished you can check out."

"I understand. Thank you, doctor," Mom said.

"Thanks for nothing," I said sullenly.

"Jackson!" Mom snapped.

I looked away from them both and stared out the window. It was gloomy and overcast. Like my future, I thought bitterly. This specialist better work absolute magic, or my career in football was done. The thought made me sick to my stomach. Football was everything.

My friends were there, my girlfriend loved me for it, and more than anything else when I was playing I felt free, alive. My entire future, from high school to my college scholarships all hinged on football. Take that away and what did I have? Not much, that was for sure. I was an okay student, but not great. I had no real talent anywhere else.

I wouldn't lose Thomas; I was sure of that. I wasn't as sure about Amber. If they diagnosed me with something that kept me from doing anything athletic, I wasn't certain she'd still be into me. She absolutely loved that I played.

The nurse came in and started fussing with my IV. It hurt, but I pointedly ignored her, and my mother who kept trying to talk to me. I flinched when the IV came out, though.

I tried to keep hoping that the specialist could give me an easy fix for the problem, but I knew something nobody else, not even the doctors, knew. I hadn't just passed out, I'd hallucinated. I didn't know what that meant, but was pretty sure it meant I was crazy. And to hallucinate something like that? Something that messed up? Definitely something wrong in my brain.

I'd probably have to tell the specialist, so they could figure out what was going on. Keeping symptoms from the doctor didn't help anyone, I was sure, but I couldn't even imagine what they, or my parents, might say when I announced I was hearing voices and hallucinating about being beaten so badly it broke bones…

We drove home, Mom chattering away and clearly trying to distract me from my problem, but I just stared out the window, unable to keep my mind from racing. My parents weren't the only ones I couldn't tell about hearing voices. My rep at school would be ruined. Amber would leave me over that for sure, even if she stuck around after learning I was basically crippled and couldn't play football.

I went straight up to my room when we got home, and lay down on my bed. I heard Mom start talking to someone on her phone. Probably the specialist's office. Come to think of it, Dr. Rasmussen hadn't mentioned what kind of specialist it was. Probably a neurologist or something, somebody to study my brain. It was probably exactly what I needed, since I'd clearly cracked. My phone buzzed. I glanced down. It was a message from Amber.

"Why haven't you messaged me?" it read. Great, I thought. I'd been worrying about her and Thomas and how they'd react to all of this all morning, and had forgotten to text her. I began typing.

"Sorry, doctor came early. Just got home."

"Can I come see you?" she replied.

"Later," I answered. "Tired."

"K, tonight?" she asked.

"Sure."

I sent a quick message to Thomas as well, letting him know I was home and that I'd see him in the morning at school. I didn't know if my mom would let me go to school, but I was going to fight for it.

…the birds today… came the whisper.

I didn't even look around this time. I shut my eyes tightly and covered my ears. It didn't help.

…hear them in the…

The whisper kept fading in and out, like someone was playing with a radio, and was just on the edge of a clear channel. But it was all clearer than it had been the day before.

"No," I muttered to the voice, willing it to be silent. "Shut up, shut up."

…inside someday. I'd like…

It was odd. The more I heard, the more I realized the voice wasn't actually speaking to me, or even about me. The whisper seemed like someone absently rambling to themselves. Even better, I thought wryly, I'm a crazy person who hears the voice of a crazy person.

"Just stop," I mumbled, hands still over my ears. I'm not sure why I kept covering them, since it didn't help, but it made me feel a little better. "No more, just stop." The voice went quiet.

Something in my room had changed. I uncovered my ears and opened my eyes, to see my mother standing in my doorway, looking extremely uncomfortable and concerned. I realized she had been standing there watching me hold my head and mutter to myself for something to stop, like I was talking to someone. Awesome, I thought with a sigh.

"Don't you knock anymore?" I asked, masking my embarrassment with anger. Her expression didn't change.

"I did," she said simply. I hadn't heard it at all, though that didn't account for much these days.

"Oh," I replied lamely. "What's up?"

"I just wanted to ask you if you wanted anything, I was going to make myself a snack." Her voice was perky and casual, but her eyes still looked worried. I bit back the guilt and shook my head.

"No, thanks. I'm not really hungry."

"Okay, hun. Let me know if you change your mind, I'll make you something."

"Thanks, Mom." She turned to go. "Mom?" She stopped and turned back around.

"Yes?"

"I want to go to school tomorrow." She considered me for a long moment before answering.

"You don't have to."

"I know."

"No football, even practice. I'm calling your school."

"I know," I replied, trying not to sound too upset. I must have succeeded, because she looked at me for another moment, then nodded.

"All right. I'll drive you." I nodded and turned away. I heard the door close behind her as she left.

...forty-one again...

"Shut up!"

Chapter Five
A New Whisper

Amber hadn't come over the night before. She'd texted and said her parents had told her she couldn't come. They thought whatever I had might be contagious.

I might be, for all I knew. It could be like, mad cow disease or something. Although I thought that might only be transmitted by eating something tainted, and I was pretty sure she wasn't a cannibal. I almost smiled at that. Almost.

I found myself wondering as I got out of the car and waved goodbye to my mom if Amber would even be at school today. I hadn't made it far before I found out.

"Jackson!" she shouted as she ran down the front steps toward me.

She didn't hesitate as she jumped up into my arms. I couldn't at that moment, or any moment after that, have described how relieved I felt. She didn't see me any differently. For now, at least. I prayed she never found out about the whisper. I held her tightly for a long minute before she let go enough to pull back and look me over.

"Jackson, are you okay?" she asked. Kind of a silly

question, I thought, since I was standing right there at school with her.

"Yeah, I'm good. I feel good," I told her, honestly. Physically, anyway. No headache or dizziness, just the pit in my stomach caused by my anxiety about it all.

"I was so scared when they put you in that ambulance."

"I was brought to the hospital in an ambulance?" I asked.

As soon as I said it, I realized that sounded stupid, but I had no idea. It made sense, of course they'd have called for an ambulance. I wished I remembered the experience, though. My first ambulance ride, and I missed it. Hopefully it was my only ambulance ride though, now that I thought about it. Some adventures just weren't worth the pain.

"Yeah," she answered simply. "They wouldn't let me close when you fell. You fell so fast, like someone flipped a switch and turned you off."

"That sounds scary. I don't remember it, though. It kind of was like someone flipped a switch."

"Don't do that again, okay?" she said, taking my hand and leading me toward the school. I couldn't help but smile. Not that I had any control over it, I thought.

"Have you seen Thomas?" I asked.

"He's by the side entrance. We weren't sure which one you'd be dropped off at, so we each watched one door."

"Cool. Let's go, I want to see him."

"You should thank him, too," she told me.

"Why?" I asked.

"He caught you when you fell, so you didn't get hurt. And he's the one who called 9-1-1 for you."

I smiled at that. Good ol' Thomas. Always there when I needed him.

"Thanks, I didn't know that."

"I have to get to first hour. Will I see you at football practice?" she asked. My heart sank.

"No," I said. I hesitated before explaining, and she paused to look at me in surprise. "The doctor says until they figure out what caused it, they want to keep me away from anything strenuous."

"What would happen if you went anyway?" she asked. I didn't like the hesitance in her gaze. She'd let go of my hand, too.

"I can't, my mom called the coach already and told him I wasn't allowed to even practice."

"I'm sorry. That really sucks," she said.

"Yeah," I replied. She looked back over her shoulder.

"I've got to go. Text me, okay?" she said. I nodded and she disappeared into the crowd.

For a moment, I just stood there. I felt completely alone in a crowd of people. I definitely didn't like how that went down. She'd been awfully quick to leave. She said she had first period, and I knew I needed to hurry too, but this felt different. Maybe it was just me.

A whisper came behind me. I didn't even look around until another whisper joined it. I glanced around curiously and saw a group of kids over by the drinking fountain whispering and pointing my way. They immediately tried to act casual when I looked around, but I knew they'd been talking about me.

Just what I needed, I thought in annoyance. What I really needed was to go see Thomas. I turned away and walked quickly down the halls.

Nobody waved. Usually a couple of kids at least said hi as I went to class in the morning. Not this time. Everyone was either whispering and looking my way, or were pointedly pretending I didn't exist. Nobody even knew I was crazy, and they were already talking about me behind my back. Guy can't even get sick at this stupid school, I thought angrily. I saw Thomas by the side entrance doors.

"Thomas!" I called. He turned around and trotted over.

"Hey man, good to see you," he said.

"Good to be seen," I answered. "Did your sister miss me?" Thomas's slightly concerned expression turned into the grin I was much more accustomed to.

"Are you kidding? She sat up all night crying for you." I laughed.

"Liar," I replied.

He started walking and I fell into step beside him. Our first period classes were next to each other, so we usually walked to class together.

"So what's the verdict, man? You going to die?" he asked casually. Only Thomas, I thought, could ask a question like that and be totally cool about it.

"No," I answered. "Doctor wouldn't have let me out if I was dying. No answers, though. They don't know what caused it."

"So you might be dying, then," he said.

I shoved him lightly. He almost knocked another kid over as he stumbled sideways. He had a point though. I hadn't thought about that. The doctors didn't actually know what the cause was, so I actually might be dying. They said it wasn't a tumor or anything like that, but did they really know? How accurate were those tests?

"Just sayin'," he said with a grin.

"I'm not dying," I replied firmly.

"That's cool. So will it happen again?"

"They don't know."

"What do they know?" he asked.

"It's not a tumor," I replied.

"Are you sure? It might be a tumor," he said. I worked hard to not shove him again.

"It's not."

"Good. Don't die on me, man. Then whose butt will I kick at practice?"

"Funny, I don't remember any butt kicking coming from you," I retorted.

"Dude, I beat you so bad I probably knocked the memory right out of your head."

"Then why am I starter?"

"Ouch, don't open that wound up," he replied with a laugh. "This is me. Catch you at lunch." With that, he turned into his classroom.

I walked into my own classroom and immediately the chatter inside stilled. I wondered how many of them had been talking about me. Most, I'd bet. This was probably the most exciting thing to happen at this school since the cheerleading squad stole Delaney's bra and panties from her gym locker and hung them on the fence posts by the track. I went to my seat and sat, without saying anything to anyone.

"So what is it?" someone behind me asked a moment after I sat.

I turned around. Speaking of Delaney, I thought wryly as I saw her waiting expectantly for my answer. I'd felt bad about the cheerleading squad's prank, a little bit anyway, but Delaney had the kind of personality it was hard not to dislike.

"Don't know," I answered.

"It might be epilepsy," another kid replied. "My aunt has epilepsy and she has seizures like that when she doesn't get her medication. Did they give you anything?"

"No, they don't know what it is. Could be dangerous giving me drugs for something I don't even really have," I told him.

"Are you contagious?" Branson asked from the desk beside mine. He was leaning back just slightly. I coughed and he flinched.

"Seriously?" I asked, giving him a look that clearly stated I thought he was a complete moron. "You think they'd let a potentially contagious, disease-ridden patient go running around a public school?" He relaxed slightly, looking a bit embarrassed.

"Enough," said Mrs. Henricks as she walked in. Everyone quieted down, though slowly. This was going to be a long day, I thought with a sigh.

True to my prediction, every class was met with the same stupid questions.

"Are you dying?"

"Is it contagious?"

"Are you quitting football?"

I was so sick of it by the end of the day that I was about to punch the next person to ask me any questions at all. I was walking to my final period of the day when it came back.

...coming. Deep breaths. Deep breaths...

I clenched my jaw so tightly it hurt to keep from shouting at the voice. I kept walking.

...with my arm... the whisper continued. It was louder again. Clearer, and closer somehow. I kept walking, my pace quickening. I almost made it to my last class. Pain flared in my arm, the one that I'd dreamt had broken during my seizure.

"No, not now," I muttered. "Not again."

"What?" Thomas asked from beside me. We shared fourth period.

"Nothing," I said, trying to keep my breathing and tone steady. He looked at me carefully.

"Doesn't look like nothing," he accused.

The edges of my vision darkened slightly. I felt a shove and wasn't sure where it came from, until I realized Thomas had shoved me into the bathroom and out of the hallway. The bathroom was empty, class was about to start.

"Deep breaths," he told me in an eerie echo of the whispered words from a moment before.

My vision darkened further as a surge of pain in my gut threatened me with a wave of nausea. I leaned over the sink, using the sides to support me. Thomas kept one hand on my arm in case he needed to catch me, and the other was patting my back like I was a baby. Amber was right, I needed to thank him.

"No," I whispered.

"Hang in there. Need me to call someone?" he asked.

"No," I said more loudly. I wasn't sure if I was saying it to him, or the voice in my head.

...three, four, five... counted the voice before the scream broke the sequence of whispered numbers.

I could see a light bulb. It was flickering madly, its sickly yellow light not providing much illumination on the damp stone wall it was hanging in. A dark silhouette moved into my line of sight.

"Stop it!" I shouted. "Stop!"

A splash of cold water on my face jerked my awareness back to the bathroom. I grabbed hold of the feeling of the icy water hitting my face and clung to it like a lifeline. After what felt far too long, my vision and focus returned.

I was still standing, I realized with surprise. Thomas's grip on my arm had tightened, his other hand splashing cold water up at my face from the running tap in the sink.

"Jacks!" Thomas was yelling. I shook my head furiously to clear it, and the darkness at the edges of my vision faded.

Another whisper spoke in my mind, but this one sounded different. It didn't sound like it was directly in my head, more off to one side. The voice wasn't the same in focus, either. This one wasn't an absent chatter. This one was intentional, directed, and dripping with malevolence.

…mine until I get bored with you. Never forget that.

Chapter Six
Diagnosis

I skipped school Monday and Tuesday. Not by choice, my parents made me stay home. They had freaked out when the school called to tell them I'd had another episode. Thomas wouldn't have told anyone, since I had come out of it, but our fourth period teacher was going to give us both detention for being late. I couldn't let him take the fall just for helping me, even though I knew my parents would hit the roof.

My appointment with the specialist was Tuesday afternoon, and my dad had insisted I stay at home, in bed, until the specialist cleared me. Having a day off of school is nice. Spending four straight days in bed when you feel plenty well enough to be up and about is mind-numbingly frustrating.

I couldn't even go to the game on Saturday. Not that I would have anyway. The idea of sitting in the stands watching my team battle our arch-rivals without me was too depressing. Amber had asked me to go with her. I told her I couldn't, so she went alone. That girl loved football.

We hadn't texted much since I'd talked with her Friday morning. Her texts had been concerned and friendly, but just not quite right. She felt distant. I didn't know if she was just scared, or if she was losing interest because I couldn't play football. Maybe it was just me, I thought. I knew I'd been a bit more distant lately as well, with everyone.

I was at last riding with both parents to my specialist appointment. Nobody had told me yet what kind of specialist. It didn't matter much to me. As long as they could fix this.

They'd been talking for some time in the front seat of the BMW, though I wasn't paying any attention. I hadn't heard the voice in days, not since the dark whisper. This worried me, though I wasn't sure why.

As we turned into a parking lot, I glanced up at the sign and felt a sinking feeling in the pit of my stomach. The sign read "Garner Mental and Behavioral Health".

"What the hell is this?" I asked, getting angry.

"Jackson, watch your language," my father said, though he didn't sound too upset.

I think he expected it. I wondered suddenly if they'd been intentionally avoiding telling me what this doctor actually specialized in. I wasn't sure whether to be furious, or terrified. I had already started to believe I was crazy. The fact that the doctor had sent us to a shrink told me he thought so, too. But why, I wondered? Nobody knew about the whisper. Nobody knew about the hallucinations.

"You guys think I'm crazy? Why would I have seizures if I'm just crazy?"

"We don't think you're crazy, Jackson," my mom said. "But the doctor thinks there's a possibility that you might have a chemical imbalance in your brain that's causing the seizures. This doctor will be able to tell us that, and can give you some medicine to help."

"Awesome, Mom. As if this whole thing hadn't completely killed my chances in school already. Wait until they hear I'm going to a shrink."

"Nobody is going to hear it. All anyone knows is you're going to a specialist, and I don't think anyone but us knows even that much," my dad told me firmly. "If it is a chemical imbalance, Dr. Garner can prescribe something to balance you back out, and the whole problem goes away. If you can make this go away taking one little pill a day, wouldn't you want to?" I thought about that for a long moment.

"Yes," I admitted, "but a shrink? Really?"

"Psychiatrist," my mother corrected.

"Whatever. Same difference."

"What does that even mean?" my dad asked. "Same difference? Think about that for a second." I rolled my eyes.

"It's just a figure of speech, Dad. It doesn't have to make sense," I argued.

"Sure it does," he replied, seeming excited that I was getting sidetracked. I wasn't, but I also wasn't getting anywhere with the shrink argument, and knew my dad had a point with the medication idea anyway.

"'From the horse's mouth', 'kicked the bucket', 'he's got a stick up his…'" I rattled off.

"Jackson!" my father said, but he was laughing. "Why don't you get better grades in English? You've got it pretty well figured out."

"Teacher hates me," I replied as we climbed out of the car.

"Oh, she does not," my mother replied.

"He," I corrected, "and yes he does. Remember when I wrote that paper for English I last year with him?"

"I don't," she answered, thoughtfully.

"The one where he told us to write about a social standard that's only true because everyone follows it?" I reminded her. "I wrote about the illusion of power in a classroom and how, like in almost any dictatorship, a revolt of the majority of the population would destroy the illusion created by the dictator that he is in control. He hasn't given me better than a C on anything ever since." My father looked impressed. My mother looked annoyed.

"Why don't you get better grades in all of your other classes, then?" my father asked.

"I get some B's," I replied defensively as we walked through the automatic doors of the office.

"No A's. You're plenty smart enough," my father replied.

"The public education system has crushed my will to study," I replied sarcastically. My father gave me a warning look. I didn't care, I was still angry that they'd hidden this from me. And scared.

I looked around. The place was done up to look cozy and comfortable, but the image was ruined both by the cold sliding glass doors, and by the terrifying woman behind the reception desk.

She seriously looked like some horrible crossover between the Wicked Witch of the West, and Captain Hook. I couldn't figure out which she looked more like. The moustache had me leaning toward the latter, though.

"May I help you?" she asked in a voice that proudly announced all fifty years of heavy chain smoking that had clearly forged it.

The rough, grating tone was almost dripping with boredom, annoyance, and that unique note of resignation that only comes from completely having given up on the world. If I closed my eyes and just listened to that voice, I might almost believe I was in Hell.

"We have an appointment with Dr. Garner," my mother replied with her polite, social smile. The woman clicked away at a computer that was probably older than I was, despite the newness of the appearance of the building.

"Jackson Holt?" the woman asked, eyes turning to me. I just nodded. "Please have a seat, and fill these out. The doctor will be with you shortly." The horrible woman handed my mother a clipboard with enough papers stuck to it to possibly be a full novel.

We moved to the chairs lining the wall and sat down. They were much less comfortable than they looked, and had obviously been chosen for appearance over comfort. I had to admit they looked nice, though.

I reached over and picked up a crisp, new magazine. It was a National Geographic, which was cool. The cover showed what was supposed to be a close-up of a strand of DNA, though I'd seen actual pictures and knew this was a CGI mock-up. Still looked cool.

I started flipping through the pages. I hadn't made it far when a pleasant-looking woman came out from a hallway behind the reception desk.

"Jackson?" she called.

I stood. My parents stood as well, which surprised me. I thought only the patient was allowed to hear what went on in a shrink's office. They followed me as I went toward the woman, though. She held out her hand to me, not my parents. I appreciated that.

"Hello, Jackson. I'm Dr. Garner." Her smile was genuine and open. Despite my better judgment, I found myself liking her.

"Hi," I replied. She turned then to my parents and shook each of their hands, stating rather than asking their names as she did so.

"Mr. Holt. Mrs. Holt. This way, please." She led us down the hallway, past a series of closed doors. Turning and opening one, she stepped aside and gestured us in.

The office didn't look anything like I'd thought a shrink's office would look. There was no wingback chair, no long couch to lay on. It was warm, comfortable, and inviting. There was a desk with a chair behind and in front, but most of the room was taken up by what looked mostly like someone's cozy little sitting room.

One chair was obviously Dr. Garner's, but there was also a really comfortable-looking chair, and a loveseat couch that looked soft and inviting. I saved the loveseat for my parents, and took the comfortable-looking chair.

I wasn't expecting much, after my encounter with the lobby chairs, but this chair was even more comfortable than it looked. I knew immediately that despite her name being on the building, this was not the woman who had chosen the décor for the lobby. My parents sat on the loveseat as Dr. Garner closed the door behind us and sat in her own chair. She smiled at all of us.

"Well, Jackson," she started, "I hear you've been having some problems."

"Just one," I corrected. She didn't glance at the notepad or file folder sitting on the small side table.

"Headaches and a seizure, right?" she asked. I nodded.

"Only one headache though, and one seizure."

"Two," my mother pointed out.

"One," I said with a glower in her direction. "The second time wasn't a full seizure. I never fell or blacked out or anything."

Dr. Garner nodded at me as if I'd been talking to her and my mother wasn't even there. Oddly, I liked that too.

"I'm going to be straight with you, Jackson," she said. "Dr. Rasmussen just wanted me to talk with you for a bit and see if I saw any indicators of a disorder called schizophrenia. I told him already I didn't think that was likely, as schizophrenia isn't generally associated with seizures. I think epilepsy is much more likely, though Dr. Rasmussen says your tests all came back clear. So what we're going to do is just chat for a while. Is that okay?"

"Sure," I replied, still not sure where this was going. I had no idea what schizophrenia was, but was quite sure I didn't want to have it.

"Great. Can you tell me about the headache?"

"It was just a headache," I told her, confused.

"Was the pain sharp or dull?" she asked.

"Dull," I said after a moment's thought, "kind of achy, I guess."

"Like a muscle soreness? Only in your head?" she asked. I shrugged. "What about the seizure? Can you tell me everything that happened right before the seizure?"

"I was at football practice. We were just running in, my friend Thomas and me, and suddenly my vision blacked out." That was all true, though wasn't nearly all of it.

"Did you hear anything right before? Smell anything? Anything seem out of place or unusual?" My glance involuntarily flickered toward my parents and back to her before I answered.

"No," I told her. She watched me for a moment, then looked at my parents with a smile. She'd caught my glance, I realized. This lady was sharp.

"Mr. and Mrs. Holt, would it be all right with you if I spoke to Jackson alone?"

"I don't think that's a very good…" my father began before she interrupted him.

"We'll be just fine, Mr. Holt. Jackson and I have become fast friends, right Jackson?" she said with a smile to me.

My parents both looked at me. I don't know what made me do it. I didn't want to be analyzed by some shrink. I didn't want to tell anyone about the whisper. But in that moment, I felt I absolutely had to.

"Yeah, Dad. We're cool," I told him.

He looked unsure, but my mom stood and ushered them both out of the room. I don't know why she did that either, but I suspected she understood I needed to share something and didn't want to share with them. Maybe she wanted me to share it with someone, even if it wasn't her. My mother was kind of a flake sometimes, but she wasn't stupid. Not by a long shot. When the door had shut behind them, Dr. Garner turned to me with a knowing smile.

"Don't worry, Jackson. I won't share anything you

don't want me to."

"Don't you have to?" I asked her suspiciously.

"No," she replied. "Well," she corrected, "I am required to report any suspicions of abuse, but I don't think that applies in this case. So, will you talk to me?"

I thought about it, for long enough that I was sure she'd talk again, but she didn't. She sat quietly, patiently, letting me work it all out.

I could tell her. She'd probably need to know, to make her own diagnosis. I probably should have told Dr. Rasmussen, but I was afraid. I had to tell someone, though. What if the voices and hallucinations really were just some chemical imbalance? What if I never told anyone, and they couldn't help me? What if I told them and they could? But what if I told them and they still couldn't help me at all?

I remembered the visions I'd had on the field, and in the bathroom at school. I had to tell her. I couldn't just live with this. It was getting worse, and fast.

"Sometimes," I started, then took a deep breath and started over. "This can't go anywhere, okay? You and me, that's it. Not Dr. Rasmussen, not my parents, nobody. Cool?" I told her. She nodded and leaned back in her chair.

"Not a word, Jackson. I'm just here to try and help. I can't help if I don't know what's going on," she told me, echoing my thoughts. I took another deep breath.

"Sometimes, I hear voices." There. I'd said it out loud. No taking it back now.

"What kind of voices?" she asked, without any trace of judgment in her tone. My relief was tremendous.

"Whispers. I can't understand them most of the time, it's too faint. But sometimes I understand a few words."

"How many voices?" she asked.

"Just one. Well, two actually. I've only heard the second one once, though."

"What do they say to you?"

"I don't think they're talking to me," I confessed.

"What do they say?"

"Just nonsense. Random words. I only hear parts of their sentences, so it's hard to understand even when I hear the words clearly. The voice talks about birds, sunsets, and the days of the week. I don't know why, but a lot of the time I think it's counting. I don't know what it's counting either, though."

"What did the other voice say?" I got a chill as I remembered the menacing, growling voice.

"Mine," I replied. "Something about 'mine'. I didn't understand that, either."

Dr. Garner considered for a long moment before speaking again.

"How long have you been hearing these voices?" she asked.

"Not long. It started last week, I think."

"Before or after the headache?" she asked.

"Same time. The headache came with the voice the first time."

One more time, you can do this, came the whisper. It was crystal clear. I heard every word. I still didn't understand it, though. Not now, I thought sharply.

"Do the voices ever tell you to do things?"

Deep breaths. Five, then go. Stop! Not now! I shouted inside my head.

"Jackson?" Dr. Garner asked. I realized I'd been quiet for several seconds.

"I'm sorry, what?" I asked.

"Are you hearing the voice right now?" she asked.

Three... two...

"I..."

...one... PULL!

My world exploded in pain.

Chapter Seven
White Coats

My head was throbbing. My left arm ached like it had been broken. Maybe it had been. It didn't hurt as badly as my right hand, though. Both burned like the skin had all been peeled away from them.

I tried to open my eyes, but they resisted. I almost panicked, but realized that I did have control of them, they were just tired and sore. I tried again. They burned a little bit, and the light was way too bright, but I got them open. A few seconds to adjust to the light and I could see okay. I looked around.

I was in a room, the brick walls painted a soft blue. The scratchy blankets covering me were a soft blue as well. There was nothing else in the room.

I looked down at my arms, but both looked totally fine. The persistent, though faint, burning sensation still kept telling me otherwise. With a start, I realized I was wearing something like green scrubs, and a pair of old, thin, green socks that weren't mine. I also wasn't wearing any shoes.

After a moment, I noticed the bed wasn't a bed at all, just a mattress on the floor. There was nothing else in the room. No window, no chair, no table, no medical equipment, nothing. This definitely wasn't the hospital again.

There was a window in the white door to the room. It looked like a hallway outside, though I couldn't see much from where I lay. The window had a metal mesh over it on the inside, preventing contact with the glass. I frowned.

What on earth was going on? This looked kind of like what I imagined prison to be like. It was only missing a small stainless steel toilet, and a second bed with a big, scary inmate named Bubba or Shiv McKenzie or something. I stood slowly, nursing my throbbing head, and moved to the door.

Looking out the window I could see I was right, it was a hallway. All pale blue brick and checkered linoleum floors, just like in this room. Several more doors like mine were in my line of sight. I tried the door. It was locked. I'm not sure why that surprised me, but it did. Was this prison, I wondered?

A man came walking past. He was wearing white scrubs. I banged loudly on the mesh of the window.

"Hey!" I shouted. "Hey, you!" The man looked my way and stopped when he saw me. He approached the window, but didn't move to open the door. "Let me out! What's going on?" I shouted.

His lips moved, but his voice was so muffled I couldn't understand. He held up one finger, indicating that I should wait, then he turned and walked away.

"Hey! Come on, man! What the hell is going on?" I shouted. I slammed my hand against the mesh again, wincing at the noise as it caused another throb in my head. The man kept walking.

I shook the mesh. It was impressively well installed. It barely rattled. It banged pretty good when I hit it, but it obviously wasn't going anywhere anytime soon.

I turned and looked at the little room again. The staining on the checkered floor told me that there used to be a night stand and a small table and chairs in the room. I didn't know why they'd been removed.

What had happened? Didn't they usually take people to hospitals when they had seizures? This was definitely not a hospital. I suddenly had the horrifying thought that maybe when I blacked out the voice had taken over. My stomach lurched as the idea took hold. What had I done? Maybe this was prison. Maybe I'd killed someone.

The sound of keys in the lock of my door spun me back around. The man on the other side was wearing a suit. It was a lousy suit, but it was a suit. Tweed, old-fashioned, very worn, a sort of dishwater brown color. The plaid tie on the pinstriped shirt didn't help the image.

I moved to stand in front of the door. As it opened, I saw two more men in white on either side of the shorter, rounder, gray-haired man in the bad suit.

"Mr. Holt," said the man with a friendly smile. I didn't buy the friendliness for a second.

"What the hell is going on?" I asked him.

"Ah," he stammered, "yes. Come with me, I'll explain everything."

I considered making a more insistent demand that he tell me now, but the two gorillas beside him shifted slightly and convinced me otherwise. I nodded, though letting the man see by my expression that I wasn't happy with this at all.

I followed the man, and his two thugs followed me, down the hallway. He took me through two sets of locked metal doors, with two little alcoves that looked for all the world like guard stations at each one. They were both empty, though.

After the second door, there was a huge room with tables, chairs, couches, and a couple of TVs mounted high up on the walls and behind little, slightly rusty cages. It was the weirdest thing.

The room had several dozen people in it, sitting on couches, or at the tables. They were playing cards, reading books, talking, just hanging out.

There were boys and girls, the youngest not much younger than I was, but there were also men and women of various ages all puttering about the room. A lady walked past us, a vacant expression in her eyes, carrying a teddy bear that looked at least twenty years older than the woman did.

Most wore the same green scrubs I did, though a handful wore t-shirts. One younger man had on a t-shirt, jeans, and some kind of hospital slippers, but nobody else had on shoes of any kind.

"What is this place?" I asked.

"Be patient, Mr. Holt. We will talk in private."

Through another metal door and we were in a very different-looking part of the building. The walls were a mild green, the floor carpeted in short, stiff, office-style carpeting, but also in a soft green. It was unsettling.

We passed a few doors, all open, showing small offices. He led me into one of these. It was nice enough, but looked just like every other one we'd passed. The short, round man gestured me toward a chair on the far side of a heavy-looking, white-painted metal desk.

The desk looked a little worse for wear, once I got a

closer look at it. The metal front plate looked to have been kicked at more than once. And hard, to leave dents in the painted metal. There was nothing on the desk within arm's reach. Pencils, paper, and various office supplies were on a small shelf behind the desk.

The short man moved behind the desk and sat, crossing his hands in front of him on the desk. I took the chair he'd pointed me toward. One of the big men in white moved around behind me where I couldn't see him without turning. I looked back at him, but the cold stare he gave back encouraged me to turn back toward the desk.

The other man closed the door behind us, himself on the outside. I could see the shadows of his shoes through the crack at the bottom of the door. He wasn't moving.

"Okay, we're in private. Will you please tell me what's going on?" I was trying hard to keep the panic out of my voice. The man smiled.

"I appreciate the manners, Mr. Holt. At Brookview, we strive for good manners. It makes all of our lives so much more pleasant, don't you think?"

"I think I really need to know what's happening," I answered. The man nodded.

"Of course, of course. I'm Dr. Fitzpatrick. I'm the psychiatrist in charge of your wing of Brookview."

"Psychiatrist?" I asked. He nodded.

"That's correct, Mr. Holt. I'll be working with you over the next few months as we try to resolve your problems."

"Months?" I squeaked out. He nodded.

"You see, when you were visiting my colleague Dr. Garner, you had another seizure. While you were under, you began screaming many… unsettling things. When the good doctor and your parents tried to get you back under control, you assaulted Dr. Garner. Sixteen stitches."

"What?" I asked in a whisper, stunned.

"Evidently, you hit her with a lamp."

"No way…" I trailed off. "What was I screaming?"

"We'll get into that. She told me about the voices you'd been hearing, Mr. Holt. That's very concerning." I felt a swell of betrayal. She'd promised not to tell anyone.

"You think?" I snapped. "That's why I went to see her, so we could fix it."

"Of course, of course. The trouble is your condition is more serious than outpatient care is equipped to deal with. So you've been given into our custody."

"I want to call my parents," I said.

"In time," Dr. Fitzpatrick said.

"Now," I replied angrily. "They'll get me out of here."

"They signed you in," replied Dr. Fitzpatrick. He seemed apologetic.

The surging feeling of betrayal this time was almost overwhelming. My breathing became rapid and my heart thumped heavily in my chest. My parents had signed me into this place? How could they do that to me… their own son, given away to be locked up for God knew how long?

"How long will I be here?" I finally managed to get out. Realizing I was totally on my own, I needed to get a handle on everything, starting with myself.

"That depends on you, and how well you respond

to your medication and therapy sessions."

"What medication?"

"We have prescribed you a number of medications that should take care of those pesky voices, prevent any further seizures, and leave you a little clearer to address your other problems."

"What other problems?" I asked, not sure I wanted to hear this.

"Your violent rages, of course."

I was too stunned to speak. I had done something one time while blacked out and they now thought I was violent and dangerous. For that matter, maybe I was. The thought was not reassuring.

"Is this a prison?" I asked. He laughed.

"Oh, no, Mr. Holt. This is a care facility for individuals like yourself with various disorders and developmental difficulties, and for a few special people who are recovering from substance abuse issues."

"A nuthouse?" I asked.

"Now, Mr. Holt, that mentality will not get you anywhere. We are all here to help, and the more you cooperate, the better we can all do our jobs and get you safe, healthy, and home. Doesn't that sound good?"

"I want to go home now," I told him.

"I wish that were possible, Mr. Holt, I really do. In due time, however." I took several long breaths as I tried to get a grip on myself.

"So now what?" I asked.

"Now, we get you acquainted with the facility. Shall we take a tour?"

"I guess," I replied, too far in shock to come up with anything more.

"That's the spirit," he said with a smile. I think he

was serious.

We stood and moved to the door. Opening it, the big orderly stepped aside and waited for us to pass before falling into step behind us.

They really must think I'm dangerous, I realized. They brought two bodyguards for the doctor, just for me. Either of these guys looked they could break me in half with one hand. I felt that two was more than a little overkill. Sort of like sending Rambo to deal with a schoolyard bully. And from the look of these two guys, it felt almost like two foxes being assigned to guard the henhouse.

We went back to the big room with all the tables and couches. Dr. Fitzpatrick gestured grandly.

"This is the rec room. Lots to do in here. We have games, and books, and TV, though the volume is kept off. Don't worry though, we have closed captioning. You are welcome to spend any of your free hours here as long as you obey the rules."

"What are the rules?" I asked. He smiled, as if that were another unexpected pleasant surprise. I wondered morbidly about the kind of kids they had in this place.

"We'll get to that, but don't worry. They're not difficult," he replied.

"Now you'll have to earn the privilege of using any of the games or cards."

"Seriously?" I asked almost numbly. This was way more than my mind could handle.

"Don't worry, it's very easy to earn privilege points. Just follow the rules and you can play games and cards, watch TV, even wear your own clothes like Mr. Turner over there."

"You mean the rules you won't tell me?" I asked.

Dr. Fitzpatrick gave me a stern look.

"I told you we would get to those, Mr. Holt."

"Uh huh. So if I'm a good little boy, I get to wear pants and play cards with the other crazies?"

"Mr. Holt," he said warningly.

"Sorry," I replied, suddenly very sure I didn't want to know what would happen if I didn't behave myself. He nodded, satisfied.

"It's all a little overwhelming at first, I certainly understand," he replied. "As I was saying, with enough points you can even join us for activities on Sundays, and movie night on Fridays. Come along." I continued following him across the large room.

I spotted a boy sitting alone on one of the uncomfortable-looking couches. He looked my age, but a little smaller than I was. His dark hair was buzzed short, and his wrists were bandaged. He was watching me. The look wasn't hostile, just… wary. I bobbed my head once his direction. He returned the gesture, but otherwise didn't move. He just kept watching as we exited the rec room.

"This is the cafeteria," Dr. Fitzpatrick said.

I glanced around. The cafeteria was a soft green like the therapy offices were. It was not an appetizing color. The smell of bleach was strong in here. I wrinkled my nose at the idea of sitting in here and eating whatever slop they called food while inhaling heavy doses of ammonia.

"Meals are at seven, twelve-thirty, and six, on the dot. If you have earned enough points, you can come in here for a snack at three in the afternoon."

"What time is it?" I asked, suddenly realizing I hadn't seen a single window. There had probably been a clock in the rec room, but I hadn't noticed. There might be one in here too, I realized and looked around for it.

"It's nine-thirty," he replied. "Too late for a breakfast today, but you'll get lunch in a few hours."

I wasn't in the least hungry. In fact, my stomach was still doing its own internal acrobatics as I tried to wrap my mind around the idea of spending the next few months in this nightmare.

Someday, the whisper came, *I'll get out.*

I looked around, instinctively checking to see if anyone else had heard it. I knew they hadn't. Dr. Fitzpatrick was rambling on something about meatloaf. I noticed one of the two big orderlies eyeing me warily. He'd noticed my reaction. I looked forward again and continued following Dr. Fitzpatrick, pretending that I wasn't listening to someone who wasn't there.

I was escorted back to my room as soon as the tour was over. There wasn't much more to it. After the cafeteria, there were the group therapy rooms, where apparently I'd be spending a lot of time, and the visitation room.

The visitation room was several big steps above any other room I'd seen here, with warm beige walls, soft carpeting, paintings and elegant decorations, even a comfortable wooden table and chairs.

Dr. Fitzpatrick had told me it would be a few weeks before I would be allowed visitation, as I needed to earn enough points for that, too. He tried to reassure me that I could call my parents once a day for fifteen minutes, if I kept my points high enough. Although that had to wait three days for my "evaluation" period to pass, so they knew if it was safe for me to call my parents. Seriously, how could calling my parents be dangerous?

I didn't understand the point system. From what he was telling me, they were completely arbitrary, and any nurse, orderly, or doctor in the place could add or remove them to my total whenever they wanted, for whatever they wanted. He was still really vague on the rules.

I didn't have to spend them to get my privileges though, which was something at least. It was more of a points-level kind of reward system. If I had twenty points, I could have snack that day. If I had fifty, I could play games in the rec room. If I had a hundred, I could join the well-behaved inmates for a movie on Friday night. With each new level I earned, I got to keep all the lower privileges as well.

Dr. Fitzpatrick promised me an actual bed if I kept my points above a hundred for a whole week. Until then, I got a blanket and an old mattress on the floor, since they didn't know if my seizures were "safe" enough for me to have hard furniture. I luckily managed to bite back my remark about a padded room. This place probably had one and I didn't want to put that idea into their heads.

I was to remain directly supervised at all times for the first seventy-two hours, while they determined my "risk level". In the meantime, I was either with an orderly, or locked in my room. Orderlies all had other things to do right now, so I was locked in my room.

I stared from just inside the locked door at my small, barren cell. I couldn't think of it any other way, no matter what spin Dr. Fitzpatrick tried to put on it.

I turned to look out the window into the empty

hallway. As the shock wore off, depression sank in immediately, threatening to overwhelm me. I put my back to the wall and slid down to the floor, putting my head in my hands.

Someday, the voice repeated.

"Shut up!" I yelled at the voice.

I'll get out, the voice continued, *and when I do…*

Chapter Eight
No Breakfast

They didn't let me eat lunch or dinner in the cafeteria. My first two meals, although calling that slop they brought me 'food' was a real stretch, were brought on a paper plate with a plastic spoon. The orderly who brought them stood there and waited for me to finish, then collected my plate and spoon and left. Not one word spoken.

Dr. Fitzpatrick wouldn't let me out of my room, even to go to the bathroom, without an orderly. I had to bang, sometimes for half an hour, to get someone's attention to let me out to use the bathroom when I had to go.

Until they got the first full round of drugs through my system, they didn't want me interacting with the other inmates. Dr. Fitzpatrick called them patients, but I had a hard time seeing this as a place people got better. One more hour staring at the checkered floor that covered my little cell and I might have gone insane. If I weren't already, that is.

It's amazing how fast you start to feel really crazy sitting in a barren room for an entire day, staring at a black and white checkered floor, with nothing to do but sit around and think about the fact that you really might actually be crazy.

When my door opened early the next morning, I jolted awake from some nightmare that I forgot the instant I opened my eyes. The panic and anxiety from the dream lingered however, my heart racing in my chest.

It was one of the orderlies. Not one I recognized, though. This one was a pleasant-looking, older, dark-skinned woman with slightly greying hair. Not super old, but possibly old enough to be my grandmother. She smiled warmly. I liked her. That was a nice change. I climbed slowly out of bed as she spoke.

"Good morning, Jackson. Is it all right if I call you Jackson?"

"Yeah, whatever," I replied groggily, still trying to shake both sleep and fear from my head.

"Breakfast is in one hour. I'll take you to the bathroom, and then to the shower, and then you can decide if you want to come back here, or if you want to go to the rec room for what time you have left before breakfast. Sound good?"

I nodded and moved toward her. She stepped back and into the hallway and started walking away. The moment I entered the hallway, one of the big bruiser orderlies fell into step behind me. Figures, I thought. They weren't about to let granny here be alone with me. I might go psychotic and kill her with a… well, with my bare hands I supposed.

She slowed so I was soon walking beside her, and smiled at me. She was a few inches shorter than I was, but that didn't seem to bother her. She didn't seem worried at all.

"I'm Mrs. Morris. I'm here in your wing every

Tuesday and Thursday from six until four, so we'll get to know each other just fine. If you need anything, just ask. I can't promise I can get it for you, but I'll sure try."

"Thanks. Right now I just need the toilet," I told her.

She kind of reminded me of my own grandmother, though Mrs. Morris was a bit younger. And obviously my grandmother wasn't this dark-skinned. I briefly considered whether Mrs. Morris was Indian or African-American, but decided it didn't really matter.

It wasn't the way she looked that reminded me of my grandmother anyway. More the way she smiled at me. It showed genuine care and attention. Like my grandmother, when Mrs. Morris looked at me, she was really *looking*. I liked that.

"Oh, I understand that," she said with a smile. "Pancakes for breakfast today," Mrs. Morris added a few steps later, giving me a look that told me she hoped that would brighten my mood.

It did, but if it were any other orderly, I wouldn't have shown it. I gave her a small smile, though I hadn't felt like smiling for quite a while now.

"You're not afraid of me," I told her, rather than asked.

The other orderlies hadn't been either, but they'd all been twice my size. Even then, they'd all seemed cautious around me. Mrs. Morris didn't seem troubled in the least to be walking along beside me. We stopped just outside the bathroom door, and she looked up at me, in a measuring fashion. After a moment, she shook her head.

"No, Jackson. I'm not afraid of you. My mother

used to always tell me I had a talent for reading people. You're a good young man. I can see it. You wouldn't hurt anyone."

"I hurt that psychiatrist."

"You had a seizure," she answered.

"I hit her with a lamp."

"Seizures come in all kinds, Jackson. But they all have one thing in common; you don't have control of your own body."

"So maybe I'd hurt you without having control," I told her. Her lack of concern was oddly unsettling. She smiled softly and reached out to pat my arm.

"You won't hurt me, Jackson. You go take care of business and then I'll take you for your shower. And don't feel rushed. You've got a whole hour, so take your time. I don't mind waiting."

I looked back at the big orderly behind me. His expression told me quite plainly that he minded waiting, but he didn't voice his objection.

I didn't take long in the bathroom, but I didn't hurry, either. When I came back out, her apparently ever-present smile was waiting.

"Ready?"

I nodded and followed her down the hallway. She moved to fall into step beside me again.

"You have kids?" I asked her suddenly. I didn't know why, but I wanted her to keep talking. I hadn't talked with anyone since the morning before and I suddenly needed it. She didn't seem to mind the personal question.

"Four," she answered. "My youngest son is about your age, I think. No grandchildren from my older children, though. Not yet, anyway. I keep hoping."

Once again, thoughts of my grandmother went through my mind. I wondered how she was handling the news that her favorite grandson was in a nuthouse.

"Do you play any sports?" she asked me. I nodded.

"Football." She nodded knowingly.

"I thought so. You have that athletic look about you, and football is very popular around here."

"Around everywhere, I'd say," I told her, a little defensively. She laughed lightly and my defensiveness slipped away.

"Oh, you'd be surprised. A lot of countries don't even consider it a real sport. We sure like it here, though. My husband watches every weekend. Seems there's always a game on someplace on Sundays."

"Do you watch?" I asked her. She shook her head.

"Not me. I appreciate the talent, but just never could sit around and watch people play on the screen. Much more fun to go in person," she winked at me.

I smiled, despite myself. My mom always said the same thing. She would never watch with me and Dad, either.

"Here you go. Everything you need is in there. Take your time, I'll be right here when you get out. Still lots of time."

I walked into the shower room. It reminded me a bit of a locker room, though without the lockers. There were some cubbies to one side, but they were all open. Clean scrubs were stacked neatly to one side, all with sizes printed on the sleeve and hem. I hadn't noticed that before on my own.

There was a dispenser built securely into one wall, behind another big metal grate, with what I assumed was a liquid soap of some kind and a gap in the grate just big enough to get a hand into for your dose of soap. That was it.

The rest of the room was tiled, with pillar showerheads, like I'd seen at a few swimming pools before, where six guys could stand around each of the three pillars to shower together. Not my favorite, but I'd done so before at away games. I was suddenly glad our school had a better shower room than this, though.

Another patient was on his way out as I came in. Otherwise, it was empty. I was relieved, but mostly because the idea of being so vulnerable in a place full of crazies wasn't my idea of the safest thing to do. After a moment, I realized the big orderly had come in behind me.

"Easy there, tiger. No free shows," I told him. He glowered at me.

"Supervised at all times, that's my orders," he told me. "Trust me, you're not my type, kid." He definitely didn't look happy about this arrangement. That actually did make me feel a little better.

"All right, do what you've gotta do, big guy. Just stay over here, okay?"

"Yup," he replied, leaning against the doorway. He pointedly looked away from me, which I appreciated.

Quickly, I turned on the water and stripped down. Getting a handful of the liquid soap, which smelled terrible, I started giving myself a quick scrub.

Mom?

Not now, I thought in annoyance.

I'm still here, the voice whispered.

Something about the tone made me pause and listen more closely. This time, the voice wasn't angry or frightened, or hurt. This time it was sad. Heartachingly, longingly sad. I wasn't sure why, but this new emotional turn caught me off guard.

Keep looking, Mom. Don't give up. I'm still right here.

The whisper was soft, but very clear. Keep looking for what? I wondered. Whose mom was supposed to keep looking?

The steady sound and feel of the warm water running over me was calming, and I found myself slipping further and further toward the voice.

It's been so long. Too long.

For the first time, I really wondered what the voice was talking about. It always seemed so random, so disjointed. Even when I understood the words, I never understood what they really meant. This time it seemed to make some sort of sense, though I still couldn't have isolated the meaning exactly.

The voice was lost. Lost where or how, I didn't know. Who, I didn't know. But they were lost. Someone should be looking for them. Their mother? Whose mother?

Get a grip, Jackson, I told myself. You're thinking about the voice in your head as a person. Knock that off or you'll never get rid of it.

I was in too deep, though. Without warning, images flooded across my mind. These images were different though. Not sharp and clear like the ones before. These were hazy and muddied.

A flash of a smiling woman, beautiful in a country kind of way. She was backlit by sunlight.

It was a beach, though I didn't know where. There were families all around. Kids laughing and playing in the sand and in the gentle surf. The woman said something, but there was no sound.

The scene shifted. The flash of police lights and the whine of a siren. This was on a street someplace, in a neighborhood. The trees were bare, and the air seemed crisp and cold. I couldn't feel it though, just see it. It was hazy and disjointed like the image of the beach had been. A blur of movement to one side, and the image changed again.

This time it was crystal clear and sharp, and felt more real. The tunnel was dark and cold, a faint and distant grayish light came from the end of the tunnel off in the distance.

The sound of water trickling slowly very nearby echoed gently in the stillness. I could feel again, and the earth below me was cold and hard. I was half-lying down, my upper body leaning against the cold, damp stone wall.

The painful, burning feeling around my wrists on my arms raised above my head made me want to look up. The sharp, steady throbbing in the middle of one of my forearms made me somewhat glad I couldn't look. I couldn't make my head obey me to look anyway.

My head turned downward without my willing it to, and I saw my legs. Only they weren't my legs. They were skinny and dirty, and the feet were too small.

My head turned again of its own volition back to the light at the end of the narrow tunnel. The sound of gravel crunching under tires echoed, and a surge of panic rose sharply in my gut.

"Hey, kid!" came the shouted voice. I felt a slap across my cheek. It stung and pulled my focus partly back to where I was.

I was lying on the wet tiles, cold and naked. Two

orderlies were standing over me, one crouching low and shaking my shoulder. He was the one who'd slapped me, I realized.

I couldn't get my focus fully back to reality. One moment I'd see the faded face of the orderly, the next I was staring at the light at the end of the tunnel, which abruptly dimmed and the sound of boots on packed earth began to echo, closer and closer. I shook my head sharply, but that made it worse. The two images swirled and blurred in my mind.

Hands touched me, and I lashed out. I felt another slap and saw the two orderlies hoisting me up, each holding one arm and another arm under each leg. They hauled me out of the shower room. The colder air of the hallway hit my wet body and I started shivering, but I didn't notice.

A sharp pain wrenched my wrists and the sharp pain in my arm flared as I was dragged by my feet from my half-reclined position on the packed earth, skin grinding on the ground below as I slid down fully to the ground. I cried out in pain.

"Jackson!" called Mrs. Morris.

My focus pulled back just enough to realize I was being carried down the hallway back toward my room. A pair of girls, other patients, I realized as I noticed their green scrubs, giggled as I was carried naked and shaking past them on their way to breakfast.

I felt teeth biting into my shoulder, and was pulled back to the tunnel. There was an immense weight on top of me, and I couldn't move. It was hard to breathe enough to cry out at the pain in my shoulder and elsewhere. Hands moved roughly across my body.

"Come on Jackson, stay with me," called Mrs.

Morris from what sounded a million miles away. I concentrated on her voice and tried to pull it to me.

There was another man passing us in the hallway. An orderly, I realized. He saw me passing by, carried by in my pitiful state, laughed and made a crude gesture at my nakedness.

Pain tried to pull me back to the tunnel, but I reached a hand out and grabbed hold of Mrs. Morris's arm. She clutched at my hand, holding it tightly and comfortingly.

"It's all right, Jackson. Just keep focusing on me. Stay focused on me. Can you hear me, Jackson?"

I tried to speak, but the sound that came out was hoarse and raw.

"There you go, just keep trying. Keep focusing on me. Here, we're at your room. Lay him down on the bed, boys."

I wouldn't let go of her hand, so they had to maneuver a bit to get me dumped onto the thin mattress. Mrs. Morris knelt down beside me, still allowing me to grip her hand. I focused on the feeling of her hand, the feeling of the cold air on my wet skin, the sound of the orderlies hollering for Dr. Fitzpatrick. All of it helped bring me back closer to reality.

Gasping as I tried to re-center, I was only half aware of Mrs. Morris pulling part of my blanket over my lower half, and beginning to towel me dry with the other half. She was still talking to me, one hand holding tightly to mine.

"... medication will help. It will just take a few days to start really having an effect. You can hang in there. Hang in there, Jackson. Dr. Fitzpatrick is on the way."

"Mrs. Morris?" I got out, my voice raw from what

must have been screaming. I was winning the battle, and the agony in the tunnel seemed further away.

"I hear you, honey," she answered.

"Are the pancakes good?" I asked. She laughed, relieved and opened her mouth to reply.

I didn't hear what she said next as a brand new and terrifying kind of pain tore into me and I was fully back in the tunnel. It was far too long before I blacked out and fell into the blissful peace of nothingness.

Chapter Nine
Cody

I missed breakfast. And lunch. By the time I woke up again, it was early afternoon. It took a long time to get anyone to come let me out to go to the bathroom. I was getting really tired of being hungry and missing all my meals.

Afraid of another seizure, the orderly came in with me. Between that and the memory of being hauled naked and shaking through the public hallways, being seen and laughed at by who knows how many people, including those two girls, I was more humiliated than I'd ever been in my life.

I vomited into the toilet. Not because of the embarrassment. What I had experienced in my mind when I'd fallen completely back into that tunnel in my mind was more than humiliating. It was painful, shameful, and sickeningly helpless. I felt violated in a way I didn't know was even possible. It was something I truly believed no man had ever experienced like that. We simply weren't equipped for it.

The girl in my mind, the one I kept becoming, was a tortured, broken, agonized soul. She couldn't be real, I knew. Nobody really experienced that kind of pain and brutalization. Nobody really felt that way.

I was more convinced that I was insane than ever. Who dreamed things like that? Who experienced those kinds of things in their minds?

I was praying they finally got my medications in and they could give me any drugs they possibly had. I couldn't live through that again. I wouldn't. I'd kill myself first.

The orderly didn't say anything as I vomited again. It was mostly dry heaves, since I hadn't actually eaten since the night before. I spat, and wiped my mouth on the back of my hand. Moving to the small, stainless steel sink, I carefully washed out my mouth and rinsed my face.

The orderly, still not saying anything, took me to the rec room. I didn't want to go there. I think he knew that, and I hated him for it.

A couple of giggles and laughs met me as I walked in. I felt my face color, and I didn't look up to meet anyone's gaze. I didn't know how many had seen my embarrassing episode in the hallway, but I was sure they'd all at least heard about it by now.

I moved to a couch and sat. I didn't have any points. I hadn't interacted enough with anyone to have earned any. The orderly stood behind the couch, a wary sentinel, ready for my next episode.

I heard the whispers around me, real ones this time, but I ignored them. I just sat, staring at that blasted checkered flooring.

Someone approached, and I tried to crawl even further inside myself. He didn't come to me though, and instead went to the small table across from the couch where I sat. There was a chessboard set up and apparently mid-game. The man made a move with a black bishop, and then walked away.

Before I could think of what to make of this, another figure approached. This one was more hesitant, and the steps seemed cautious. I looked up. It was the boy from the day before, with the buzz cut.

"Hey," he said uncertainly. I looked down again. "Can I sit?" he asked.

"I guess," I muttered. The boy sat on the shorter, totally mismatched couch at a right angle the one I was currently trying to become one with.

"I'm Cody," he said. He started to hold out his hand, but hesitated, and pulled it back.

"Hi," I replied, not giving him my own name.

"How you doing?" he asked.

"That's a stupid question," I replied, looking up and growing angry. He held up both hands in a calming gesture.

"I know, I'm sorry. It's habit, you know? You say hi, then you ask how it's going. Obviously you're not doing great, or you wouldn't be in this over-sized outhouse." The boy gave a dark look to the orderly behind me. I noticed the two girls from the hallway to one side, pointing, whispering and giggling. Cody noticed my gaze and looked back to me.

"Don't mind them. Those two really are nuts," he said with a smile. I looked down. I could feel my cheeks flushing again. "What's your name?" Cody tried again.

"What do you care? Need to know what name to use when making fun of me?" I snapped.

"Easy, bro," he said. "No, you just seem like one of the only other really lucid guys in here, and I'm hoping to, you know, have someone to kind of help watch my back. I'd do the same for you, of course." I frowned. This really did sound like prison talk.

"Watch your back? What, you afraid you're going to get shanked?" I asked, jokingly. The look on Cody's face killed any humor I had left in me at that moment. "Are you kidding me?!" I almost yelped.

"Dude, some of the people here are okay, just a bit shaken by whatever. Like you and me. We're fine. You just have seizures, and I'm…" he hesitated and looked down at his bandaged wrists. "I'm self-destructive. No harm to anyone else," he assured me quickly.

Someone made a weird, guttural call across the room. Nobody seemed to notice but me, so I glanced at Cody for reassurance. He made a face.

"That's Louis. Tourette's or something. He does that sometimes. He's okay, though. Wouldn't hurt a fly. Some of the people here though," he glanced around, "would open your neck just to feel the spray of blood on their face."

"If you came over here to make me feel better, you suck at it," I told him, horrified. He gave me an apologetic smile.

"Yeah, sorry. Just want to make sure you know what you're getting into. I've been here a while and know most of these guys, and what to watch out for. That guy, for example?" Cody pointed at a middle-aged guy playing solitaire.

"Yeah?" I urged, despite myself.

"That guy killed someone. With his bare hands. No joke, he beat the guy until his head was just a pile of mush."

"Seriously? Why isn't he in prison?"

"Insanity plea," Cody said with a shrug.

"They seriously put me in here to get help, and instead I'm in here with a bunch of lunatics and psychopaths?"

"Welcome to Brookview," Cody said with a wry smile. I sat quietly for a moment, digesting this before he interrupted my thoughts.

"Anyway, I really just wanted to see if you'd be cool watching my back. I know most of the people here, but we get new ones in all the time, and I really don't want someone to stab me in the back with a filed-down plastic spoon," he said.

"A plastic spoon?" I asked incredulously.

"Seriously. Saw it happen myself two months ago. Some crazy girl stabbed an old guy five times in the back with a plastic spoon she'd filed down into a blade. Killed him."

"Where is she now?" I asked, looking around and behind myself. The orderly still standing behind me had an unpleasant smile on his face. He was enjoying this. I put him on my rapidly growing list of people I hated.

"She got let out."

"What?!" I blurted.

"No, really!" Cody said. "Her insurance ran out, so they sent her home."

"But she killed someone! Shouldn't she be in jail?"

"Probably. But no, the people in here get different rules applied to them. Stab someone to death outside and you get life in prison. Do it here, and you get your points taken away." His voice took on a mocking, acting tone. "No Friday night movie for you, you crazy psycho killer! We were going to watch Titanic. And no dessert for a month! That'll teach you!"

I laughed in disbelief. This place was unreal. I had a medical condition needing treatment, and they sent me to a place where people stab each other to death with plastic-ware. What kind of system was this country running?

"This is insane," I said.

"Yes, and so is almost everyone here. I can teach you who to avoid, and who's cool."

"How do you know I'm not a crazy person you should avoid? I attacked my therapist, you know."

"Nah," Cody said dismissively, "Mrs. Morris said you were cool. Listen, all I'm asking is that we can maybe hang together in rec, and in the cafeteria so neither of us gets stabbed in the back. What do you say, that cool?"

"Yeah, I guess. You seem okay. Except," I hesitated and looked down to the bandages.

"I have depression issues, that okay with you?" he snapped defensively.

"Yeah, cool, but you said you saw someone stabbed to death here two months ago. If you'd tried to cut your wrists before that they'd be healed by now, right?" Cody looked down, simultaneously ashamed and defensive.

"That was last time I was in here. I've only been in here two weeks this time."

"You've been here twice?" I asked, surprised. After one day here, I'd happily vow to never again to say or do anything to ever land myself in a place like this, if I had any say in the matter. Cody shifted uncomfortably.

"This fool's been here six times," said the orderly behind me with a laugh. I gave him a dirty look and turned some of my growing fear into anger.

"Hey, do you mind? Bad enough you pervs are always checking us out in the shower and bathroom. Think you could leave us crazies to at least have a conversation without you getting up in our business?" I said angrily. The orderly chuckled, but didn't say anything.

"It's cool, but thanks," Cody said with a slight smile. "He's right though. Six times. Like I said, depression issues."

"Life that bad?" I asked. He looked down at his wrists, then shrugged.

"Sometimes."

"Sorry, man," I said simply.

I thought about it for a while. I'd just finished thinking I'd have killed myself before going through what I just went through that morning. Maybe what Cody was dealing with outside this place was just as bad. Bad enough that he'd risk failing suicide and ending up in a place like this again.

"Can I ask something without you getting all pissed at me? You don't have to answer." I asked.

"Maybe," he said warily.

"If you tried to kill yourself by cutting your wrists, why does the thought of someone stabbing you to death bother you? Isn't that kind of what you want?"

I watched as his expression went from surprise, to amusement, to an oddly amused defiance.

"My life, my terms," he said firmly.

"I can respect that," I told him.

It made an odd sort of sense. He might have wanted to end his life, but he wanted it done his way, in his own time. He didn't want someone taking it from him. I could definitely respect that.

"That's cool," I said. He looked relieved I wasn't going to argue it.

"Hey, it's about time for dinner. You got my back?" he asked.

I returned the smile and nodded, holding out a hand to him. He grinned and slapped it. Together, we stood and headed for the cafeteria, my own private stalker in white walking quietly behind us.

Chapter Ten
Group Therapy

The next morning after breakfast I had my first group therapy session. I had no idea what to expect, but had seen movies where they did this. I was morbidly curious to see if it was anything like I'd seen on screen.

The group therapy room was a soft green, down the hall from Dr. Fitzpatrick's office. I hadn't seen him, or this room, since he gave me his tour.

The room had old inspirational posters all over the place, mixed with random inspirational sayings in cutout letters. Some of them looked like they were thirty or forty years old. There was a semi-circle of folding metal chairs facing the wall with the door, with one chair near the wall and not far from the door facing the semi-circle.

A couple of people were already in their chairs when I got there. Cody wasn't one of them, I was disappointed to see. Several empty chairs left though, I reminded myself. He seemed like he'd be a good person to be friends with in here. He really knew his way around.

I moved to a chair, but before I could sit down, the woman sitting beside the empty chair shrieked at me, clawing at the air in front of me threateningly.

"Hey kid," the guy on the other side of the empty chair said.

I glanced over and took an involuntary step back. It was the guy Cody had said had beaten a man to death.

"Don't sit on Martin," he said.

"I'm sorry, Martin?" I asked, confused. The woman was now stroking the empty air and muttering apologies to nothing.

"Martin is Lynette's husband. Deceased," he clarified.

I looked back at the empty chair and the woman, then back to the killer. He shrugged, almost apologetically. I nodded slowly, and moved across the semi-circle to sit in a chair with nobody on either side of it.

After several seconds of thinking how crazy that poor lady Lynette was for thinking she could see and talk to her dead husband, I realized I was currently in no position to judge. I heard voices that weren't there, and hallucinated more horrible things than I could possibly have imagined before all this started. I felt a sudden surge of sympathy for the lady.

Lynette caught me looking and glared at me. I mouthed the words "I'm sorry," to her, then again to the empty seat beside her. Lynette's expression softened a little. Better than nothing, I thought.

A few more people came in, but no Cody. Finally, at nine o'clock on the dot, a man in a purple button-up shirt with no tie walked in. Right behind him came a big orderly. I already had mine standing behind me. This one took up post just inside the doorway as the man sat in the single chair facing us.

"Good morning, everyone," he said with just the barest trace of a Mexican accent.

"Good morning," mumbled a couple of my group mates. Most of them ignored him.

"We have a new friend with us here today, so we'll start our session by introducing ourselves." The man looked directly at me. Great, I thought. "I'm Dr. Sanchez," he said. "I organize this group session each morning, and am here to help facilitate open communication, and respect of one another's boundaries."

"Even Martin's?" one greasy-looking teen boy asked with a snicker.

"Even Martin's," Dr. Sanchez said with a warning look. He looked back to me. "Why don't you tell us your name, a little about yourself, and what brings you to us here at Brookview."

I hesitated, not sure I wanted to talk at all here, with these people, in this place. Dr. Sanchez gave me an encouraging smile and someone snickered.

"I'm Jackson," I started. "I play football for my school." There was a moment of doubt as I realized I wasn't at all sure beyond that how to describe myself.

"And what brings you to us, Jackson?" Dr. Sanchez urged.

"I guess I…" I looked around. I was going to get teased for this, probably from the greasy-looking kid, but Lynette seemed fine with Martin, and they expected everyone to be crazy here, so why not? "I hear voices." Sure enough, grease-boy snickered. Dr. Sanchez shot him another warning look.

"I heard you pass out in the shower, too," said the greasy kid.

"I have seizures sometimes," I replied defensively.

"All the girls got to check you out as they carried you crying like a baby down the hallway, your junk hanging out." The kid said.

"Greg, that's enough. Twenty points deducted." Dr. Sanchez said, making a note on his notepad.

"Hey, it's not my fault he ain't got much to look at." It was a totally pointless insult, but with everything else, it was just enough to push me beyond caring about my own consequences.

"Just because it's not as big as the one your dad shows you every night…" I snapped back.

Greg went past red rage in an instant as his face flushed white and he shook with fury. He leapt out of his chair and charged at me. We weren't more than ten feet apart to begin with, but the speed with which the orderlies got to him was awe-inspiring.

As someone who both tackled and was tackled by others on a frequent basis in my daily life, watching these two men move was almost poetic in speed and efficiency. Terrible as the moment was, I had to admire them.

My personal orderly had his massive arms locked tightly around me from behind before I knew what was happening, and the one near the door covered the few feet from there to Greg's fast-moving form before he could cut the distance between us in half, and took him down in a full flying tackle that would have made my coach weep tears of joy.

The pair went down through the metal chairs, knocking them out of the way as they fell. People dove in all directions to get out of their way. It can't have been more than two full seconds from my retaliatory remark and the orderlies' complete and total physical control of Greg and myself. For a long moment, everyone sat, or lay, perfectly still.

"That," I couldn't help but say, "was awesome…"

Lynette, far on the other side of the circle, grinned. The man who'd beat another man to death burst into laughter. Most of the others just got up and backed slowly away, hands up. I looked around for Sanchez. He was back in the doorway, eyes wide and his face almost as white as mine was. He looked ready to bolt.

I immediately realized that this man was terrified of us. He talked a good talk and played the game, but at the first sign of any trouble, he was ready to cut and run. My respect for him dropped several notches.

Meanwhile, my respect for the orderlies jumped up. The man who'd floored Greg stood, still holding the flailing boy, and moved for the door. Sanchez got out of his way awfully fast.

My own personal vice grip held me tightly enough that I had to keep my breaths shallow, until Greg was gone and the door shut behind him. The huge man's dark arms didn't even look like they were trying hard to hold me tightly enough to make my ribs ache.

"We cool?" asked the orderly in my ear. I nodded. I hadn't given him any resistance at all the whole time.

"Don't worry about me," I told him. "I'm cool."

Slowly the big man eased his grip and let me go. For several seconds he looked ready to come at me again if I so much as sneezed. After a moment, he relaxed.

"Thanks," he said.

"For what?" I asked, confused.

"For not fighting me. I hate when they fight me. Then I have to get rough."

I turned enough to look back at the burly black man squarely in the eyes.

"Trust me dude," I told him, "the absolute last thing on my list is to make you have to get rough with me. You guys are hardcore…" The guy gave me a slightly smug smile and nodded.

"All right kid, back to the rec room for you."

Once back in the rec room, I spotted Cody. He looked surprised to see me back.

"What's up? Thought you had group." he asked.

"I did. It let out early."

"Nothing lets out early around here. Or late. These people live and die by their schedules."

"Some kid named Greg tried to attack me."

"Are you serious?" Cody asked, suddenly very interested. I laughed at his sudden attention. Looked like a hound dog that had just caught a scent.

"Serious as a heart attack," I replied.

"What for?" he asked. I shrugged noncommittally. "Come on, man!" he urged with a laugh. "All I've got is gossip, don't rob me of my one remaining joy in life!" I couldn't help but laugh.

"Okay, okay! Don't be so dramatic." I said, grinning. "He made some stupid crack about my seizure yesterday morning. He wasn't even there and he was trying to make jokes about size. So I threw it back in his face. The joke, not my size," I clarified. Cody laughed.

"Thank God, you had me worried for a second there."

"Nah, he's not my type."

"Do you have a type?" he asked. I eyed him sidelong and he gave me a light shove.

"Oh come off it, I'm not into dudes," he said.

"I have a girlfriend," I told him, answering his question. "Blonde, hot, loves watching me play football."

"Pretty clear type. She a cheerleader?" he asked. I shook my head and he nodded, considering me. "Not the stereotype though. That's cool."

"Yeah, she's very cool," I replied. "How about you?" He shook his head.

"Too much time in a place like this doesn't do much for your chances at getting a good girl."

"You're looking for a good girl? Well there's your problem," I teased. He laughed, but shook his head.

"Yeah, I want a good girl," he affirmed. "I want love, not just sex. You got a problem with that?"

"Not me," I replied. "I'm with you, all jokes aside. Amber's like that for me."

"All love, no sex?" he asked, with a glint of mischief in his eye. I laughed.

"That's not what I meant. Just that I love her."

"That's cool. You're lucky."

"Not lucky enough to stay out of this joint," I said with a sigh.

"Makes two of us," he said, looking at his bandages. "If I'd been lucky, they wouldn't have found me for another fifteen minutes. Then I wouldn't be here either."

"Okay, so I know we haven't known each other that long, so it's cool if you don't want to talk about it, but I have to ask what was so bad that it pushed you to try and kill yourself?"

"You're right, we don't know each other that well," he said, looking away. He looked back again a moment later. "Besides, you never talk about you, either."

"What do you mean? You know I have seizures."

"You didn't mention the voices in your head," he replied. I hesitated. He had a point.

"It's kind of uncomfortable," I answered.

"Exactly."

"Okay, fine. I hear a voice. Not voices. It's the same voice all the time."

"Does it tell you to do things?" he asked with a grin. I ignored his poor attempt at a joke. The idea gave me chills.

"No, it doesn't talk directly to me. It's like it doesn't know I can hear it, like I'm eavesdropping on a conversation. Only the voice is only talking to itself."

"That's weird. I thought schizophrenics always involved themselves in their delusions."

"Schiziowhat?" I asked, thrown off track. I remembered Dr. Garner had used the same word, but I still didn't know what it meant.

"Schizophrenic," he explained. "It's what most people who hear voices or see people who aren't there and stuff have. Chemical imbalance in the brain, I think. Like Lynette."

"Like Lynette with Martin," I replied, thoughtfully. I wondered for a moment if that's what I had. It felt weird to potentially have a name for it. I didn't know if I should be reassured because it happened often, or discouraged. Sure didn't help Lynette. Maybe it was incurable, I thought. Maybe not.

"Yeah," he interrupted my thoughts. "Anyway, so this voice doesn't talk to you, or really to anyone else. Just itself. What does it say?"

"I don't know," I replied. "I mean, I know what it's

saying most of the time, even though it's really faint, like a whisper, but it's really random and broken. Like one minute she's talking about the season, the next she's talking about the flickering light. Then she turns around and counts down, and when she gets to one, I suddenly felt like my hands had been run over by a truck."

"She?" Cody asked, his mischievous grin back.

"That's the part in all of that you fixated on?" I asked him with a laugh. He laughed in return.

"Just messing with you, bro. Seriously though, that's really weird. It's almost like you really are hearing someone else. Weird circumstances. A flickering light? Sudden pain in the hands?"

"That's impossible. I'm sure it's schizophra-something, like you said. People don't hear other people unless they're right there."

"Cell phones," he replied. I rolled my eyes.

"That's not what I meant," I told him, annoyed.

"No, no, hear me out. Cell phones work by taking sound and converting it to a high-frequency signal, right? Then it transmits it out?" I nodded and he continued. "Then your phone, on the receiving end, picks up that signal, and translates it back into sound."

"Okay, so?" I asked, not sure where he was going with this train of thought, but interested despite myself.

"So what if something about this mystery girl's brain translates her thoughts or whatever into a high-frequency signal, that somehow your brain is then picking up, and translating back into sound?"

"That's not possible," I told him. "You need machines to do things like that. Devices, like phones."

"Not necessarily. Our eyes pick up light, which then

gets converted into an electrical signal, like digital, you know? Then our brains read the signal, and translate it into an image. Our brains do things like that all the time with all kinds of different input." I stared at him.

"You did really well in biology class, didn't you?" I stated more than asked. He laughed.

"I did really well in all of my classes until… you know."

"You can't seriously think I'm like reading someone's mind, can you?" I asked him. He shrugged.

"I used to watch this show that looked for people with unusual and superhuman powers."

"Your mother never taught you that TV isn't real?"

"This wasn't that kind of show. It was a documentary, sort of. Real people, real powers. Not like flight or invincibility or anything, but some were getting close. There was a guy who could hold his breath underwater for ten minutes. And one who could run forever without getting tired. Another guy could roll a metal frying pan up into a tight little burrito with his bare hands. And one guy could hold a bare wire plugged into the wall, and hold a light bulb in the other hand and it would light up. Freaky stuff."

"Wow," I told him dryly. "I think you belong in here." He shoved me in mock outrage. I laughed.

"Well, you can either believe that maybe you're actually a superhero or something with psychic powers, or you can believe that your brain is short circuiting and you're hearing things that aren't there. Your call, boss."

"I can't get better if I don't admit I'm sick."

"Boy, they got that one into you awfully fast," he replied, shaking his head.

"What?"

"'Step one to resolving a problem is admitting there's a problem'," he said in an impressive imitation of Dr. Fitzpatrick.

"I never heard anyone say that," I argued. "I just think that fighting against it will just make it harder to cure me."

"No cure for schizophrenia, my friend. Just drugs to help dull the hallucinations."

"Thanks, that's exactly what I needed to hear."

"Sorry," he said. I could tell he actually meant it, and I softened.

We sat quietly for a while, both lost in our own thoughts. Suddenly, he spoke again.

"So just humor me. What if you're hearing a real girl?"

"And seeing," I replied.

"What?" he asked, pausing at the new revelation.

"When I have my seizures. That only happens when I see her, too. Well, I don't actually see her, it's like I'm seeing through her eyes. See what she sees, hear what she hears," I hesitated. "Feel what she feels," I finished, waiting for the joke. It didn't come, and in that moment I recognized that Cody could be the kind of friend I desperately needed right then. He seemed to instinctively know when it was okay to tease.

"What do you see?" he asked somberly. For a moment, I thought that was the joke, but I looked at him for a long moment and could tell he was being completely serious.

"A tunnel. Long and dark, stone with packed earth on the bottom. There's a light in a little glass case with a metal frame. It's really faint and yellow, and flickers. I can see light at the end of the tunnel, but only during the day. It's totally dark when I see it at night. I can hear birds, and dripping water. And a couple of times I saw a man, but not very clearly. I couldn't like, see his face or anything."

"Is it always the tunnel?"

I was grateful he still hadn't asked what I felt when my mind went to that dark place.

"Always. Well, okay, not always," I corrected, remembering the oddly hazy visions when my whisper had started talking about her mother. "Once I saw a beach, and a street in a neighborhood, but those were different. I wasn't seeing it through her eyes, exactly. It was different, but I don't know how to explain it."

"Okay, so why is it always the tunnel?" he asked.

"I don't know," I replied, but that wasn't true. "I think, maybe, she might be handcuffed down there or something."

"Oh my God, Jackson…" Cody stared at me.

"What?"

"Okay, so we admit that what you see might be hallucinations caused by schizophrenia or something like that, right?"

"Right. It has to be, there's no other answer," I stubbornly argued.

"What if you've somehow tapped into the mind of someone in trouble? What if she's being held captive, and she's trapped there right now and needs your help? What if he's hurting her?" That hit a sore spot with me, in more ways than one.

"What if I'm just crazy, and I'm exactly where I belong?" I retorted defensively.

"Dude, what if you're not?"

Chapter Eleven
Miss Lewis

This was ridiculous, I thought. I stared at page fifteen of the insanely long "personality evaluation" they'd given me. It was hundreds of questions long, and they were weird, random questions. And they repeated with a slight rephrase with frustrating regularity.

One would ask if I preferred chocolate or vanilla ice cream. The very next page, twenty questions later, it would ask if I preferred vanilla or chocolate. Three more pages later and it would ask if my favorite ice cream flavor was chocolate or vanilla.

If I wasn't crazy before coming into this nightmare, this stupid test and those blasted checkered floors would have driven me there by now. Looking down the hallways, or staring at the floor in any of the rooms was alarmingly disorienting. Whoever had the bright idea to pick the most crazy-making floor pattern on the face of the planet was either an evil genius, or a complete moron.

This test was supposed to "help them help me", Dr. Fitzpatrick had told me. I had no idea how asking me my favorite ice cream flavor over and over, but only giving me the same two choices every time, was going to help them, but Dr. Fitzpatrick was insistent. What if I liked strawberry? Or butter pecan?

I'd been at this for over an hour already, and had another ten pages to go. Sighing deeply, I kept answering. I was tempted to just start picking answers randomly, but had a nagging suspicion that doing so would land me on another medication. They had me on three already, and they made my brain feel fuzzy, and my mouth dry.

They wouldn't give me free access to water, either. Like I was going to try and drown myself with the three ounces of water those tiny cups would hold. Three times a day they'd started giving me two of those cups. One of water, one with my pills in it.

The orderly, always one of the big guys, would stand and watch me take them, then make me open my mouth and stick my tongue out to prove I'd swallowed them. I'd been behaving and taking them without a fuss, for two reasons.

First, I hadn't heard the voice in two days, since my third dose. Second, I needed the points for good behavior to finally call my parents.

Four days in this place and I was completely convinced that my parents signing me out was the only way I was ever getting out of here. It had become painfully obvious to me already that this was not a place where people were sent to get better.

I had another group therapy session in an hour, I knew. I had to finish this test first, though. They'd removed Greg from the group and moved him elsewhere as he apparently became violent any time someone even suggested he come back to my group.

The fact that they moved him and not me told me

he'd probably had issues with more than just me in the group. With an attitude like his, that wasn't too surprising.

I felt like I should be agitated at the idea of running into him in the rec room, but at least one of the pills was making it hard for me to get emotionally worked up at all. Other than mild annoyance, like I currently felt while filling out this stupid evaluation, I was having trouble feeling much of anything besides hopelessness and depression.

Dr. Fitzpatrick told me one of the pills was for my depression, but it either wasn't working at all, or my depression was so intense that even a dulled-down version was worse than anything I'd ever experienced in my life.

I reminded myself that I could call my parents today, if I kept my points up. I hadn't lost points for anything since my first group therapy session when I got Greg all riled, where I hadn't actually earned any yet so they couldn't take any away anyway.

By the time I finished the test, my brain felt partially melted, just like the chocolate or vanilla ice cream that test seemed obsessed with. The poor orderly had been watching me the whole time I filled out the test, because apparently the short, dull little pencil they'd given me was a potential weapon. Death by golf pencil, I thought, would look awesome on an obituary. He immediately came over and took the pencil from me when I indicated I was finished.

"How do you do it, man?" I asked him. It was the big black guy from my first group session, so I felt a little more comfortable trying to talk to him than many of the others.

"Do what?" he asked.

"Sit there for two and a half hours, staring at someone to make sure they don't try to stab themselves to death with a golf pencil?"

"Gotta keep you guys safe," he replied with a shrug.

"I'm not going to hurt myself," I told him.

"I know," he told me, sounding sincere, "but it's my job to make sure."

I nodded and stood slowly, stretching. They'd given me my own socks, which felt a lot better than the hospital socks I'd started with. These gave me less traction on the crazy-making checkered linoleum, though. I headed for the door, which the orderly had opened for me.

"What's your name?" I asked him.

"Call me Rip," he replied simply as he fell into step behind me. "Group therapy in five," he added.

"Hi, Rip. Thanks for being cool," I told him. I didn't really know the guy, but he seemed a lot more chill than most of the orderlies around here.

"I'm cool as long as you are," he answered. I laughed as I headed for the group therapy room.

"Are you kidding? I'm the coolest guy in here."

"That's depressing," he told me with a slight smile.

"Ouch!" I replied, laughing again. "All right, I see how it's going to be."

I walked into the group therapy room to see Dr. Sanchez. He was still leading my first group therapy session each day, even though I was pretty sure that as skittish as he was he'd have a complete mental breakdown in a month.

"Hello everyone," Dr. Sanchez said with his annoyingly fake smile. "Today, we're going to talk about children. Jackson, why don't you start." I hesitated, confused.

"Umm… what?" I replied brilliantly.

"Children, Jackson. Our topic today is children. Tell us how you feel about children."

The new woman who'd started in our group yesterday was singing something softly. It was a creepy tune, and she sang it non-stop. Literally non-stop. She didn't even sleep, or so I'd heard. It was unsettling.

"I don't know," I replied, not sure what he wanted. "I'm fifteen, I don't have kids. I don't have any little brothers or sisters, either. I have an older brother, but he's in college and definitely doesn't count as a child. I guess I don't really care one way or the other."

"That's very interesting, Jackson," Dr. Sanchez said, turning to Alan, the man who'd supposedly killed someone with his bare hands. "Why don't you share your thoughts, Alan?"

He'd been really quiet and calm every time I'd seen him, in group and in rec. I was starting to doubt the rumors about what he'd been sent here for. This place was really bad about rumors. He looked upset right now, though. Controlled, but not happy about this subject at all.

"I don't want to talk," Alan replied.

"Come now, Alan," Dr. Sanchez urged in his most condescending tone, like he was trying to talk a three-year-old into eating his Cheerios. "It's important that we all share and connect here. This is a safe place."

Alan snorted, and folded his arms. They stared each other down for several long, boring minutes before Dr. Sanchez caved and started talking to someone else.

We spent the whole hour with everyone just talking

about how they felt about children. I was baffled. I had no idea how this was supposed to be helpful. Nobody was allowed to talk more than a few minutes before Dr. Sanchez cut them off and started asking how everyone felt about what they had just said.

Just another aspect of this place that was enough to drive someone crazy, I thought to myself. I had to close my eyes to keep from staring at the floor in boredom. When I did stare at the floor for longer than a few seconds, I started getting dizzy and disoriented. I wasn't sure if that was all the floor, or if that was due partly to the medications, but either way it wasn't a pleasant feeling.

After group, I got to go to the rec room. I knew Cody would be there. He was sitting at the chess board, moving a piece when I walked in. That chess board was another weird thing I'd never seen before. Not a chess board, I'd seen plenty of those, but a chess board where nobody seemed to actually be playing it. Randomly, people would walk past and make a move.

It was never the same person who made the move either, and I figured by this point ten or twelve different people were all playing this game, just picking which side they wanted to move at random, regardless of turn order.

Singing lady walked past me on the way into the room. She always watched the tiny, caged, closed-captioned TVs, all while still singing. Gave me chills when she walked past, that eerie tune on her lips.

Cody saw me and waved with a smile. I headed over and sat down. I wasn't followed this time by an orderly. I'd passed my seventy-two-hour observation period, so was allowed to be unescorted, though only in public areas like this.

"'Sup," I said as I sat next to him on the couch in front of the chess board.

"Hey," he replied, studying the board.

"Dude, what's with the chess board?" I asked him.

"It's a chess board. What about it?" he asked.

"Who's playing?"

"Whoever wants to, I guess."

"Who's winning?" I asked.

"I am," he replied.

I looked at the board. It didn't make much sense to me. I knew how to play chess, basically, but I wasn't one of those prodigies who could see like eight moves ahead. Even the idea of that blew my mind.

"Which one are you?" I asked, not looking away from the board.

"Whichever one is winning," he answered. I looked up at him and he laughed.

"I don't know, man. It's just one of the weird quirks around here. This game has been going on for weeks. When someone finally wins, someone will reset the board. I think an orderly does it at night, because I've never seen it get reset. It just happens. People just come by and play a move. I don't know why."

"You just played a move," I told him.

"Yeah."

"Why?" I asked.

"I don't know," he replied. I laughed and gave him a light shove.

"You are crazy," I told him. He nodded.

"Yeah. I love chess, though."

"Really?" I asked, curious. Cody didn't share much about himself, so this was a nice opening.

"Yeah," he replied. "I used to compete."

"Like professional chess?" I asked, not sure there was such a thing.

"No, just at my school club. We'd play against other school clubs."

"I get it, so you were a nerd," I teased. He gave me a look and I knew he didn't appreciate the joke.

"Just because you're a jock doesn't give you the right to make fun of the kids who aren't," he snapped defensively. I held up both hands in surrender.

"Sorry, I was just joking. I don't have anything against it."

"Then don't joke about it."

"No problem," I replied.

We were quiet for several moments, and I could feel his anger was still there. I didn't want to leave it like that.

"Seriously though," I told him, "I'm sorry. I didn't mean anything by it. I might be a jock, but I don't bully anyone, and I don't make fun of people. Not my scene. I was just teasing you a little because we're friends."

"Are we?" he asked, looking over at me. It sounded challenging, but I could see the hope in his eyes.

"Sure, bro," I told him. "We've got each other's backs, right?" He nodded. "And we hang out together, right?" He nodded again. "There ya go. That's friends."

"Yeah, it is." He smiled at me. It started to feel a little uncomfortable, so I turned back to the board. I was about to say something when Dr. Tilton, my after-lunch solo session therapist, appeared and interrupted.

"Mr. Holt?" she said. I looked up. "You may make your phone call now." I looked to Cody, who nodded encouragingly as I stood. He stood as well, and Dr.

Tilton misinterpreted the movement. "You can remain here, Miss Lewis."

I frowned at the psychiatrist as I followed her, glancing back at Cody, sure I'd misunderstood. If I hadn't, that was a really lousy thing for a shrink to make fun of a patient like that. Sure, Cody wasn't the most butch kid I'd ever met, but he was all right. This placed sucked, I thought for possibly the millionth time since waking up that morning.

Chapter Twelve
Phone Call

Walking into her office, she sat down and pulled an old rotary phone out from under the desk. I stared at the thing.

"What's that?" I asked.

"A telephone," she replied, like she was talking to a very small child. The staff did that a lot around here, I'd noticed.

"Thank you, Captain Obvious," I replied. She frowned.

"Careful, Mr. Holt. I can take you to zero just like that," she threatened. She meant my points, and that would take away my phone call.

"Sorry," I replied, preferring to swallow my pride than lose my phone call. I'd waited four days for this call. "I just have no idea how to use one of these kinds of phones."

"I have your parents' number here. I'll dial for you. Fifteen minutes, and not a second longer," she told me as she began dialing the number written in the open file on the desk in front of her. Those files looked an awful lot like the criminal record files I'd seen in cop shows, I thought. I didn't like the comparison.

Watching her dial the antique phone was

fascinating. She'd put her finger in a little hole on the numbered circle and spin the circle all the way around and let go. The disc would then spin slowly back to its starting position with a rapid clicking noise.

She started a little stopwatch to one side the moment the first ring sounded. She pressed a button on the phone and a small speaker built into the front clicked on.

I wouldn't even have privacy on my parents' end, I realized. Not that I really expected any different. Privacy wasn't exactly in ample supply around here.

The phone rang four times, several seconds each time, several seconds delay between. I watched the stopwatch tick down. I suddenly realized they may not answer. They may not know I was going to be able to call them today at all. I had no idea how much they'd been told about the rules and my status here. A click on the other end sounded.

"Hello?" came my mother's voice.

"Mom?" I asked, suddenly feeling my throat tighten and tears come to my eyes. I hadn't realized how much I'd missed her until that moment. I was desperate to be back home with her again.

"Jackson!" she cried. She didn't hold back. I heard her gasp out a sob as she said my name. "How are you, baby?" she asked me, fighting through the tears to speak.

"I'm okay, Mom," I reassured her. I didn't think I was at all, but I needed to ease her into it. I swallowed hard to get control of my own tears.

"Are they taking good care of you?" she asked.

"I'm fed, clean, and clothed, Mom."

"That's not what I mean, but it's good to hear

anyway."

"I want to come home," I told her plainly.

"I know, baby. I want you home too. We have to get you better first, though."

"This place won't make me better."

"Come on now, Jackson, you haven't even given it a chance. It's not that bad, is it?"

"Remember Camp Holloway?" I said. She laughed in surprise.

"I remember."

"This is worse," I told her seriously. Her laughter died almost immediately.

"Oh, honey. It'll get better as you get better," she said naïvely. I didn't respond for a while. I watched the timer tick several more precious seconds away.

"How's Dad?" I finally asked.

"He's fine. He misses you, too."

"And Brent?" I asked about my older brother.

"He's doing well, too. Says he always knew you were crazy," she said in a tone that made it clear she didn't approve of the message. I laughed. That was Brent, all right.

"Tell him he's the one that should be in here. Met a great gal in here, by the way. She'd make him a great girlfriend. Lovely singing voice."

"Oh, you two!" Mom said with an uncertain laugh.

"Seriously though, Mom," I said after another awkward pause, "please get me out of here. I can keep taking the medication they're giving me. I haven't had an episode since they started me on these. They work great. I'll just keep taking the medications and we'll all be fine. I don't need to be here." The last few sentences came out in an almost panicked rush. She didn't respond for a long while.

"Jackson, I know you hate it there. But they're all there to help you. We are here to help you. You have to stick it out, just like Camp Holloway. You can do it. I know you can. Just focus on getting better, so you can come home."

"I can come home now, Mom! Just come get me!"

"I can't, baby," she said, crying again.

"Mom!" I shouted. Dr. Tilton started to gesture toward the door. "This place is crazier than I am! They won't even let me pee in privacy, and some kid attacked me in group! You've got to come ge…"

"Jackson," she interrupted in her no-nonsense mom voice, "you will be fine. Just focus on getting better. Dr. Fitzpatrick says we can come visit you in a few weeks. You can hold on until then."

"Mom, I…"

"Goodbye Jackson. I love you," she said.

"Mom, wait!" I heard the line go dead, then the dull tone of the phone rang long and steady. I looked at the timer. I still had seven minutes left. I looked back to Dr. Tilton.

"I have seven minutes left. Can I make another call?"

"I'm sorry Mr. Holt, but you're already overly excited. We'll try again another day."

I stared at her, stunned, as the orderly came in behind me and took me by the arm, helping me rather forcefully to my feet and out the door. He escorted me back to the rec room. Cody looked up as I came in, but his eyes went down again quickly. That was weird, I thought. Moving over to him, I sat down beside him again.

"That was fast," he said. He didn't sound quite right. I almost missed it though, focused on that call.

"She hung up on me," I told him, still in shock.

"Who did? Your girlfriend?" he said with a slightly teasing, but still uncomfortable tone.

"My Mom," I told him, still too shaken to make a joke, or to respond to his. His awkward smile faded.

"Oh man, I'm sorry. I remember the first time my dad did that when I first got here."

"Seriously?" I asked, looking over at him. He nodded, not looking at me.

"Yeah. I freaked out a little, demanded he come get me out. Shut me down cold."

"That's exactly what my mom did," I said, surprised. He nodded.

"They say it's for our own good, putting us here. They don't know what it's like though, and they won't let us tell them."

"What do you mean?" I asked, a feeling of dread sinking in.

"Any time you start to badmouth this place, the doctors cut off phone calls and visits, saying you're getting too emotional. Your parents let them do it, because the doctors tell them you need to not get so emotionally excited. I hate to say it, Jackson, but you're stuck here."

I sat back against the couch, overwhelmed. I was stuck here. Possibly forever.

"You said you'd been in here a couple of times. How did you get out?"

"Insurance ran out," he said. I stared at him, open-mouthed.

"You've got to be kidding me. Seriously? So as long

as my insurance still pays them, they'll keep me here forever?"

"Pretty much."

"They can't do that!" I almost shouted. Cody looked around nervously and made a shushing gesture with his hand.

"Easy, Jackson. Going to get yourself on lockdown."

"I'm stuck here forever," I said, half to myself as I put my head in my hands. "My dad says our insurance is awesome."

"I'm sorry," Cody said quietly.

We sat quietly for several minutes before heading in to lunch together. We'd gotten our food and been eating for a few minutes, me stewing in the hopelessness of my situation before something random came back to me, interrupting my self-pity session.

"Hey, so what was with Dr. Tilton? Pretty lousy thing to say, calling you a girl like that," I told him. He didn't look at me, and his face flushed.

"Not that bad," he said.

"Why is that not bad?" I asked, confused and suddenly sure I was missing something. I took another bite of something that was either macaroni and cheese, or taco salad.

"Because I am a girl, sort of," he told me, voice forlorn. I stared at him, stunned into silence for the third time in ten minutes.

"What?" I finally got out.

"I'm trans," Cody said. "I'm biologically female, but I identify as male. The flak I get all the time over it are what cause my depression. The doctors here insist everyone refer to me by the 'correct' gender. They won't acknowledge that I'm male. It's so hard being stuck in the wrong body, Jackson. You have no idea."

"No, I really don't," I answered honestly.

It explained the depression, for sure. I'd never actually met anyone who was trans before. Cody didn't look anything like the few I'd seen on TV, though. He looked like a boy. Like a normal fifteen-year-old boy.

"I understand if you don't want to be friends anymore," he said in the smallest, saddest voice I think I'd ever heard.

"Are you attracted to me?" I asked him after another pause for thought. His eyes snapped up sharply, flashing angry. His plastic spoon snapped in half on the table as he slammed it down.

"What the hell, Jackson? Don't think so much of yourself. I'm not into dudes, and definitely wouldn't be into you even if I were."

"I'm not into you either," I said simply.

"What the hell do I care? I told you I'm not into you!" he was getting angrier, and totally missing my point. I realized my teasing was too much and I'd better clarify fast, before he got into trouble. He'd attracted the attention of one of the orderlies who was easing toward us. I leaned across the table toward him and spoke very clearly, and softly enough that only he could hear.

"Cody, if you're not into me, and I'm not into you, what do I care what you've got in your pants?"

Cody froze, staring at me for several long seconds. I watched in amused fascination as the emotions played across his face. First shock, then confusion, then realization, then amusement. He broke into laughter.

"Jackson, you're an asshole," he said breathlessly. I

laughed with him.

"Wait, I'm an asshole? Why, because I don't care that you're trans? I'll bet you'd have called me the same thing if I'd told you I thought it was wrong or unnatural or some other junk. A guy can't win around here!" I exclaimed in mock-exasperation. He laughed again.

"Sorry man, but you really had me going there. I thought you were going to be like everyone else."

"Cody, if I were like everyone else, I wouldn't be in this dive." I watched the orderly pause, watch us for a moment, then go back to his position near the door. Crisis averted, I thought with relief.

"Good point," he replied, taking a bite of the mysterious substance we were being fed. "So we're cool?"

"Yeah, we're cool," I told him. "Should I still call you bro?"

"It would mean a lot if you did," he answered, a little awkwardly.

"Don't get all sappy on me, now. Bro it is, then. Just making sure that was cool," I told him. He nodded gratefully, and went back to his food.

"You going to call your mom again tomorrow?" he asked, changing subjects.

His whole demeanor had changed. He seemed suddenly so much more open and relaxed than he ever had before. I couldn't imagine, him trying to keep that secret from me, even for only a few days, because he was afraid I'd turn on him the moment I found out. Blew my mind that some people could be that cruel.

"No," I replied.

"I'm sorry," he said somberly. I nodded.

"I think I'll call my girlfriend, though. Maybe try my dad day after tomorrow."

"Good idea," he told me, brightening.

"It'll be good to hear her voice."

"I'm jealous. Not about your girlfriend; unless she's seriously hot, anyway. Just of what you've got with her. It's cool. Must be really nice."

"Well, she is all kinds of hot, so be jealous about her all you want. I hear you, though. She's amazing, and it's really a comfort to know she's out there waiting for me, if I ever get out of here."

"Don't worry. If you go long enough without any episodes, they'll have to send you home, because insurance will stop paying out. Just keep reminding your parents how much better you're doing." I took a bite and thought for a while.

"So I have to ask," I started, changing subjects. Cody paused with his broken spoon halfway to his mouth. "If you're biologically female but identify as male and are into girls, does that make you gay or straight? And if you identify as a guy and you actually were into guys, would *that* make you gay, or straight? Very confusing."

Cody laughed and shook his head.

"Asshole."

Chapter Thirteen
Night Terrors

It took three days to get to talk to Amber. The orderlies had decided they were out to get everyone all riled up, and there were several fights and incidents between patients the previous two days.

I tried to intervene and break up the first one, and they took away my points for it. I stayed out of the second one entirely… and they took away my points for it. I was learning awfully fast which orderlies were dangerous, and which were safe. They were sometimes harder to tell apart than my fellow patients.

On that third day after my phone call to my mother, Mrs. Morris was on duty. I was reminded once more why I liked her. It really was remarkable how the entire rec room calmed way down when she was on duty.

I didn't know what it was about her, but she just made everyone feel safer, less agitated. Some of the other orderlies, like those on duty the past few days, seemed to get a sick pleasure from getting the patients agitated and unsettled.

I'd watched one laughing as he beat a patient with his billy club. The patient had attacked him, but only because the orderly had been intentionally aggravating the guy.

With her on duty, it was really easy for almost everyone to earn enough points to get their privileges for the day. I sat with Dr. Tilton in her office, as the stern woman dialed the rotary phone. I'd had to give her the number, since it wasn't in my file. Luckily, I'd memorized it months ago. Even more luckily, Amber's name was on the list of approved contacts my mother had apparently given them.

One ring. Two rings. Then the click of a picked up line.

"Hello?" she asked, in a voice that told me she hadn't recognized the number on the caller ID.

"Hi, Amber," I said, suddenly nervous now that I was actually talking with her.

"Jacks!" she said enthusiastically. There was something off, though. I couldn't quite place it.

"How's it going?" I asked.

"Good, thanks. You?" she replied.

"Been better. It sure is good to hear your voice, though."

"You too," she agreed, though again something sounded off.

"Is this a bad time?" I asked her, trying to figure out what was going on.

"No, no, this is fine," she said hesitantly.

"What's wrong?" I asked, now certain something was up.

"Nothing. It's just that…"

"Just that what?"

"I didn't want to do it like this," she muttered to herself. "Jackson, we need to break up."

"What?!" I looked up at Dr. Tilton, embarrassed. She was casually pretending she couldn't hear the call at all. Small favors, I thought.

"I'm sorry Jacks, I didn't mean for it to go this way."

"What way? That I'd get locked up against my will for a week and you'd immediately ditch me?"

"It's not like that, Jacks," she said pleadingly.

"Is there someone else?" I asked.

"Of course not!" she said firmly. "It's just that… you don't know what people are saying."

"Are you seriously breaking up with me because of what people are saying about me?"

"Not just you!" she insisted. I felt ill.

"Oh. I get it. You're not breaking up with me because of what they're saying about me. You're breaking up with me because of what they're saying about you for being with me."

"It's really hard…"

"You think it's a cakewalk over here? I've been working all week to *earn* the right to call you, just to hear your voice! You have no idea what it's like in this place, Amber."

"I'm sorry, Jackson."

"Me too. Well, enjoy your life, then."

"What we had…" she began, before I interrupted.

"If you're ending it like this because of something like that, we didn't have what I thought we had anyway. Later, Amber."

I reached out and pressed the button on top to hang up. Dr. Tilton nodded to the side and the orderly moved right in. I still had ten minutes left. I didn't even bother to try and ask. I just stood and went with him back to the rec room. Cody had gone for his personal session, so I was alone, relatively speaking, once I got there. Mrs. Morris saw me, and presumably my expression, and came over within moments, however.

"You okay, honey?" she asked. I shrugged. "Come on, now. You can tell me."

"Girlfriend just dumped me. Been in here a lousy week and she's had enough."

"Oh, that's a shame," Mrs. Morris said sincerely. I just nodded. "I'm sorry, honey. Sometimes things just don't work out. My mother used to always tell me that you find out awful quick who your real friends were when things get bad."

"She wasn't as good a friend as I thought, I guess."

"Hard way to learn it, but better now than ten years down the road."

"That's true, I suppose." I looked up at her.

"Mrs. Morris?"

"Hmm?"

"Thanks," I told her. She smiled and nodded.

"Sure thing. You just let me know if you need anything."

"I will."

It wasn't long after that I asked to be taken to my room. It was still early, before dinner, but I wasn't hungry anyway. My parents had abandoned me, my girlfriend had dumped me, and I was destined to spend the rest of my life slowly becoming the old guy who always sat in a wheelchair in one corner in a shirt soaked with his own drool. I lay down on the bed.

To my surprise, I fell asleep and began to dream almost immediately.

———

I was walking through the park with my friend Rachel, we hugged and said goodbye as we reached the far end, each of us going a different route home from there.

I had made it several blocks further down the road when someone had come around from an alley that I usually passed by on the way home, even though it was technically a shortcut.

It was a sheriff. He saw me, and frantically gestured me over. I broke into a run and approached him.

"What's wrong?" I asked, noting the urgency in his manner.

"Hana, your little brother is hurt. He needs your help." The sheriff said.

I didn't hesitate. I ran right alongside him as he ducked back into the alley to head toward my house. He knew my name, he knew my brother, he knew where I lived, and he was a sheriff. I never hesitated.

Not far from the end of the alley, something struck me in the back of the head. As I fell, I could see the sheriff, who had fallen slightly behind me, holding his billy club.

Confused, stunned, and hurt, I hit the ground hard. In less than a second, he was on me, and a black bag went down over my head and cuffs snapped tightly on my wrists pulled violently behind my back.

All I could think in that instant was whether my family was okay. Another sharp blow to the head, then everything went dark.

In what seemed an instant, I was somewhere else. I could hear a faint trickle of water right next to me. The floor was cold and hard.

As I shifted position to sit up, the sound of the

clinking chain at my wrists echoed through the dark tunnel. There was only a small, yellow bulb a few yards down the stone tunnel I seemed to be in.

Movement to one side caused me to yelp. It took me only a moment to recognize the man who crouched beside me. It was him. He was staring at me with hatred and loathing in his eyes.

"What's going on?" I whimpered.

"You think you're better than me," he stated.

"What? I don't even…" my head rocked as he slapped me, quick as a snake.

"Don't talk back to me, girl. You belong to me now, and I'm going to teach you how much better than you I am."

"You can't…" I began, but another sickeningly hard slap shook my skull.

"Shut up!" he yelled.

"Help!" I screamed when I could catch my breath. Another slap and my vision blurred for a moment.

"Nobody can hear you, Hana. Nobody but me will ever hear you again," he said, leaning in to whisper the sinister words. The hatred in his eyes was terrifying.

"What are you going to do?" I asked. I braced for the expected slap. Surprisingly, he let me finish the question.

"I'm going to make you scream, Hana. For the rest of your life, all you'll know is the pain I bring you. Just a taste of the suffering I've endured in my life."

"Is my family…" I tasted blood this time as my head rocked, and for a moment I wondered if he'd loosened some of my teeth with that last slap. I sobbed a choking, gasping noise at the pain.

"Your family will suffer too, their precious little

princess taken from them." Thank God, I thought. They were okay. They would find me. "They'll get over it, though. Nobody will miss you for long. Your pain, Hana, is just beginning."

He stood, slowly, and began to remove his belt. I stared at the rattlesnake etched into the silver of the over-sized buckle. I didn't comprehend what was happening. At least not until he drew a knife and began cutting away my clothing.

Realization began to dawn. I screamed, and the lonely echo of the sound rang back to me from the long, empty tunnel.

He was right. My pain was only beginning.

———

I woke up still screaming. I gasped for breath and I rolled off my mattress on the floor and onto my hands and knees as I tried to keep myself from vomiting.

My heart raced in my chest, seeming faster than any heavy metal drum riff I'd ever heard. I was covered in sweat, and was dizzy and nauseated. Despite the sweat, I was shaking like I was freezing.

I waited for a moment to hear the keys in the door, but nobody came. I didn't know what time it was, but someone should have been on duty.

It took a moment to realize I wasn't the only one screaming in this hallway. Distantly, muffled as it came through the sound-dampening door, I could hear at least two others screaming as well. No help would be coming tonight.

I pulled the blanket from the damp mattress and curled up on top of it on the cold, bare floor. Shaking, afraid, lost and alone, I had lost everything. But now I knew something I hadn't known before. Something that somehow changed everything.

Her name was Hana.

Chapter Fourteen
Allies

The next morning, after lying awake all night thinking about her, I had the beginnings of a plan. Everything I had dreamt, everything I experienced while having my seizures before the medication, had all felt so real.

The more I thought about it, the more convinced I became that the whisper in my mind wasn't an illness, or an imbalance. Somehow, just like Cody had said, I was certain that I was connecting with someone. Someone that needed my help.

The nightmare from the night before kept replaying in my head. She was a girl, quite a bit younger than I was. Maybe eleven years old, judging from what her friend, Rachel, had looked like. She had parents and a little brother. And she had been abducted by a sheriff.

Held captive, she was being tortured. Violently, sexually, psychologically tortured. Nobody knew where she was. I didn't know either, I had to remind myself. They could be clear across the country. Definitely an American sheriff, but beyond that I had no idea. I knew she was in a tunnel, but that could be any of millions of places.

I had a two bigger problems to deal with first,

however. First, I was locked in this place and drugged out so I couldn't hear her. Second, even if I weren't already diagnosed insane and stuck in a nuthouse, nobody would believe me even if I told them.

Someone would believe me though, I thought with hope. I knew who would believe me.

"Cody!" I called out as I went into the cafeteria and saw him sitting in his usual spot. He smiled and waved.

"Pancakes today," he said with an enthusiastic nod.

They only did pancakes once a week or so, seemingly at random, and oddly they were pretty good. I mean, I wouldn't take them over any restaurant or home-cooked pancakes, but I'd take them every single time over the garbage they normally served. I wouldn't touch the scrambled eggs alongside the pancakes on Cody's plate to save my life, for example.

"Nice!" I said, heading to grab some food before returning to sit across from my friend.

"So how's the girlfriend?" he asked. I almost choked on my first bite of pancake. "Woah, easy. That good, huh?"

"She broke up with me."

"Seriously?" he asked incredulously. "Man, you can't catch a break!"

"You're telling me."

"So what now?" he asked.

I knew what he meant, but I chose to take it as a lead in to what I really wanted to talk to him about. I glanced around to make sure nobody could overhear. I leaned in close to him just in case.

"Now I escape," I told him. His eyes got wide and he looked around us in a panic.

"Are you insane?" he asked in a harsh whisper that

probably carried much further than his regular voice would have.

"Apparently," I answered with a smirk.

"Dude, seriously, you can't do that!"

"I have to, Cody."

"They'll chase you to the ends of the earth! They'll drop you like a bad habit if your insurance runs out, but bolt before their checks stop coming in and it'll be worse than escaping from prison!"

"Cody, listen to me." Cody stopped and listened, to my mild surprise. "You were right."

"I often am. About what?"

"The girl. The one I hear in my head."

"How do you mean?" he asked, appearing confused, but I could see the excitement of his realization building in his face. He wasn't stupid, that was for sure.

"She's real. I dreamt about her last night."

"Not to play devil's advocate, Jackson, but I dream about a lot of hot girls. Doesn't mean they're real."

"No, this was different. She really was kidnapped. I saw the whole thing through her eyes." My tone was getting more and more intense and anxious. "She was walking home from school and some psycho kidnapped her. A cop, Cody! A frickin' cop!"

"No way…" he said in awe.

"The guy lured her into an alley and clubbed her over the head. How messed up is that! He's got her locked in that tunnel I kept seeing. He hurts her, Cody. Bad. I need to find her and help her."

"Okay, so say I believe you," he began. I could see it in his eyes. He not only believed me, he was already trying to figure out how to help me escape. "How do we get you out of here?"

"Well the easiest ways are either to get my parents to let me out of here, or wait for my insurance to run out. Insurance probably won't run out for a while, but I might be able to get my parents to get me out when they come visit in a couple of weeks. That's a long time for her to wait, though. She's hurting bad, Cody."

"Okay, so we'll use your parents as a backup then, while we come up with another plan. Can you talk to the girl? Tell her to hold on?"

"I don't think she can hear me," I told him. "I hear her, or used to before they started drugging me up, but she can't hear me."

"Have you ever tried?"

"Well, no. But I couldn't do it now anyway, with these drugs in my system. I don't know how she reached me last night. I don't hear her anymore during the day."

"So stop taking the pills, man," he told me, like it was the easiest thing in the world.

"How am I supposed to do that? They watch me take them, then make me open my mouth and show them under my tongue to be sure I swallowed them."

Instead of answering me directly, Cody picked up a bean from his plate, put it in his mouth, and swallowed. He then opened his mouth, and stuck out his tongue, moving it around so I could see he didn't have the bean hiding anywhere. He then closed his mouth for a moment, then opened it again and the bean was just sitting there on his tongue.

"How did you do that?" I asked, impressed. He demonstrated how he'd stashed the bean between his upper cheek and the upper gums on one side. "That's a bit scary." He smirked.

"I've never had to do it myself, but I've been around enough to know several of the people here do. No idea why the staff hasn't caught on. Maybe they have, and just don't care, I don't know."

"Either way, it helps. What do I do with the pills after, though?"

"Spit them in the toilet next time you go to take a leak."

"They watch me all the time. They even come in and watch me pee," I told him, my expression clearly showing my disgust. He made a similar face.

"That's nasty."

"Yeah."

"Okay, well you know the buttons on your mattress?" I stretched uncomfortably to show I did indeed.

"Yeah, I hate those things. Who designed those mattresses?"

"Right? Anyway, right where the button is stitched onto the fabric there's a hole just big enough to stuff a pill into the mattress. You can't do that forever, but you could probably manage it for a few weeks before someone noticed. Hopefully we'll have you out of here long before it becomes a problem."

"I'm starting to seriously worry about you," I laughed. He shrugged.

"Time in the joint changes a man," he said with a grin.

"I'll say," I agreed.

"I'll help," came a deeper voice from behind me. Alan, the bare-handed killer, sat down beside us.

"What?" I asked, trying to ask casual.

"You need out. I need a favor. You help me, I help you."

"I don't know what you're talking about," Cody said.

"Save it, kid. I have ears like a bat, and you two suck at being quiet. Luckily it's pretty active in here today, since I doubt anyone else heard you."

"If you tell anyone," Cody started to threaten, but Alan interrupted.

"I don't want to tell anyone, kid. I want your help. You help me, I'll help you. It's that simple."

"Why should we trust you? You killed a guy with your bare hands," I said, probably foolishly.

Cody's eyes went wide as I said it. Alan leaned close to me, his dark brown eyes looking almost black, and very menacing.

"Yeah, kid. I did. And I'd do it again if that situation ever came up. Maybe one of these days I'll tell you about it, but for now, you have two choices. You can ditch the escape idea altogether because you don't trust me and I might sell you out, or you can have a little faith in me based on the facts that I'm just as stuck here as you are, and that I'm not asking to go with you."

"You're not?" Cody asked in surprise.

"No, I'm not."

"What do you want, then?" I asked, confused.

"Take a letter to my daughter."

"That's it?" I asked, surprised.

"That's it," he agreed. "Promise me you'll deliver my letter to my daughter before you go off and do whatever else it is you're planning. Promise me that, and I'll help you get out of here."

I looked at Cody, and we wordlessly swapped a few messages back and forth. Cody was not in favor of this plan. Something about Alan's voice when he talked about his daughter made me disagree, however.

"Deal," I told him, holding out my hand. Cody made an exasperated sound. Alan grinned and shook my hand.

"Deal," he repeated. "I know how to do this, but it'll take a couple of weeks."

"We can't wait that long!" I protested.

"Kid, do you want out or not? If you try anything before a week from Sunday, I can practically guarantee you'll get busted. Did you hear that Lucille tried to kill herself two days ago? Broke the sink in one of the bathrooms and tried to stab herself to death with a piece of the porcelain. No idea how she broke it, those things aren't fragile. Anyway, her whole wing is on double security, which means all the other wings are on alert, too. Besides, I already have a perfect plan, but it will only work a week from Sunday."

"Fine, we'll wait. But I want to hear the plan," Cody said.

Alan opened his mouth to speak, but a horrible shrieking from across the cafeteria pulled all three of our gazes. One of the older women was screaming an awful, ear-splitting, inhuman sound.

She suddenly spun and began slamming her head face-first against the brick wall. She only got three hits in before the orderly tackled her, but there was a splattering of blood on the wall when she went down.

"What the…" I shouted in a panic as I scrambled to my feet and backed away.

"Easy," Alan told me, putting a hand on my

shoulder. Rather than threatening, the gesture felt very comforting. I appreciated the gesture, but I was still pretty freaked out.

"Wh… why?" I stammered, horrified.

"Some people are broken, kid. That's all there is to it. This world is hard, and very scary. Her husband committed suicide last week. It was gruesome, and she found him. Word is, she was unstable to begin with, and that sent her way over the edge. I imagine right now, she's just trying to get back to her husband the only way she knows how."

"How do you know that?" I asked him, surprised. We watched as she was carried, unconscious, out of the room.

"Something you need to understand about people, kid. Everyone has a story. Some are funny. Some are tragic, or unbelievable. Some barely make any sense. But everyone has a story. The people in here aren't in here for no reason, and most of them were normal at one point. Bad things happened to bring most of us here. Remember that, kid. Just slapping the crazy label on someone as a way to ignore the problem doesn't do anyone any good. We're so much more complex than that. That lady is hurting inside, and nobody is helping her, they've just locked her away and threw drugs at her brain. Welcome to the system, kid. We'll talk about the plan later. You two just make sure you have enough points to go to the activity a week from Sunday, or the whole plan is blown."

He walked away as a veritable army of psychiatrists and orderlies flooded into the room to escort people back to their own rooms.

"I can't believe we just had a conversation with the

dude that crushes heads with his bare hands," Cody said, "and he's going to *help* us."

"He's in my therapy group," I explained. "We haven't ever talked before, and he doesn't talk much in group, but whatever he did to get put in this place, I think he did it for her."

"For who?" Cody asked, confused.

"His daughter."

Chapter Fifteen
Complications

After that lady had tried to bash her own face in, we were all banned from rec time for the next few days as everyone underwent emergency counseling to help them deal with the trauma. It was crazy how much the tension built without the one, incredibly small comfort of being allowed time in the rec room.

The emergency counseling was a joke, like everything else around this place. It had been fifteen minutes with one of the interns, who had tried to determine how I felt about the incident, offered to let me talk about it if I wanted to, then making a few notes on her notepad, she told me to remember to discuss my feelings with my therapist at my next session.

My sessions, with Dr. Tilton, were just as much of a waste of time. She never actually asked me what I thought about anything. Her questions were always the same.

"How are you feeling?"

"Fine, I guess."

"Just fine?"

"Yeah."

"Do you feel like the medications are helping you?"

"I guess. I don't hear the voice anymore." I didn't

explain to her about the dream.

"That's good. Any side effects?"

"I get dizzy if I stand up too fast, and my mouth is always dry. Can I have some water?"

"After your session," she answered.

"Okay."

"Have you had any violent tendencies this week?"

"I had the urge to punch President Kennedy," I told her, bored and frustrated. She started writing. "Wow, I was kidding. No, no violent tendencies." She looked up at me and considered me a long moment before crossing out the line she'd just written.

"How has it been talking with your family?"

"You're always here, why do you even need to ask that?"

"Just trying to learn how you feel about talking with them," she explained. I rolled my eyes.

"Fine, I guess. I've only talked to my mom twice now. I don't know what you guys told her after my first call with her, but she won't talk to me about anything real. It's all superficial."

"We haven't spoken to her, Mr. Holt."

"Not even to let her know how I'm doing?"

"That's what your phone calls are for."

"Do I get to see them a week from Saturday?"

"That's entirely up to you. So what would you like to talk about?"

"What was up with the lady trying to kill herself in the cafeteria yesterday?"

"She's doing much better now."

"Yeah, but what was going on there?"

"She's struggling to cope with a personal loss, Mr. Holt."

"The emergency counselor said I should talk to you about it."

"I don't really think that's appropriate, and not really any of your business." I was shocked, though by this point I shouldn't have been. There wasn't a single thing about this place that was designed to actually help anyone. Emergency counselor told me to talk to my therapist, my therapist said it wasn't my business.

"Not even talking about how I feel about it?"

"How do you feel about it?" she asked. Useless woman, I thought in annoyance. It was a shame that Mrs. Morris wasn't a therapist here. She'd actually care enough to listen.

"Upset, obviously. There I was having breakfast with a few friends and this lady tried to head-butt herself into a closed-casket funeral."

"Do you feel that you were traumatized in any way by this?"

"It was even more traumatizing than the macaroni and cheese," I retorted. She frowned.

"Careful, Mr. Holt. I can put you to zero just like that. This is not the way to earn a phone call today, let alone a visit in a week and a half."

"Sorry."

"Is there anything else you'd like to talk about?"

"Actually, yes. Is there a structured recovery plan for me to get released?"

"Yes, we have a detailed treatment plan for you, Mr. Holt. We'll have to discuss it another time, however, as it seems we're out of time for this session. Hold that thought and we'll see you tomorrow."

"Can I make my phone call now?"

"We're done for now, Mr. Holt. Please return to the

rec room."

I followed the orderly to the rec room. We passed my second-favorite orderly, Rip, on the way in. I held up a hand and he slapped it with a small smile as he passed us going the other way.

In the rec room, I didn't see Cody. With a sigh, I moved to sit and watch TV. The screen of the ancient TV was covered by a metal grate. I assumed that was to keep anyone from breaking it. It was also small, high on the wall, and muted. The closed captions were mostly readable, but sometimes if the captioning had more than two lines, the bottom line went below the edge of the TV cage and was hidden by the wider metal frame of the box.

I didn't recognize the show, but it was in black and white. I lost interest fast, but suddenly found reason to focus on it again when Greg came and sat down on the other couch facing this TV.

"'Sup, loser," he said.

"I'm sorry," I told him.

The sincerity in my tone brought his gaze straight around to me. I'd been thinking a lot about what Alan had said. I truly had no idea what Greg was dealing with to get put in here, but I had no right to taunt him like I had. For all I knew, he might actually have been molested by his father which would make my insult not only unnecessary, but downright cruel.

"What did you say?" he asked, suspiciously.

"I'm sorry, dude. I shouldn't have said what I did."

"Why?" he asked. I wasn't expecting that question.

"It was my first day in here, and I was pretty defensive. I don't know you or your story, and I had no call to bag on you like that."

"You're right, you don't know me," he snarled. "But I promise you, if I can figure out how to break you without getting busted, I'm all over you."

"Why?" I asked him, annoyed. "You insulted me, I insulted you, I apologized, now you're threatening me? Dude, what happened to you?" For the briefest of moments, the anger in his eyes slipped before snapping back to full intensity.

"Just watch your back," he snarled and stood, storming away.

Awesome, I thought. Figures I'd make one stupid mistake on day one and make an enemy for life in here. Greg didn't scare me, but he could cause problems for me down the road. I would have to watch my back, like he suggested.

"Hey, man," Cody said, dropping into the seat beside me. Or, I thought with a smile, I could have Cody watch it for me.

"Greg apparently wants to 'break' me."

"Aw, he's got a crush!" Cody said with a teasing grin.

"Shut up!" I laughed. "Seriously though, what's his deal?"

"Who knows. That guy doesn't share anything but insults and punches," Cody sighed. "If he wants to get at you though, we'll have to keep an eye out."

"Looks like I got the better end of this back-watching deal," I told him. "Unless there's a psycho after you too?" I said questioningly. He shook his head.

"Nah, everyone loves me. I mean, who would blame them?"

"Craft time!" came a sing-song voice.

I turned and looked, and some overly perky, middle

aged blonde stood in the entryway of the rec room, holding up a large basket of something colorful. She started listing names out loud. People stood and headed toward her and her over-sized orderly bodyguard as she called their names.

"What's that all about?"

"Craft time," Cody mimicked her high pitched voice. I laughed. "Every so often they do what they call 'occupational therapy'. At least this lady calls it what it is. It's like, finger-paints and basket weaving and junk."

"How is that occupational?" I asked.

"Beats me. I've never heard of a professional Play-Doh artist."

"Jackson Holt," the perky lady called.

"Hey, looks like I've got enough points!" I said in mock enthusiasm.

"Michelle Lewis," she called. Cody cringed. It took me a second, but I made the connection.

"Michelle?" I asked him, making sure I had no trace of mocking or amusement in my voice or face.

"Cody," he said, threateningly.

"Just making sure," I answered. "Why do they all call you Michelle here?"

"They think that there's something wrong with me, and…"

"There's not?" I asked, teasingly. He gave me a warning look.

"Yeah, depression. That's it. But they think that my being a boy means there's something wrong with me. All the staff here thinks that calling me by my given name and referring to me as a she will help me realize my identity, I guess. They don't seem to understand that I have realized my identity. And it isn't Michelle."

"They don't seem to listen well here," I answered with a sigh.

"They'll probably get mad at you if they catch you calling my Cody," he cautioned. I shrugged.

"So? You are Cody. Why wouldn't I call you that?" I replied. He smiled and nodded his appreciation. "Shall we go crafting?"

"I guess. I've seen this movie twenty-seven times," he said, gesturing at the screen.

If that wasn't depressing, I didn't know what was, I thought as I watched another few seconds of the old black and white picture.

We stood and headed for the cafeteria with the rest of the well-behaved psychos.

"Actually, Mr. Holt, I'd like to meet with you now," said another woman from the side. She was in decent shape, but the severe business skirt and jacket removed any possibility of an appealing figure. Interestingly, her heart-shaped face was the same. Plenty of potential for attractiveness, but her stern expression killed it.

"Who are you?" I asked, surprised.

"I'm Darcy Moon with Social Services," she replied. "I'm your court-appointed caseworker."

"Caseworker?" I asked, confused.

"Yes, Mr. Holt, caseworker. Dr. Garner has decided to press assault charges, and I've been appointed by the court to assess your mental state and determine if you're competent to stand trial. Obviously you will be tried as a juvenile, but considering the circumstances, we need to determine if even that much is viable. Come with me?" she asked as she gestured down a hallway.

I noticed she did not have an orderly with her. I

looked at Cody, who had paused to wait for me. I shrugged. He shrugged. I turned and went with her. That crazy psychiatrist I'd first gone to see was pressing assault charges? Because I'd had a seizure and she'd gotten hurt? This was insane. A psychiatrist, more than anyone else, should understand the circumstances weren't in my control.

"No bodyguard?" I asked halfway down the hallway.

"That's not necessary, Mr. Holt. All of your records and doctor's reports indicate that you're only violent when having a seizure, and those have stopped entirely since you started your medication. Do you feel I should have a bodyguard present?"

"No, ma'am." Something about her manner practically demanded to be addressed formally. She nodded once, curtly.

"Then I think having an orderly at the guard station within calling distance is more than sufficient."

"Thanks," I told her. She nodded once again, and gestured me into an office. I went in and sat. She moved behind the table and opened her large, leather satchel.

"They let you in unsupervised," I said, realizing how weird that suddenly seemed. She gave me a small smile.

"Most of my clients are assigned to me from this facility," she explained. "I'm well known here and have full clearance. Not to worry, Mr. Holt."

"Jackson. It gets real old having everyone call me Mr. Holt around here," I corrected her. She looked up for a moment, and nodded.

"Jackson, then."

"Thanks, Mrs. Moon."

"Miss," she corrected. I nodded.

She continued pulling out papers. Opening the file she set on top, she clicked a ballpoint pen and poised her hand above the paper, ready to start writing.

"Shall we begin?"

Chapter Sixteen
Plans Inside and Out

I liked Miss Moon. She was serious and very much a no-nonsense kind of lady, but I figured out really quickly that she meant well and really was there to help.

She was certain that the charges were more a nuisance than a real problem, since the very fact that Dr. Garner herself had been the one to submit recommendation for my admittance at this facility made it clear she believed I wasn't mentally competent enough to continue normal life.

That was likely enough to get the charges dismissed entirely, though would likely draw a mandate from the judge that I remain here for a certain period of time.

When I asked how long that would be, Miss Moon had told me it would likely be six months to a year. So I was essentially being sentenced anyway for the assault, just in this place instead of a juvenile detention facility. Miss Moon insisted this was the better option, but I wasn't at all certain I believed her.

I'd told her all about the voice and the seizures. She had it all in the files in front of her anyway. I didn't tell her about the dream, or my conclusion about Hana.

We'd left on positive terms, though with me more discouraged than ever. Miss Moon had said she would come back again in a week to assess my progress. She promised she was going to push for my release as early as possible once the charges were dismissed.

The whole situation sucked, but she was trying. I appreciated that much, at least. I'd been able to make my phone call shortly after my meeting with Miss Moon.

I decided this time I needed to call Thomas. I couldn't believe I'd wasted one of my three phone calls on Amber. I swallowed my bitterness and gave Dr. Tilton the number. My parents had approved Thomas on my call list, but that was a no-brainer.

"Hello?" I heard Thomas answer.

"Hey, Thomas!" I said excitedly.

"Jacks!" he returned, just as excited as I was. "Did you get out?"

"No, man, I'm still stuck here. I get a phone call every couple of days, though. If I'm a good boy, anyway."

"I'm surprised you got a call, then," he retorted. I laughed.

"I can play nice when I need to."

"You know, I always knew one of us would snap one day. Gotta be honest, I always thought it would be me, buddy."

"That makes two of us," I teased with a laugh. "Hey listen, do you remember that assignment we got just before I got sent in here? The one about ways society works together?" I was trying to be as careful as possible, with Dr. Tilton there listening. I prayed Thomas was on his game today. He hesitated long enough before answering that I started to worry.

"Yeah, for social sciences," he replied. I barely

restrained my sigh of relief.

"I thought maybe that since we were assigned to do it together and I'm in here for a while, that maybe I could help by giving you a topic."

"Okay, cool. Shoot," he said. I loved that guy, I thought with a smile. I could always count on Thomas to conspire with me in mischief of any sort.

"I heard about a girl who was kidnapped within the last few years. Her name was Hana. I didn't get a last name. They never found her. I thought maybe we could do the report on her, and maybe on the search efforts of her community. Maybe you could do some research and find out more information and mail it to me here, and I can write my part and mail it back. What do you think?"

"Yeah, I guess that'd work," he said.

I could hear in his voice that he was trying to figure out my play. I hoped I'd given him enough to understand what I was asking of him. All I needed was more information on Hana's kidnapping. If I could find proof that she existed, that might help me to get help to her. Or to help her myself, if nobody would listen. Nobody would listen, I knew.

"Do you know where?"

"No, man, sorry. Not too far away though, I don't think."

This was a recent theory of mine. The town I'd seen in what I believed to be her memories looked vaguely familiar. I thought I might have been there before, and I'd never really been anywhere beyond a hundred miles or so from our house. Even a hundred miles was considered a 'big vacation' to my parents.

Besides, I didn't know how mind reading worked,

but it seemed to me that it couldn't work from that far away. She had to be kind of close. That was my theory, anyway.

"It's cool," he said. "I'll do some digging and see. Hana?"

"Yeah. Probably at least six months ago."

"All right, I'll see what I can find. Is it cool if I go a different way if I can't find anything on her?" He was asking me how important this was, I recognized.

"I kind of really want to do it on this," I told him. He was quiet another long moment.

"All right, I'll see what I can do. Hey Jacks? Sorry about Amber."

"Thanks."

"Don't let it get to you, bro. She doesn't deserve you."

"I know."

We talked a bit about the team, and the game I'd missed. We'd crushed our rival team so badly that Thomas said they had run home with their tails between their legs and wouldn't ever come back. Heartache for the game I loved, for the friends I loved, for the family I loved, all surged.

We talked about school, and the new girl Thomas had met last week. He was really into her. We talked about all the normal stuff, like he was just catching me up. He was, and I appreciated that that's all it was.

Thomas was ready and waiting for me to step right back into life when I got out of here. It was a sharp reminder that good friends are hard to find, and so important to keep.

"Hey, maybe you can come visit one of these weeks with my parents."

"Yeah, I'll ask my dad," he said.

"Don't wear one of those old rock shirts, though. Got a guy here who thinks Megadeth is a band of aliens who are conspiring to steal his soul. Seriously."

"Now that's jacked," he said.

"You're telling me."

Dr. Tilton tapped the stop watch. One minute left on the countdown. Time to wrap it up.

"Hey, I've got to go, bro. Tell your dad I said hi."

"He hates you," Thomas said. I laughed.

"I know. That's why it's fun to be polite to him."

"You're twisted."

"I know that, too. Hey, send me what you find on that Hana girl as soon as you finish your research. I'd like to start that project right away. Catch you later."

"You got it. Later."

Dr. Tilton hung up the phone and I stood. She nodded and the orderly let me out, following me back to the rec room.

Man, I was getting sick of this room, I thought as I walked in. Cody waved to me from a table where he was sitting with Alan. Well this would be interesting, I thought. I moved over and joined them.

"Hey," Cody said. I nodded to him, then to Alan.

"Plan time," Alan said. "You still up for this?"

I nodded. Cody hesitated.

"Look kid," Alan said to Cody, "we need you for this to work. And if we play this right, you can leave with him."

"What?" Cody said, surprised. "I can get out, too?"

"If we all do our jobs, yes."

"What if I don't want to go?" Cody asked. I stared at him.

"You wouldn't want to get out of here?"

"They'll come after us when we do. Besides, it's not any better for me out there than it is in here."

"It would be an epic adventure!" I told him. "Can you imagine, breaking out of this place, going on a road trip, and rescuing some poor girl? You'd be a hero!"

"I don't…" Cody started, but Alan interrupted.

"You're serious, aren't you." I looked over at him.

"Yeah, why?"

"Not many people would break out of a mental institution to rescue a girl they only hear in their heads. How do you know she's real?"

"She's real," Cody and I both said at the same time. I gave him a smile.

"Schizophrenia can be really convincing. Heard about a guy once who became so convinced that he'd been recruited as a secret government operative that he broke into an abandoned warehouse every day for three months, believing it was his operation's secret headquarters. When they finally found the guy, he had cut out a big piece of his own arm because he believed the enemy had planted a tracker there. He was almost dead from infection from the wound."

"This is different," I insisted. His story shook me, but I never would have admitted that out loud. Doubt once again burrowed its way into my mind.

"You sure?" Alan asked. I hesitated. Cody kicked me under the table.

"Yes, I'm sure," I said. Alan shrugged.

"Suit yourself. I don't care what you do, as long as you get the letter to my daughter. I'll slip you the letter in the morning when the day comes. It will have her name and address on the outside. If you open it and read it, I will kill you. Clear?"

"Crystal," I said, leaning back involuntarily away from him. It was generally good practice to not upset men known for turning their enemies' heads into pulp, I thought.

"Good. Here's the plan. Rip and Frank will be the two orderlies on duty for the Sunday activity. Rip will do his best to keep things from getting out of hand, but Frank loves to incite fights. Gives him an excuse to beat on people and not get into trouble for it. We have a local choir coming in to perform for our special activity in the meeting hall. With me so far?"

Cody and I both nodded.

"Okay, so I'll sit in the back row, near the door leading back here to the rec room, where Frank will be standing. Rip will be by the front door, where the choir will enter and exit from. Frank will start antagonizing me."

"How do you know that?"

"Because Frank is a jerk, and he'd love the chance to rob the entire room full of patients of their special activity just because he can. Especially if it means he gets to pound on me in the process. He'll keep pushing until he gets a rise out of me. I'm going to go after him."

"After Frank?" Cody squeaked out. "That guy is twice your size, and loves to fight! He'll tear you apart!"

"It'll be worth it, as long as you get that letter to my baby girl. They haven't let me talk to her in two years."

"I can't even imagine. Alan, I'm sorry," I said. He continued like I hadn't spoken.

"When I do, everyone will panic. Several of the other patients will jump in, but most will be scrambling for the exits. Rip will start by helping get the choir out, but I'll make sure he has to come back and help Frank instead."

"Seriously?" Cody asked again in disbelief.

"I used to do MMA," Alan said by way of explanation. "Mixed martial arts," he clarified at Cody's blank stare. I certainly knew what that was, but apparently Cody didn't. I looked Alan over. Now that he said that, I could believe it.

"Awesome," Cody said to himself with a grin.

"Now Jackson, you and Cody will have to be top-notch best behavior, because you both need to not only get invited to the activity, and you have to have earned your street clothes."

"What?" Cody said, instantly discouraged. "I haven't earned my street clothes since I've been here."

"You need to," he said. "This choir all have matching jackets and hats. They've been here before. They'll take their jackets off and leave them near the front door. Jackson, you need to steal a pair of jackets and hats during the commotion. Should be plenty of chances, with the panic several will get dropped and a lot of these guys will ignore the jackets in order to get away from the rioting crazies. With their jackets and hats, and a pair of jeans and street shoes, you'll make it out the door without a problem."

"Okay," I said, thinking about how that was going to work. I wasn't sure I could do it, but I had to. For her, I had to.

"Cody, you have to get Rip's keys."

"Come on!" Cody exclaimed. "Are you kidding me? Rip would kill me!"

"Rip will be distracted. You'll need them, though."

"How am I supposed to do that?" Cody asked, frustrated.

"Your job, kid. Figure it out," Alan said. Cody threw up both hands in exasperation and Alan continued. "Once you have the hats and jackets, mix yourselves in among the choir as they try to push out the door to safety. Another orderly will be on duty outside, and will be helping get the choir out. With the hats and jackets, they'll escort you out with the choir. Follow them until they get to the big metal gate. The guard on the other side will be signing them each out, checking IDs. When they start to line up, sneak out of line and run down the hallway to the left. Take it all the way to the end, it'll turn a few times. When you get there, there's a maintenance door that requires a key to get in or out. That's where Rip's keys come in."

"We use the key to get out the maintenance door," I said, trying to feel like I was contributing even though I knew it was a pointless repetition of exactly what he'd just said.

"Right," Alan answered. "Get through that door and run straight out from there. If you're fast, you'll beat the choir to their bus in the parking lot and can hide on it. They'll drive you straight out. Boom," Alan finished, leaning back and looking smug.

"That's..." Cody hesitated, looking for the right word, "insane," he finished, glaring at Alan.

"If you've got a better idea, I'd love to hear it," he said calmly.

"Jackson, your parents are coming the day before that, right?" Cody asked. "Just ask them to sign you out. Then you get out free and clear, and we don't have to risk anything on a crazy plan."

"And what if they won't?" I asked him softly.

"They're your parents, they won't sign you out when you tell them how bad it is?"

"They might, but didn't you say they wouldn't let me tell?"

"You can get a few sentences out before the orderlies interrupt. If the lines you get out are good ones, your parents can sign you out on the spot. Boom," Cody said, looking smugly at Alan.

"And when that fails, and it will," Alan said with a glare at Cody, "we go with my plan on Sunday. Deal?"

"That sounds pretty good, Cody," I said, trying to convince my friend. He didn't look convinced. "Come on, man. I'll try my parents first. It won't cost us anything for me to try. If that doesn't work, we go with Alan's plan. It's solid. You don't have to come with me if you're scared, but I need your help. Hana needs me, Cody. I don't know why she's talking to me, but maybe I'm the only person in the world that can hear her. That guy is a real psycho, and he won't keep her there forever. She may not have another chance. She may have nobody else in the world that can help her, except for us." I waited, as did Alan, as Cody mulled this over in his mind.

"Okay, fine," he finally said in resignation. I grinned and reached out to grip his shoulder.

"Awesome! You rock, bro." Cody smiled at me.

"Okay, so for now all we have to do is behave ourselves. Concert privilege for all three of us, and street clothes privileges for you two. Got it?" Alan reminded us. We both nodded.

"Got it," I said. This was going to be a long week and a half.

Chapter Seventeen
Interference

I'd managed it. I wasn't sure how, but I'd done it, and it had only taken me eight days. I still had two left before the choir performance. I walked into the rec room in my own t-shirt, my own jeans, my own socks and sneakers, and thank God, my own underwear.

I'd been hiding pills for six days as well, and my mind felt clearer than it had ever been. I hadn't realized how the medications had been slowly, but surely, fogging my brain. I felt like a million bucks.

Cody was already there, wearing his own street clothes. Jeans, a white t-shirt and an open, short-sleeved button-up. He had on his own socks, but hadn't earned his sneakers yet. I'd had a good morning the day before with Mrs. Morris, and she'd slipped me a few extra points.

"Hey man," Cody said as I approached. He was sitting at the chess board again.

"Hey. Want to play a game?" I asked, pointing at the board. He looked up at me in surprise and laughed. I made a point to look offended. "What? You'll win, I know, but I'd bet every stitch of clothing I'm wearing right now that you haven't played a real game since you got sent here."

"You've got that right."

"So come on, show a newbie how it's done," I urged. He laughed, and gestured me to the seat across from him at the board.

"All right, but you're going to regret this."

"Bring it on. I'm betting you're all talk," I accused.

As he began resetting the board, I noticed something surprising.

"Hey, what happened to your bandages?" I pointed at his wrists. He had been careful to turn them down and away from me, I noticed.

"Doc said they were healed enough to remove the bandages. They took them off last night. About time too, the itching was driving me… well, you know." He grinned at me.

"Is it too weird if I asked if I could see?" He hesitated a long moment before responding.

"I guess it's only fair. I've seen you naked, after all." His grin was very mocking.

"You what?" I asked, surprised and confused. Then it dawned on me. "Oh man, you saw them haul me out of the shower room my first morning…"

I could feel my cheeks flush. It shouldn't bother me, since he was a guy, but the awareness that biologically he was female seemed to make a difference. I frowned at my own reaction and shook it loose.

Cody wasn't into guys, so it really wasn't any different than any other guy having seen me. I was angry at myself for the irrational reaction, and hated that even someone as non-judgmental as I liked to think I was had some biases still lurking in the back of my mind.

"Yeah, don't worry though. I've shut everyone up about it."

"Hey, I did notice nobody really said much, except for Greg."

"I told everyone you'd dropped him when he mentioned it in group, and that's why your first group was canceled early. I also told them that's why Mitchel requested a different group. Everyone bought it, and nobody wants to mention it to you since they already think you're violent."

I was shocked. I had no idea he'd been the reason nobody but Greg had really made fun of me over the incident. The idea that he'd basically reinforced the rumors that I was violent was a little unsettling though.

"Dude, I don't know whether to hug you, or hit you."

"See?" he retorted as he continued setting up pieces. "Dangerous and unpredictable." I laughed.

"Well?" I asked after a moment.

"Well what?" he asked.

"Are you going to let me see? It really is okay if you're not comfortable," I told him, realizing how uncomfortable it actually might be for him. For a moment, I felt bad for even asking. He shrugged though, and held up his wrists for me to see.

The wounds had mostly healed over, but there were still a pair of angry red lines running from his wrists toward his forearms, about four inches long. The lines were wide and jagged.

"Oh my God, Cody. What did you use, a hacksaw?"

"Broken mirror," he replied.

"Dude, that's messed up."

"I know."

"Looks like they're healing well, though," I said. He nodded and went back to setting up pieces.

"Okay, you remember how to play?" he asked. I shrugged slightly, letting him change the subject, and he smiled patiently. Explaining the game took a while, but it was nice to focus on something other than depression, frustration, and anxiety. Not to mention insanity.

Once we started playing, it became painfully obvious how much better than me he was. He beat me in six moves the first game. Laughing, he set it up again. I was more careful the second game, and I suspect he went easy, so it lasted a lot longer.

"Have you heard her?" he asked, moving his first pawn.

I knew who he meant, and shook my head. We had both thought once the drugs were out of my system, I'd start hearing her again. I'd actually been terrified the seizures would start up again and ruin the entire plan, which was why I'd waited a few days to start hiding pills.

However, in six days without the drugs, I had still heard nothing. Not one whisper. I didn't like thinking that it was possible that the reason I didn't hear her anymore is because the sheriff had finally killed her. The thought had crossed my mind a hundred times, and it still gave me chills.

"You will," Cody said reassuringly, as if reading my thoughts.

"I hope so. Hearing her at first was seriously scary. But the more I heard her, the more I started to understand. Then she stopped talking to me, probably because of the drugs, and I realized how much I miss hearing her. Is that weird?"

"The fact that you can hear her is weird," Cody clarified, moving a rook and taking my queen. "The fact that you miss her isn't. She was literally inside your head, dude. Girl gets inside your head and you're done for."

"It's not like that," I told him, a little annoyed at the inference.

"Oh, I don't mean that," he hastily amended, "but any girl gets into your head and it's hard to let go. Mothers, sisters, friends, girlfriends, wives, whatever. Once you let them in deep enough like that, they'll always be there, one way or another. That's why so many guys are still mama's boys when they grow up."

"Makes sense, I guess."

"It'll be such a cool moment when we find her and set her free," Cody said with a smile as he moved a bishop. "Can you even imagine what that'd be like? Being rescued after so long? Man, I don't even know how long she has been held, but even after only a few days of that it's got to be incredible to suddenly be free again."

"I don't know how long either," I said, thinking more about the girl than the game as I made my move. "I really hope it hasn't been that long, but I know it's been at least several months. It just sort of feels like it's been a long time, you know?"

"Nope. But I'll take your word for it. Check."

"Come on," I grumbled as I tried to find a way out. "I actually can sort of imagine. Not only have I been imprisoned here for weeks, under torture of therapy and constant, old, black and white TV shows in closed captioning, but you forget I've been in her head when he's hurting her. She won't know what to do when she's freed. It's like when you've been obsessing over something for months, and then suddenly it's time, and then suddenly over. It's hard to sort of reset your life, you know? It's going to be really hard for her, even once she's out. A lot to recover from, a life to reconnect with, and for a while anyway the media definitely won't leave her alone. Those news reporters will be all over her for weeks, maybe months, after she comes back. I sure don't envy that."

"I hadn't even thought about that," he said softly. "I just kept thinking how awesome it would be to get free after something like that. It's scary that there's so much more struggle she has to go through after that."

"Yeah. This is going to impact her whole life, even years after she's been rescued. I've only been through a few of her encounters, and there are parts of me that won't ever be the same," I finished in a tone just above a whisper. I had a momentary flash of the way it felt when… I shuddered and pushed back the nausea.

"Well, even that will be better than spending the rest of her life where she is."

"No doubt, bro. That's why I have to help her," I smiled smugly as I moved my piece and got out of check. Cody casually crushed my smugness when he moved a single bishop a single space.

"Checkmate."

"Let's go again, if you want," I told him.

He nodded with an eager smile. I could tell he was loving getting back into his game. That's about how I'd feel when I got to play football again.

I may not get why he was so into chess, but he wouldn't ever understand why I loved football, either.

We didn't really have to. We just had to understand that the other felt that way. I'd take another beating or two on the chess board to give him a taste of that again. Maybe someday I'd get him on a field for some flag football and I could get back at him for the chess beatings.

"Excited to see your parents again?" he asked as he reset the board.

"Sort of," I replied. "My dad still hasn't talked to me since I got in here. Mom keeps saying he's busy. I think he's ashamed that his son is in a looney bin. He might not even come."

"Seriously? That sucks," he said, gesturing for me to go first.

"Yeah. He's always been a high-pride kind of guy. He probably thinks having a crazy son will hurt his standing in his social group."

"Maybe. People are weird about that," he said. "My parents lost a lot of friends when I came out. And even more the first time I ended up in here. They still think it's a psychological disorder making me trans."

"What does make you trans?" I asked him as I made my move. He looked up at me in annoyance.

"What makes you straight?"

I thought about that. I supposed I got what he meant. It was kind of a dumb question. A lot of little things went into forming your identity, both biologically and environmentally. The nature vs nurture argument was the wrong debate, according to my social sciences teacher last semester.

He said that the human psyche was so complex that there were an almost infinite number of variables coming from a person's genetics, environment, and their personal experiences that all mixed together to make a person who they were. Blaming any single thing for any single trait was short-sighted and ignorant. Just like I was, apparently.

"Sorry, man. Didn't mean to insult you. Just trying to understand. That was a fair point."

"It's cool," he said, calm once more. "I appreciate that you're even trying. Most people don't want to even make the effort. You've given me a lot more effort than most people do, actually. You're a good friend."

"Thanks, man. You are too. I mean, it'd take a good friend to risk getting busted like this to help your literally certified crazy friend escape from a mental hospital to rescue the voice in his head," I said casually. Cody moved a piece as he laughed.

"I know it. I must be crazy. Wait…" We both laughed.

"Hey girls," a voice came from the side. It was Greg. Our good humor immediately died.

"What do you want, Greg?" I asked.

"Oh, nothing," he said. Casually he reached his foot out and nudged the table. The pieces wobbled and slid slightly out of place.

"Hey!" Cody cried, glaring at the kid while he put the pieces back centered in their squares.

I started to stand up, just as Greg kicked the table hard. Pieces went everywhere. I opened my mouth to say something, but Cody leapt at Greg, and dragged him down roughly to the ground.

"Cody!" I shouted. The pair grappled for only a moment before Cody landed a solid punch and Greg let him go.

Cody got back to his feet as Greg was still trying to

stand. Greg stumbled backward as he stood, out of the way of Cody's kick. He lunged in behind the kick to hit Cody, and would have landed the blow if I hadn't shoved Cody out of the way, putting myself in the line of fire.

The punch just grazed my cheekbone. It probably wouldn't bruise, but it burned a bit. I slammed my own fist into Greg's face, dropping him solidly to the ground. Gated doors clattered as orderlies rushed in. Why none of them had gotten there sooner, I had no idea. Those guys sure liked to pick their battles.

"Jackson!" shouted Mrs. Morris as she rushed in, two big orderlies right behind her. Rip was one of them, I didn't know the other guy. Cody had managed to get back between me and Greg.

"Sorry, Mrs. Morris," Cody said, poised in a stance like he'd just thrown a punch. "Greg started it."

Reaching the trio of patients, Rip immediately grabbed Cody and gripped him tightly. Cody didn't resist. The other one grabbed and held me, while Mrs. Morris bent down to check on Greg, who was totally unmoving.

"Jackson, I…" Mrs. Morris started.

"Jackson tried to stop us, Mrs. Morris," Cody interrupted quickly. "He wasn't fighting, it was me and Greg."

Mrs. Morris hesitated, long enough that I knew she hadn't actually seen the fight. She looked at Cody and then down to Greg. Rip looked over at me. I saw his eyes go to my cheek where Greg had grazed me and he frowned. He looked up at me, but I looked away. I waited for him to rat me out, but nothing came.

"All right, Michelle," she said. I watched Cody

flinch at the use of his given name. "I have to reset you and Greg back down to zero for fighting. Jackson, I have to dock you twenty for getting involved at all. I appreciate that you tried to stop it, but it wasn't your place."

"Mrs. Morris, I'll lose my shoes and jeans!" I protested. She shook her head.

"I know, Jackson. I'm sorry, but you made your choice." I bit back my sarcastic retort, knowing it would probably cost me more points.

"I need…" I started, then rephrased. "I was really hoping to visit my parents tomorrow with my street clothes."

"Losing twenty won't allow you your visit tomorrow, Jackson. Unless you bust tail tonight and tomorrow morning earning points back. You won't be able to get your street clothes all back by then, but you should have them back by Sunday for the activity if you really work hard. You need to not get involved, Jackson. That's for your own safety."

"I understand, Mrs. Morris."

"Let the boys go," she said. The two men did so, but Rip stayed close to Cody.

"Back to your rooms, both of you. We have to take Greg to the infirmary."

I didn't protest, and went back to my room. The orderly who followed me locked the door behind me. If I didn't get my jeans and street shoes back by Sunday, the plan wouldn't work. No matter how distracted the orderly outside the activity room is, he'd notice the green scrubs and bare feet.

Cody wouldn't make it to the activity at all. Not in two days. I had no idea how I'd get Rip's keys without him. I still had to get a jacket and hat, too. I didn't know how I'd find Hana once I made it out without him, either. So much of this had hinged on Cody having my back.

Cody did have my back, I reminded myself. His taking the full heat had made it so I could still make the activity, and my parent visit, if I pushed the next few days. Cody had lost his visitation this weekend and the chance to go with me, all because he'd taken the fall for my knocking Greg flat on his back.

The punk had it coming, though, I grumbled to myself as I lay down on my bed. I started upright a moment later as I heard it. It had been weeks.

Are you there? came the whisper.

Chapter Eighteen
Confessions to the Moon

"Hello, Miss Moon," I said as she walked toward me. She'd said she would be back sometime this week, but I'd all but forgotten about her.

"Hello, Jackson. Good to see you again. Shall we go visit?" she said. Her outfit was blue this time, a better color for her than the brown she'd worn the last week.

"Sure," I replied. I stood and moved to follow her. Cody was in group therapy, so now was as good a time as any. We went to the same office, and I waited as she got her papers out and got situated.

"So, how have things been going?" she asked me. It was the same as the 'how are you feeling' line my psychiatrist kept giving me, only Miss Moon seemed to actually want to hear the answer.

"Okay," I told her. "Kid tried to pick a fight with me and my friend yesterday. Got us all in a bit of trouble." She nodded and made a note.

"Did you fight?" she asked.

"No," I lied.

I had to keep the story straight though, if the orderlies found out I had actually been fighting, they'd kick me back to zero so fast my head would spin. She nodded and made a note.

"And what about the schizophrenia?" she asked. "Any relapses or episodes?"

"That the official diagnosis?" I asked her, surprised. Nobody had told me anything about it. Nobody told me much of anything, actually. She glanced back down at the file through the glasses perched near the end of her nose.

"That's what I have here, yes."

"No relapses," I lied again. "I haven't had an episode since they started me on my meds."

"That's good," she said, making a note. "Jackson, I really wanted to talk to you about your symptoms."

"Why? It's all in the file," I pointed at the offending object.

"I know, and I've read it, but I'd rather hear it from you. Can you tell me about it?"

"I guess. What do you want to know?"

"Just tell me about it. When you first heard the voice, what it said, when you had your first seizure and what you saw."

"I don't know," I said, thinking. "I heard it after a football game first. Just a whisper. I don't remember what she said. I don't remember most of what she says, actually. Most of it doesn't make sense."

"She?" Miss Moon asked, making a note. I sighed.

"Yeah. She. It's a girl's voice."

"Is it someone you know?"

"No."

"You say it doesn't make any sense. Is it gibberish?"

"No, the words make sense, just not the… what's the word…"

"Context?"

"Yeah, exactly. It's like I hear little pieces of a

conversation, and it's all out of context so I don't understand it."

"I understand," she said, making another note. "So when she talks to you…"

"She doesn't talk to me," I corrected. "When I hear her, it really is like I'm overhearing someone else's conversation."

"Who is she talking to?"

"Herself, mostly. Sometimes to a man."

"Do you hear the man, too?"

"Only when she does. Like I can hear what she hears."

"Do you ever become this girl?" she asked.

"Sort of," I hesitated. "More like I'm a passenger in her body, and only when I have the seizures."

"Does she make you do things?"

"What? No, she doesn't control my body. I don't control hers, either. I just see, hear and… feel what she feels."

"What does she feel?" Miss Moon asked. This time I paused long enough that Miss Moon's brow furrowed. Someone finally asked the question I was most afraid of.

"Cold. And pain. The man hurts her."

"Do you enjoy that?"

"Being hurt? Seriously?"

"Seriously," Miss Moon asked. I stared at her for a moment in disgust.

"No, I don't enjoy being hurt. And certainly not like he hurts her."

"How does he hurt her?" I suddenly realized that Miss Moon had already gotten more out of me in ten minutes than a team of shrinks had managed in weeks.

I had to respect that.

"You know," I hedged.

"No, I don't. Please tell me," she said.

"He beats her, cuts her… rapes her." I couldn't believe I'd said it out loud. I felt dirty and sick.

"And you feel all of this?"

"Yes. Can we talk about something else?"

"I'm sorry, Jackson. I know this is uncomfortable for you. It's really important for me to understand. I'm meeting with the judge later this afternoon. I know this isn't fun. Help me out so I can help you out." I took a deep, shaky breath and nodded.

"Does she or the man ever ask you to do things?"

"No, neither of them talk to me. She talks mostly to herself, and he only talks to her."

"When you have your seizures, are the images inside your head or outside?"

"I don't know, outside I guess. When I'm in her mind, it's just like her body is my body, only I can't control it. I don't know if that even makes sense."

"I think I understand. Has anyone ever hurt you, the way this man hurts the girl?"

"No!" I said firmly. "Nobody has ever done anything to me like what he does to her."

"When he does these things, do you become aroused?"

"What the hell!" I snapped out, moving to stand.

"Jackson, I really am sorry. I have to fully understand what's going on so I can give my best recommendation to the judge."

"You're giving the recommendation to the judge? About whether to keep me here?" I asked, slowly sitting back down. She nodded. "You're talking to me and asking questions like you think I might be the dangerous one. I'm not dangerous, Miss Moon. That psycho cop is." She frowned and I realized I'd given away too much again.

"What cop?" she asked.

"The man who's holding her captive. He's a cop."

"He's kidnapped her?" she asked, curious.

"Yeah, he has. He's got her chained up in some cave or tunnel or something somewhere."

"Jackson, do you believe this girl is real?" There was a weight to this question that I hadn't felt in any of the others she had asked.

My stomach felt like I'd just been hit. I suddenly became aware that I'd been talking about her and the cop like it was all real. I believed it was, but I wasn't supposed to let anyone else know that. I sighed and leaned back, closing and rubbing my eyes.

"No, Miss Moon. People don't just hear others talking from miles away, or see and feel through their bodies. Miss Moon, I haven't experienced any of this since they got me on my medication. That's a clear sign that the whole thing is a chemical imbalance, right? Just a symptom of something not wiring right in my head, and the medication fixes it, right?" She didn't answer, so I looked over at her. Her expression was one of concern.

"I'm not the one to make that call, Jackson. I wish I were in a better position to help you, but the fact remains that you assaulted a psychiatrist, and your file here shows you've attacked orderlies here as well, not to mention a fellow patient in a group therapy session."

"What!" I exclaimed, leaning forward. "That's a lie! I had one seizure, the day after they brought me in.

They came in and grabbed me. If any of them got hit while I was in my seizure or whatever, it's their own fault for coming in. Aren't you supposed to give seizure victims room? I didn't *attack* anyone. And the kid in group? He attacked me. I never even stood up from my chair, and you can ask the orderly Rip. I didn't move so much as a muscle the whole time. If that file says otherwise, I'd have a major sit-down with whoever is writing that garbage."

Her expression was one of doubt, and uncertainty. She wanted to believe me, I realized. But she was mentally pitting the word of an emotionally, and chemically, unbalanced teenager against a licensed professional.

"Miss Moon, I'm not dangerous, to myself or anyone else. The medications have taken care of the problem. Please, ask Rip about the group therapy thing. Don't take my word for it, talk to Rip."

She leaned back and took a deep breath.

"I will, Jackson." She removed her glasses and set them on the table.

"You will?" I asked, not sure I believed her.

"I promise I will ask Rip about the group therapy incident. But you promise me, Jackson. Promise me that you're shooting me straight. I really and truly want to help you, but I can't help you if you're lying to me."

Her gaze was intense. I held it through sheer force of will, knowing that I was lying to her, but not about what she thought I might be.

"I promise, Miss Moon." I said steadily. She watched me another long moment, then nodded.

"Okay, Jackson. Okay. I'll talk to Rip. Not because I don't believe you, but because the additional witness will help when I try to tell the judge you're not dangerous and that the medications have stabilized your condition to a manageable level. Assuming I don't hear a wildly different story from the orderly, I'm going to recommend that when he drops the charges at the pretrial next week that he not mandate a length of stay for you here. That way you can leave whenever your parents and your doctors feel it's appropriate. It's the best I can do."

"Thank you, Miss Moon," I said sincerely. "I'd hug you if there weren't a table between us. And, you know, if I didn't think you'd punch me if I tried." She cracked a smile.

"That wouldn't be appropriate, Jackson, but I appreciate the thought. You're welcome. I have to be going, but I appreciate you being so open with me. It really does help."

"You're welcome."

We went back to the rec room, where I watched her turn and go out through the gated door, unsure if I'd just sealed my own fate.

Not that it mattered, I knew. One way or another, I'd be out of here in less than two days.

Chapter Nineteen
Parents

I walked into the visitation room. It was by far the most elegant, well designed room in the entire place. And of course it had its own entrance from the main visitor entry area and a separate one for the patients so this room, and probably the lobby outside, gave the illusion that the whole place was this nice. I made a mental note not to mention the cockroaches.

Both of my parents were there, to my surprise. What was more, my brother Brent was there with them. They all stood from the chairs they were sharing along one side of the long table in the middle of the room. My mother ran to me.

"Oh, my boy!" she wept as she clung to me.

I held her tightly, drinking in everything about her. I'd been here only a few weeks and I already felt I had begun to lose connection to who I was. Or who I was before this all happened, at any rate. I didn't think I'd ever be the same person again.

She smelled of her best perfume, and wore her best business skirt and blouse. Dad was all dressed up too, though Brent wore his college t-shirt and a pair of jeans with holes in the knees. I sure wasn't worth dressing up for, his entire demeanor cried out. He meant it in fun though, and I could see his relief at seeing me in his eyes.

"Hi, Mom," I said.

"Oh, honey, how are you? I've missed you so much!" she gushed. She kissed my cheek, and I rubbed it absently.

"Easy, Mom, I only have forty-five minutes," I said with a smile.

She nodded and stepped back, wiping at her eyes. My dad stepped up awkwardly. He started to go for a hug, then hesitated, moved to shake my hand, then stopped altogether. It was the most awkward encounter I'd ever had with my father.

"Hello, Jackson," he said, reservedly.

"Hi, Dad. How are you?"

"I'm doing well, thank you."

His emotional distance was almost physically painful. My relationship with my father had never been great, but had always been decent. I was always much closer to my mother, though. That said, he and I got along just fine most of the time. This distance was new, and very uncomfortable.

"Hey, Brent," I said, turning to my brother to break the awkward tension with my father, "I can't believe they got you out from under whatever rock you've been hiding under."

"Well, crazy brothers call for crazy measures," he snapped back, grabbing me in a solid hug.

I hugged him back. We were always jabbing at one another, but we loved each other. It was always in fun. It was just sort of how we related, since in our family the men simply weren't affectionate or even very emotionally open with each other. Mom gave us all a hard time about it pretty regularly. It was guy stuff though, she wouldn't understand.

"If they wanted crazy measures, they sure found the right guy," I said as we both stepped back. He grinned at me.

"Dude, you look terrible. They feeding you okay?"

"Brent!" our mother chastised him, but we both ignored her.

"Define 'feeding'," I replied. I saw the dark look on the orderly on the far side of the room and changed tactics. "No, seriously they feed us fine. Not like Mom does, but it's not bad."

Brent nodded as we all sat down. I noticed all three of them sat on one side of the table, with me across from them in the middle. It felt like a prison visit, complete with guards.

"So…" I tried to begin, but tapered off. I suddenly felt like I had no idea how to interact with my own family.

"How's treatment going?" my mom asked. With a glance at the orderly, I again bit back my first remark.

"Great!" I said, deciding to play the 'all cured' angle in hopes they'd sign me out. I reminded myself that these people here had the ability to get me out of here before the end of the day if they decided I was better. "No episodes at all since they started my medication."

"That's wonderful, sweetie!" my mom said, giving my father a sidelong look.

"The doctor told us sometimes episodes can be months between," he said.

He was giving me his overly critical 'the doctor knows best and you need professional care' look. Of course Dr. Fitzpatrick would tell him that. He wanted to keep his rooms full so the money kept flowing in. Losing me was losing a cash source.

No symptoms? No problem! All he had to do was invent an imaginary and unnaturally long timeline under which I needed to remain under observation.

"Are you serious? Before the medication I was having symptoms every few hours. Then with medication I don't have any for weeks? Do you really want my academic career to suffer for *months* when I don't even have any symptoms anymore? Doesn't seem like a very wise, or economically sound move."

Playing on his money sense and concern for my academic wellbeing was a cheap shot, and I knew it, but I was desperate. It was either this or a very risky escape attempt tomorrow. I truly didn't know if my whisper girl would survive another few months while I waited calmly for them to let me out.

My only reassurance came from her speaking to me again last night. And this time it almost felt like she really was speaking to me, asking if I was there. She wasn't talking to herself. Maybe she was talking to me, I wondered. Although she hadn't responded when I'd tried to speak back to her.

Maybe she was talking to her mother. She'd called out to her before. It didn't matter though, she had spoken again and I had heard her. She was still alive. For now.

My dad gave me a considering look and I could tell he was giving serious merit to what I'd told him. My mother looked hopeful. I knew immediately that my dad was the only reason I was still in this place. His paranoia and desperation to ensure his children got the best medical care available for anything from a papercut to a splinter was what truly held me captive.

"I think," he finally said, "that maybe if we wait just a few more…"

"Come on, Dad!" I interrupted. "Did the doctor give you anything other than a glowing review of my behavior and progress here?" This was a dangerous question, since I didn't know which doctor he'd talked to, and which had been putting bad marks in my file.

"Well, no," he said, to my relief. "He did strongly urge we keep you here for a few more months to ensure the long-term viability of the medication."

"The doctor just wants to keep me here so the insurance checks keep rolling in," I said.

It was a mistake, and I knew it the instant the words escaped my lips. I clapped my mouth shut in horror at what I'd just done. My father's gaze turned steely, as it always did when anyone questioned his precious professional medical care providers. I knew better than that. So stupid, I berated myself. My mother's eyes closed in resignation. She knew as well as I did that I'd just nailed my own coffin shut. Brent was slowly shaking his head.

"Son, these doctors here have undergone extensive training, specializing them in exactly the kinds of medical conditions you're experiencing." I could have quoted this speech. I'd certainly heard it often enough. "Years of higher education have been dedicated specifically to learning about and understanding maladies exactly like yours. If you think you know better than they do, perhaps you should spend the next eight years in medical school."

"I can't, Dad," I retorted, angry at both him and myself. "I'm going to be here for the next eight years, taking my medication and sitting around with *no symptoms* as I wait to get too old for your insurance to cover me. Then these people will kick me out so hard I won't land for a week."

The orderly was moving toward me.

"No, not yet!" I begged him.

"I'm sorry, Mr. Holt, you're becoming overly emotional. I think it's time your family went home. They can visit again next week if you keep your points up," he told me.

"Next week might be too late! She needs my help!" I shouted, once more losing control over my mouth. I really needed to fix that little problem.

"Too late for what?" asked my mother, suddenly alarmed.

I didn't get a chance to clarify. The orderly grabbed my arm and hauled me out of the room. As the door shut on my family, my last image of them was my mother's look of concern and distress, my father's expression of stony resolve, and my older brother's intensely focused gaze. He stared at me, eyes filled with something I couldn't identify.

He was trying to tell me something, I realized at the last moment before I lost sight. I didn't know what, though.

I immediately stopped resisting, realizing that if I fought the orderly, he could drop my points back to zero on a whim. I'd lose my street clothes, my activity privileges, and my opportunity.

I walked calmly back to the rec room alongside the orderly. He let go of my arm about halfway down the hallway, but remained ready in case I tried to bolt back to the visitors' room. I didn't. My chance to bolt was coming.

Steeling my resolve, I mentally reviewed the plan for the next day. I wouldn't have Cody to help me, but I thought I could do it. I just had to figure out how to get Rip's keys. I had to do it, for Hana.

Are you there? the whisper came again.

I'm here, I thought back to her, as hard as I could. I'm coming, I promised her. I didn't know if she could hear me. I didn't know if I could even find her if, no when, I got out of here, but I had to try.

<h1>Chapter Twenty
The Great Escape</h1>

Morning came slowly. I'd been lying awake for hours, staring at the ceiling. I hadn't been able to sleep much the night before, my nervousness and excitement about the planned escape keeping me on edge and my mind racing. Mostly with everything that could possibly go wrong, despite my best efforts to stay positive.

I sat quietly with Cody at breakfast, neither of us saying much. I could tell his nerves were on edge too. We exchanged a casual greeting, a not-so-casual look, and ate in relative quiet.

The room was noisy, as always, with sounds ranging from the noisy eating of the people at the table behind us, to idle chatter, to the louder-than-usual singing of the creepy singing lady. I looked her way. She was looking back at me.

"Woah," I said softly to Cody, "creepy singing lady is staring at me." Cody glanced that way and grinned.

"Maybe she's into you. You're single now, right?"

"Shut up!" I laughed.

"You're right though, that is creepy. I thought that song of hers was weird. She's just sitting there now, staring at you. No, wait, she's singing and rocking back and forth again. Spooky, dude."

"The last thing we need is something weird and unexpected to happen today," I told him.

"That's for sure. I wish I could come and help," he said sadly. I nodded.

"I know. Thanks for making sure I could still do this, though."

"Yeah, someone's gotta help that girl," he replied. I nodded.

"Well, I've got group therapy pretty soon here. I need to get going."

"Yeah, I'm done here too. Going to go see if I can get the lady with the teddy bear to tell me the bear's name."

I laughed and we stood, placed our dishes in the bins, and headed to the door. Mrs. Morris came in while we were a dozen feet from the door. She smiled at us.

"Hello Jackson, hello Michelle." Cody twitched again at the sound of his name. I wished the orderlies would quit doing that to him.

"Hi, Mrs. Morris," we both said.

"I'm very sorry things played out the way they did for the choir performance today," she said sincerely.

"I know," Cody said. "Thanks."

"They're coming back in December. They're going to give us a Christmas show," she said with a smile. "Perhaps you'd like to go to that one?" she asked Cody.

"That sounds nice, thanks Mrs. Morris. Let me know when they're coming and I'll be sure to keep my points up."

"Oh, I'm sure you'll keep your points anyway, Michelle. You're a good kid. You've done such a wonderful job rebuilding your lost points the last two days. If you'd had just one more day you'd have been able to attend. It's a shame there isn't an opportunity to earn a nice bonus before the show." Something in her tone caught my ear, but I couldn't place it. "Well, perhaps next time."

We smiled and nodded, and Mrs. Morris moved to go around us, on Cody's side. Suddenly, she stumbled and began to fall. Cody reached out reflexively and caught her, helping to steady her on her feet. The other orderly rushed forward, but Mrs. Morris waved him back.

"No, no," she said to the approaching orderly. "I'm fine, I just slipped is all. Michelle here just saved me a nasty spill, let me tell you!" The orderly nodded and turned to go back to the doorway. "Well," Mrs. Morris said to Cody, "what a kind act! Thank you so much, that could have been a terrible fall. I'd like to give you a few extra points for your help. Say, fifteen?"

I looked sharply at Cody. From his surprised, excited expression I knew that, conveniently, was exactly the amount of points he still needed in order to go to the show. He wouldn't have enough for street clothes, but we could figure something out, I was sure.

"Thank you, Mrs. Morris!" Cody exclaimed. She nodded and smiled, patting his hand still on her arm.

"You're welcome dear, now go and enjoy your day. I'll see you two at lunch." As she moved to pass by again, she whispered just loudly enough for the two of us to hear. "Don't make me regret that."

I felt like I'd been kicked in the chest. She was very much going to regret that. Her incredibly kind gesture had opened the doorway for Cody to escape right alongside me. There was no help for it, but it killed me to know that we were going to seriously abuse that act of kindness. For a good cause, I knew, but still…

"I have group in a few minutes," I told him as we ducked out of the cafeteria and into the rec room.

"That's okay, I have something I need to do. What are we going to do about the pants and shoes?" he asked.

"I have an idea, but I'll have to see if I can pull it off. We'll talk after group."

"Okay, meet you here in an hour. Later."

This was going to work, I thought as I headed to my group session.

…no birds today… the voice faded in and out.

Hang in there. I'm coming, I told her.

Too windy… she whispered.

I could hear wind, faintly in the background. Looking out at the treetops barely visible outside the high, narrow, barred windows I saw no movement. No wind. Where are you, Hana? I asked her. There was no response.

Group therapy was agonizingly slow. It seemed to take forever. This was even one of the rare sessions where we could discuss whatever we wanted, which was always more entertaining at least. Alan looked just as anxious as I did, thankfully. Neither of us spoke much. I hoped nobody else noticed.

He met my gaze and raised a brow in question. I nodded once, subtly, and he returned the gesture. Looking back to Dr. Sanchez, I watched him go through his fake little smiles and encouraging questions. The false friendliness really annoyed me.

I looked down at his pants pocket. He kept a

permanent marker in that pocket, and it always poked out slightly while he sat down, and for a few moments when he stood.

My plan was simple, but required a skill I probably didn't have. With a little luck, though… I just had to wait until group was over.

When the time came and the end of group was announced, I stood before Dr. Sanchez could and headed for the door. I'd chosen a seat furthest from the door, and had to pass directly by him to get out.

My timing was perfect. He stood just as I began to pass him. I sidestepped slightly and bumped into him, jarring him just enough to distract him as I slipped the permanent marker from his pocket and into my sleeve just before it would have slipped deeper down into his pocket.

"Jackson!" he snapped at me.

"I'm very sorry, Dr. Sanchez, I wasn't watching where I was going. Are you okay?" I asked, patting his arm.

"I'm fine, Jackson, just stop touching me. Go back to rec."

"Yes, sir."

Heart pounding a mile a minute, I slipped out into the hall, where I transferred the marker into the waist of my pants and under my shirt. I couldn't believe I'd just pulled that off. I'd seen it done in movies, but despite popular belief, watching something in a movie did not in any way make one an expert in real life.

And yet here I was, a master pickpocket. I mentally congratulated myself on my own high degree of awesome, begged my own forgiveness for an abject lack of humility, and smugly returned to the rec room.

Cody was already there, a slightly smug grin on his own face.

"What are you so pleased about?" I asked him.

"Oh, nothing. Just solved our little key problem."

"What? What did you do?" He smirked and shook his head.

"You'll see," was all he'd give me.

"Fine then, keep your little surprise," I laughed. "I have one of my own. I need your feet."

"What? Why?"

"I solved our little shoe problem."

"Well aren't we just a couple of geniuses," he said.

"You got that right. Now, feet."

Cody pulled his feet up under him and to one side on the couch in the most feminine posture I'd ever seen from him. I'd seen countless girls sit like this before, but I'd never seen a guy do it. I could also tell the move didn't come naturally to him, which I thought was interesting.

"Nice," I said, casually slipping the black marker out and beginning to draw on his white socks. He immediately figured out what I was doing and laughed.

He kept a lookout while I transformed his white socks into a pair of black and white Nikes, complete with the swoosh. He'd glance down every minute or so to watch my progress before returning to lookout duty.

"You've got skills," he said at one point.

"Yeah, drawing shoes is real hard core."

"Beats Play-Doh sculpting."

"That's for sure," I laughed.

When finished, any inspection beyond a passing glance would reveal the fraud, but a casual look from a distance would pass well enough.

"I think this'll work," I told him. He nodded his agreement.

"What about pants? I'm still stuck in these scrubs."

"Can't help you on that one. I think though that if you walk out on the far side of me from the orderly, the shoes, jacket, and hat will be enough. We don't have much choice, can't hide that green color."

"Okay, we'll just have to try it. Concert is in ten minutes, you ready for this?" He looked excited. I felt terrified.

"I wish the choir was coming after lunch," I said regretfully as I put a hand on my stomach. "Who knows when we'll eat next."

"Aw man, why'd you have to go and bring that up?" he protested. "That's it, we're calling it off."

"Shut up!" I laughed. "Come on, let's join the crowd."

A group of my fellow inmates was gathering near the gated door that would lead them to the activity room. We fell into the crowd, mingling in far enough that it would be difficult to notice his socks.

Something pressed into my hand. Glancing down, it was a folded note. On the front in surprisingly precise handwriting was an address and a name; Lily Polaski. I glanced up, but didn't see who'd pressed it into my hand. It had to be Alan, but I didn't see him in the crowd. I slipped the note into my pocket.

The address was in Springfield, not too far away I thought, but I didn't know if that was in the right direction for Hana. I still hadn't figured out how to find her once I made it out. Thomas hadn't delivered, and I had no more information about her than I'd had before.

Springfield was as good a direction as any, I decided. Besides, I'd promised Alan. And if he was willing to take a beating to help me out of here, I was certainly willing to take a day to deliver his note.

The orderlies, Frank and Rip, began ushering us into the activity room. True to his word, Alan appeared and slipped into a spot in the back corner. He winked at us as we passed. Cody and I pushed hard to get a spot near the front. We couldn't get the front row, but we got an end on the second row back. It would do, I decided.

Once we were all seated and under control, Rip went to the door near the side sectioned off for the performance; the door nearest our seats. The choir came in, all smiles and waves. I could see the nervousness in their eyes.

I felt a surge of regret, knowing these people were coming in to bring us a little brightness in a dark place, volunteering their time to make our lives a little bit better in the only way they could. They were afraid of us, that much was clear, and we were about to reinforce that fear.

I shoved the guilt down. This choir would probably never come back, but there would be others. A small price to pay for saving a girl's life, I reminded myself.

The choir hung their jackets across the rail on the back of the room, and lined up in neat little rows.

Nobody applauded. I felt bad about that too, but I couldn't draw attention to myself by being the only one to clap.

They were a mix of ages. No teens, but a couple of them didn't look far past that. We could probably get by unnoticed in the commotion. I took a quick look at the group's clothing. They all had matching red jackets, all hanging on the back rail at the moment, and all currently wore blue shirts. I had on a red t-shirt, but figured I could pull the jacket closed in front as we left so that wouldn't be obvious.

They all wore yellow fedoras too, the hats I was supposed to steal in the commotion. I hoped a few of these guys dropped their hats in the dash to get out when the fists started flying. If they didn't, I had no idea how I'd get them.

I looked at Cody. He looked more excited than ever. I grinned as the thought crossed my mind that this kid really was crazy, but not for the reasons they thought he was. I glanced around one last time, this time at the room full of patients.

Creepy singing lady was there. And she wasn't singing, she was staring at me again. It was unnerving, that steady, focused, unblinking stare. Then I saw something that really stopped me cold. There was a third orderly in the room.

He had just moved into position on the other side of the room across from Rip, the pair of them making an invisible barrier between us and the choir. I glanced back at Alan, and hoped his commotion would be enough to draw all three orderlies. This would be a short escape if it didn't.

The choir began to sing. It was a bright and happy song, and I had to smile. It was the first song I'd heard in three weeks, not counting creepy singing lady's tune. I glanced back at her as the thought of her crossed my mind. She was still staring. I firmly turned my gaze back forward.

Listening carefully, I could just hear Frank mutter

something to Alan in the back. Alan didn't respond. As the song ended, I heard Frank mutter something again, and Alan made some remark back. I couldn't quite make it out.

Another song, another bright and happy tune. They'd no doubt keep them all like that, to keep the patients calm and happy. Can't risk a sad or intense tune in a room full of crazies, I thought wryly. I turned my focus back to Alan, listening as closely as I could. The tone in Alan's harsh whisper made it clear that he was nearing breaking point. I glanced back, and saw Frank grinning a nasty little grin.

Looking up at Rip and the other orderly, they were both paying more attention to the choir than anything else. Neither seemed to notice the building tension in the back of the room. The song ended just in time for me to make out what Frank said next.

"She probably loved it. Begged for it. The little…"

That was as far as Frank made it. I heard a sudden crash and looked back, like everyone else in the room. Alan had vaulted his row, bringing his chair with him, slamming it hard into Frank. Frank got an arm up, so it didn't hit him in the head, but the force of the blow rocked him to the side. Alan was on him like lightning.

The room exploded into motion, everyone suddenly rushing to get as far as possible away from the building fight. Two other patients immediately jumped to help Alan, an unexpected twist.

I heard Rip curse loudly and he moved to race down the side of the room to the aid of his coworker. Cody, already standing, stepped past me and in a move as smooth as melting butter, reached out and grabbed Rip's keys from his belt.

The retractable cord tethering them to his belt extended quickly as Rip ran past, but not missing a beat, Cody raised his other hand, which were to my astonishment holding a pair of wire cutters, and neatly snipped the cord before it hit its limit and alerted Rip to the theft.

I stared in awe, and Cody gave me the most self-satisfied, cat-got-the-mouse grin I've ever seen in my life. I couldn't help it, I laughed.

"Boom," he said, jingling the keys in front of me.

"Where did you…"

"I slept with the maintenance guy!" he snapped sarcastically. "You really want to talk about this now?"

He had a point, I knew. I looked up to see the other orderly, arms spread wide, trying to barricade the choir from the patients as the fairly large choir tried to force their way through a single-person door. That was going to be a big problem, I realized.

Someone moved in front of me, and I realized it was creepy singing lady. She held two hats and two jackets. I had no idea how she'd gotten them, or how she knew we needed them, but here she was. She pushed them into our hands.

"Go," her surprisingly melodic voice said softly. "Help her."

For a long moment, I stood stunned. She knew about Hana and our plan? How did she know? What did she know?

"Come on!" Cody shouted, pulling on my arm.

I looked up and saw the other orderly, still guarding the choir. Creepy singing lady turned and ran at him, shrieking like a psychotic cat. Leaping at him, she clung to him, clawing and biting as he frantically tried to pry her free.

This served two purposes for us. First, it more than distracted orderly number three. Second, it sent the choir into such a chaotic frenzy of screams and shoves trying to force their way out the door that it was effortless to slip on our jackets and hats and work comfortably into the throng.

I glanced back at Alan. Rip was fending off three patients, and Frank had Alan on the ground and was beating him fiercely with his billy club. I hesitated, but Cody pulled me harder, not letting go of my arm.

"That was the plan!" he shouted in my ear.

Even with him shouting so close, I could barely hear him in the ruckus and chaos. Clenching my teeth, I followed my loyal friend.

Through the door, there was a fourth orderly, our last guarded point before our escape, assuming we didn't run into anyone else in the hallway to the maintenance door. He was rushing people past and pointing them straight down the long hallway running parallel to the length of the room.

Cody and I both ducked our heads slightly, hoping the narrow brims of the fedoras would be enough cover. We both held our breaths as we passed the orderly. He never glanced twice at us. We ran with the crowd down the hallway.

Around a single turn, we saw the gated, guarded door where the choir was being ID checked on the way out. A lot of them had made it through already, and I worried we wouldn't have time to get to the bus before they did.

"This way," Cody whispered sharply.

The sounds of the commotion in the activity room

had faded quickly as we went down the hallway, and it was almost eerily quiet down here. We slowed enough to let everyone else pass us, bottlenecking at the gate and waiting to be ID checked. Cody and I turned left and raced down a side hall.

"We made it!" Cody said excitedly.

"Not yet, don't jinx us!" I snapped back.

We ran hard. Cody was quick, but not as fast as I was. I slowed just enough for him to keep pace. A few turns down the blessedly-empty corridor, and we saw our objective. A heavy, metal maintenance door, with a thick, probably bulletproof, glass window in it.

Cody tossed me the keys, since I was again just slightly ahead. I put the key in the lock. There was no handle, just the heavy lock. The key wouldn't turn.

"It's not working!" I cried, panic rising.

"Wrong key!" he said, pushing me aside. He switched keys quickly, going through two more before finding the right one.

"Hey! Stop!" came a shout down the hallway. We both looked back to see two orderlies charging full speed toward us. Cody shoved the door open and pushed me through.

"Go, go!" he yelled.

I took three steps when I heard the door slam shut. I glanced back, expecting to see Cody right on my heels. His face instead greeted me from the other side of the window. I ran back, but the door was, of course, locked. I shook it hard.

"Cody!" I yelled.

I watched through the window as he forcefully broke the key off in the lock, effectively sealing the door. The two orderlies hit him hard from behind, pressing his face against the glass. He looked sidelong at me and mouthed a single word, once more.

"Go."

I hesitated a moment, but had no choice. One of the orderlies turned and sprinted back down the hallway as the other threw Cody to the ground and pinned him there. I ran.

Disoriented at first, having never seen this place from the outside, it took me a moment to find the front parking lot. I spotted the bus, and the eight people already climbing into it. I was too late. Cursing, I looked around. I could see the parking lot exit to the road beyond. I'd have to go on foot.

Ditching the jacket and hat, I ran. The sound of a highly modified small car engine thrummed up beside me. Ready to bolt, I heard a voice.

"Hey! Aren't the cuckoos supposed to stay inside their cage?"

I knew that voice. Looking back, I broke into a grin.

"Brent!" I cried.

He jerked his head, indicating that I should get in. I ran to the car, sliding across the hood of his tricked-out, lightning blue Honda, and dove into the passenger seat. Calmly and easily, he drove us out onto the road and away from my prison, slowly enough to not arouse any suspicion.

As we rounded onto the road, I could hear an alarm blaring from the facility.

I'd made it.

Chapter Twenty-One
Runaway

"What the hell are you doing here?" I asked him.

"Grateful, much?" he asked, sarcastically.

"I'm sorry, I really do appreciate it, but seriously…"

"Are you kidding? I can read you like a book. The moment they started hauling you away from the meeting room yesterday, I knew you'd be making an escape attempt. Figured you could use a getaway car. I came by today and planned to come every day until I saw you next. I knew it wouldn't be long, but wow Jack-O, you don't waste time!"

"You could get so busted for this. Way worse than the wine cooler incident," I told him. He nodded soberly.

"I know. You wouldn't be breaking out if there weren't a reason. You're my brother, I've got you."

"Thanks, Brent. Can you take me to Springfield?"

"Sure thing, boss. So? What is it?"

"What's what?"

"Your reason, dummy. What is so important that you broke out of the big house for it?"

"I'm saving a life."

"Sounds big."

"It is. She was kidnapped." Brent frowned and

looked at me hard at this.

"Seriously?"

"Seriously. By a cop."

"Oh man, you don't do anything half-assed, do you. Even your crazy missions are hardcore serious. So how'd you find out about her?" he asked, glancing over at me. I hesitated. "Come on, spill it. I'm committing a felony for you, here. You owe me."

"Okay, fine. But I'm not crazy."

"Fair enough. Let's hear it."

"She's the girl I hear whispering in my head."

"Dude," he said.

"Zip it, Brent! Think what you want, but she's real, and she's really in trouble."

"Okay, okay. Stand down, soldier. I'm helping, aren't I?"

"Yeah. Thanks."

"So she's in Springfield?"

"No. Someone helped me get out. Another patient. He made me promise to bring a letter to his daughter for him if he helped. I have to go there first."

"Where's your girl, then?"

"I… I don't know," I admitted. He whistled long and low.

"Well this won't be easy. Any leads? Got a name, or where she was taken from?"

"Her name is Hana. That's all I've got."

"Can't she tell you where she is? You know, in your head?"

"I don't think she knows I can hear her."

"So you're looking for a girl whose last name you don't know, who may or may not have been kidnapped by a cop an unknown time ago, from an unknown place somewhere in the world, being held in another, secret unknown place also somewhere in the world." His tone was dry and critical.

"Yes," I said in a small voice. "She's in the US though. Definitely an American girl and an American sheriff."

"Well, that narrows it down some," he said with a sigh. "Okay, so we get you to this girl's house to deliver the letter, then we have to, what, do some research?"

Thomas! I thought. He was supposed to have already been doing research. We could save days of work if he'd already found something.

"My friend Thomas was going to do some research for me, like a week ago."

"You still hanging with that punk?"

"Not a good time, Brent."

"Sorry. Okay, so we deliver a letter, then go find Thomas and hit him up for information. Sounds solid."

"It's a start, at least," I said.

"So what's the address?" I gave it to him and he made a turn. He handed me his phone, and I punched up his GPS with the address.

"You should call Thomas too, while you've got it. See if he's found anything worth risking going to see him."

I nodded and dialed. It rang long enough that I was sure it was about to go to his voicemail.

"Hello?" he asked.

"Thomas!" I said, trying to convey my urgency. I switched him to speaker so Brent could hear him.

"Jacks! What's going on, man? Another good behavior phone call? Aren't I special!"

"Not now, Thomas," I stopped him. "This is code

red.”

“What’s the sit-rep?” he asked immediately. It was funny how we fell right back into our old secret agent games we used to play when we were little.

“I’ve escaped custody and…”

“You what?” he said, his voice a panicked squeak.

“Code red, dude! Shut up and let me finish! I’m out, and moving fast. Please tell me what you’ve found on Hana.”

“Oh man, I mailed that stuff to you. You didn’t get it? I sent it like five days ago.”

“No. Figures, it’ll probably show up tomorrow,” I sighed. “You found something then? What did you find?” I asked, suddenly excited.

“You’re one lucky punk, you know that?” Thomas asked. “I ran a search for someone named Hana going missing. Name is spelled weird, so that slowed me down. I thought it would take forever, but once I had the right search, it came right up. Guess why. She disappeared from Harbor Glen.”

“What? That’s only like ten miles from our neighborhood.”

“Exactly. Found a couple of articles in the local paper about it. You said kidnapping, so that’s what I searched first, and nothing came up. She’s just listed as missing in every article I found. Cops said they think she might have run away.”

“Bull. A cop is the one who took her,” I replied.

“No way!”

“Yeah. Up against the big guns here. Okay, so Harbor Glen, that’s a good start. What else do you have?”

“Not much. She disappeared three years ago,

and…"

"Three years? Oh my God…" I trailed off. Three years. Hana had been abducted, and held prisoner and tortured for three… long… years. I felt sick.

"Yeah, three years. They searched for ages. The whole town was out looking for her."

"Why didn't we ever hear about this?"

"Umm, we were twelve? And weren't all that interested in current events? She was twelve too, by the way."

"Wow," I replied, a little surprised that learning she was my age didn't surprise me. Her friend Rachel had looked so young. But then, that was three years ago. "Okay, so Harbor Glen, three years ago. Do you have anything else?"

"Just that her parents were devastated, of course. Word is they're still putting up posters around their neighborhood and take trips on the weekends to nearby major cities for the same thing. Parents' names are John and Vivian. Last name is Daily. As in, 'every day'. Weird name, huh?"

"I guess. Hana Daily. Okay, that's a lot more than I had before. Thomas, you rock, bro."

"I know it. And you owe me. So on the run, huh? Know what you're doing?"

"Got a solid plan."

"You with anyone?"

"No," I lied. "Stole a phone."

I knew I could trust Thomas completely, but I didn't know if anyone could trace this call and listen to the conversation later. Thomas probably is one of the first people they'd check when they realized I was missing. Besides, then he could tell them I'd said I was alone with complete deniability. I had to protect Brent.

"Need anything else?"

"Not now. Maybe later. I'll be in touch if I do. Thanks, man. Seriously, I owe you."

"No way, man. We're square, as always."

"Thanks." I hung up the phone.

"Okay, so maybe he's not such a punk," Brent admitted when I hung up. I gave him my best told-you-so grin.

"Thomas is awesome. Solid guy, loyal friend. Can't ask for more."

"There actually is a kidnapped girl." he said in wonder. I nodded. "That's… awesome."

"What?" I asked him, looking at him with concern.

"Not that she was kidnapped, that seriously sucks, but it looks like you're actually not crazy. You're psychic, little brother! Now that's awesome!"

The phone rang in my hand, causing me to startle, and I dropped it. Scrambling around on the floor for it, I finally grabbed it and felt my stomach lurch as I saw the caller ID. It was Mom.

"Not psychic enough to know when a phone is going to ring though," he said with a laugh. I handed the phone to him, and he made a face when he saw who it was. He answered the phone.

"Hey, Mom," he said, casual and slick. I envied him that ability. He was always cool as ice under pressure. "No, just heading to a party. Why?"

He paused for a long moment. I could hear her talking on the other end, but without her on speaker I couldn't make it out.

"No way, are you frickin' kidding me? Stupid kid. When?" He winked at me.

Mom had just told him I'd escaped, I realized. They hadn't wasted time alerting her. And probably the authorities. He switched it to speaker for me.

"…half an hour ago. He has no idea what he's doing. My poor baby boy, he's going to get himself hurt! He's not well, Brent. He hasn't contacted you?"

"No, he doesn't have my new number, remember? Does he even have a phone to make calls with?"

"I don't know. He might have stolen one by now. Who knows where he is and what trouble he's in. We have to find him…" she trailed off, crying.

"It's okay, Mom. I'm sure he's fine. He's a smart kid, he'll be okay. We'll find him soon."

"I need you to come home, Brent."

"Okay, Mom. I'll be there tonight."

"You'll be here in fifteen minutes, young man!" she snapped.

"Mom, I'm heading to…" Brent tried to argue. We both knew resistance was futile.

"Brent, this is your brother we're talking about! Your *sick* brother! You get home right now!"

"Okay, Mom, calm down."

"I'll calm down when my baby boy is back safe and sound and getting proper care! Fifteen minutes!" She hung up.

"You know, she's the scariest nice person I know," I told him. He just nodded. She was an absolute sweetheart, but when she got angry it could get near-apocalyptic.

"It's going to take ten more minutes to get you to that girl's house for the letter."

"Lily," I told him.

"Yeah."

"Drop me off up here. You can make it home in fifteen minutes if you go now."

"I'm not going to leave you on the side of the road, moron," he argued.

"If you're not home in fifteen minutes, Mom will get suspicious. She might not rat you out to the cops herself, but she'd tell Dad and he certainly would. You've done enough for me already, I'm way farther away than they'd guess I could have made it. Nobody will be looking for me this far out, yet. Leave me up here, I'll walk to Lily's, then head to Harbor Glen. I need to try and find Hana's parents. Maybe I can get more information from them."

"You sure?" he asked, glancing at me uncertainly.

"Totally."

"Okay, little brother. This is your rodeo. I'll get away as soon as I can and try to find you on the road to Harbor Glen."

"Awesome. Thanks, Brent."

He pulled the car over, passing right by the gas station I'd have expected him to stop at, and pulling in front of a random house. I gave him a questioning look.

"Those gas stations always have lot cameras. Gotta fly under the radar."

"Thanks," I said. I hadn't thought of that. I needed to remember little details like that. I wasn't used to being a wanted criminal.

"Hey," he said as I started to get out. I paused and looked over. "Here." He handed me a wad of cash.

"Dude, this has to be like two hundred bucks!"

"Almost three. You need money for food and stuff. And don't thank me, it's a loan. I expect it back with interest."

"You got it," I said gratefully. He grinned at me.

"Fly free, little jailbird," he said teasingly.

"Shove it, Brent. And thanks."

Chapter Twenty-Two
Lily Polaski

It took me an hour and a half to make the run on foot to Lily's house, and another half an hour to find the exact house in her maze of a neighborhood. It was a lot further than I'd thought it was. Most of the drive would have been on the highway, I'd realized.

When I finally found her house, I was surprised by how small and worn it looked. I shouldn't really have been surprised. When Alan got locked up, his income would have disappeared. Lily and her mother were probably struggling to make ends meet without him.

I hesitated a long moment before knocking on the door. I waited another long moment to hear any movement inside. Finally, a run-down looking woman answered the door. She looked me over critically.

"What?" she asked.

"Is… is Lily home?" I asked.

"Why?"

"I just… needed to talk to her. I'm a friend of hers from school."

"I don't know you," she said, giving me a dark look. Wow, I thought, what a grouchy lady. She looked too old to be Alan's wife, I realized.

"Lily does. Can you ask her if she'll come talk to

me?" I was gambling again. Lily didn't know me at all, and I might not be anywhere near her age.

"Lily!" the lady shouted over her shoulder after a long, considering stare.

"Yeah?" I heard a girl call.

"Visitor!"

It was a long moment before the girl appeared. She was a little older than I was, but not much. And very cute, I couldn't help but notice. She frowned at me, but I gave her a pleading look.

"Says he's a friend of yours from school," the woman said. Lily looked at me another moment before breaking into a bright smile.

"Oh, hi David," she said and stepped past the woman onto the porch. "Thanks, Aunt Jude, I've got this."

The woman eyed me suspiciously again, but then turned and went into the house. The girl looked at me questioningly. I waited until the woman was gone before I spoke.

"Hi, Lily. I know you don't know me. Thanks for covering." She just nodded and waited. "This is going to sound weird, but I'm a friend of your father's…" She quickly looked behind her and carefully shut the door. Taking my hand, she walked me further away from the house, out to the sidewalk.

"You know my father?" she asked, suddenly very intense.

"Yeah, we were at the same… facility together," I explained, more than a little embarrassed to be telling a hot older girl I just got out of a nuthouse.

"What facility?" she asked, almost urgently.

"Brookview," I replied confused, "over in

Middleton." How did she not know where her father was?

"Thank you!" she said sincerely, touching my arm. "Nobody will tell me where he is. They don't want me to write to him, or see him, or talk to him."

"Why not?" I asked, surprised.

"They say he's dangerous. Nobody believes what happened."

"Nobody will tell anyone in the facility what happened," I told her.

"My boyfriend's dad tried to…" she trailed off, awkwardly. "My dad walked in and just went nuts. He used to do MMA," she explained.

"I know, he told me," I replied with a smile.

"Anyway, the guy didn't make it. The two of them had argued pretty bad two days before over a tool he'd borrowed from my dad, so everyone said it was 'motive', or something stupid like that. The guy was some upstanding pillar of society, so nobody believed he would have done that to me. My dad saved me, and they locked him up for it."

"I'm so sorry. He's really a good guy," I told her. I wasn't sure, but she sure seemed to think so, and he'd certainly helped me out, so I wasn't about to ruin her image of him. Besides, if what she said was true, I was behind Alan a hundred percent and respected him all the more for it. "Helped me a lot while I was in there."

"Thank you so much for telling me where he is," she said. "I might be able to sneak letters to him now."

"I have a letter," I replied, a little uncomfortable.

She put a hand to her mouth, and her eyes welled. I handed her the note, slightly crumpled from my pocket. She took it and started reading. It was two full pages, so I awkwardly stood there and waited while she read it, unsure if I should just leave her to it.

Her tears ran freely as she read. When she finished, she carefully folded the letter, and kissed it before putting it in her pocket. Lily leaned forward and pulled me into a tight hug.

"Thank you…" she said softly.

She smelled like strawberries, I couldn't help but notice. I hugged her back, because it seemed like the right thing to do, but I was too uncomfortable to do it right. Lightly kissing my cheek, she let me go.

"I don't even know your name," she said.

"Jackson," I told her.

"Thank you, Jackson. You don't know how much it means to me," she said, wiping her eyes.

"I know how much it meant to him," I replied.

"Do you need anything?" she asked suddenly. "Are you hungry or thirsty? I can get you a sandwich and some iced tea or something."

"Actually," I started, then changed my mind. "No, I am kind of in a hurry. I have to be somewhere soon." My stomach betrayed me, with a loud rumble. She smiled at me.

"Can you wait five minutes? I'll bring you a sandwich and a bottle of sweet tea. Do you have a ride coming?"

"No, but it's not far. You really don't have to…"

"Let me do something for you," she insisted. I considered a moment, then nodded as my stomach again protested. "Wait here," she said, running into the house.

I waited for not five, but ten minutes. I was starting to consider that something might be wrong and whether I should just run for it, when she came out. Not from the front door, but from the garage. She was carrying a backpack and pushing a bike.

"What…" I started to ask. She pushed the backpack at me. It was crammed full.

"I just got an Amber Alert on my phone. Some kid got away from Brookview and they think some adult in a blue Honda might have taken him. That's you, isn't it." She didn't say it in an accusing manner, just very matter-of-factly. I just nodded.

"Take that," she pointed at the backpack. "There's a stack of peanut butter sandwiches in there, wrapped so they'll keep a few days. There's also a few t-shirts that might fit you and don't look too girly. I don't have any pants that might fit you, I'm sorry. There's also a ball cap that belonged to my dad, and a sleeping bag crammed in there in the bottom. It's a kids' sleeping bag, I'm sorry. It's all I've got. A couple of water bottles on the sides there, too."

"Why would you do that?" I asked, stunned. "You just found out I escaped from a mental institution."

"You're a friend of my dad's, and you need my help. That's enough for me. Here," she said, pushing the bike toward me. "I don't have a car, they won't let me drive, but this will be better than walking."

"This is too much," I told her.

"Hey, I'm not the only one who got that alert, Jackson. You need to get rolling."

I set the kickstand and perched the bike, then set the backpack down and hugged her, right this time.

"Thank you, Lily. You and your Dad are solid people."

"So are you. Take care of yourself, Jackson. I hope

you make it wherever you're going."

"I have to," I told her. "She needs my help." Lily didn't ask as I put on the backpack and climbed on the bike. I appreciated that. Giving her one last smile, I pedaled away.

I couldn't believe how much people were helping me. I couldn't help but have my faith in humanity a bit bolstered. Although, part of me nagged, all these people are helping an asylum escapee. Maybe that doesn't speak so well for humanity, I thought wryly.

Lily was right however, and I made much better time with the bike. I figured it would still take me a couple more hours to get to Harbor Glen from Lily's house. Every car that passed me, I tensed. Who knows who else had received that alert that might know enough to be suspicious of me.

I stopped and pulled out the blue ball cap and pulled it low. I changed my t-shirt as well, knowing that a lot of people had seen me at the hospital in the t-shirt I'd escaped in. Grabbing a swig from one of the water bottles, I mentally thanked Lily again. I pulled out a sandwich, and ate it as I got back on the bike and kept pedaling, steering one-handed.

I knew the general direction of Harbor Glen, but worried I'd get lost long before I got there. It struck me just how dependent on my GPS I'd become. I wished I had a phone. Except they could trace me with a phone, I reminded myself.

I finally found a frontage road, and followed it along the highway. The highway signs kept me on the right track. It felt good to be outside again. Good to have the wind blowing in my face, the sun warming my body. The breeze was almost hot, a portent of the approaching summer.

I didn't know how long I'd stay this way, but for now, I was free.

Where are you, Hana? I asked mentally.

Are you there? the whisper came immediately. I screeched the bike to a halt and focused on the voice excitedly.

"I'm here." I said aloud, trying to project it in my mind.

Is anyone there? she called.

"I'm here, Hana. Where are you?"

…the birds…

I sighed. She couldn't hear me, and I had no more clues to her location. I kept pedaling. An hour later, I came across a road sign on the frontage road at a T-junction. There was a piece of paper folded and taped to it. It had the letter J written on the front.

Looking around in a panic, I saw and heard no one. Approaching carefully, I took the note down, expecting an ambush of some kind. Nothing happened.

I opened the note, still carefully looking around before reading it.

Ran the road looking for you. No sign. Hope you're okay. Parents suspicious, have to go back home. Can't help more. I'll try and keep them off your trail.

~B

P.S. Dig below.

Brent had already been here looking for me. It had taken longer than I thought to get to Lily's. Of course, it had taken less time than I'd thought to get this far thanks to the bike, but I'd obviously already missed my brother.

I looked down at the ground below the pole. There was a spot where the gravel and dirt looked freshly turned. In a small Ziploc bag was a lighter, an emergency blanket, a small roll of para-cord, a cheap plastic poncho, and my brother's cherished Swiss Army knife. He'd gotten it in the scouts when he was ten and it was among his prized possessions.

Smiling, I packed the compactly folded blanket and poncho into the bag, along with the para-cord. The lighter and knife went into my pocket. Who knew what I'd need, but between Brent and Lily, I had far more than I thought I'd ever have on this crazy mission of mine.

Back on the bike, I kept pedaling. Another hour to Harbor Glen.

There, I would find Hana's parents.

Chapter Twenty-Three
Harbor Glen

It wasn't hard to get to Harbor Glen, thankfully, though after two hours of walking followed by two hours on the bike, I was definitely exhausted. It was crazy how fast you lost an athletic edge when you stopped exercising every day.

I stopped the bike in front of a library. I'd be able to get to a computer there and could look up John and Vivian Daily. I put the bike in the bike rack, and paused as I realized I had no lock. No help for it, I thought with a sigh.

The library felt amazing. Air conditioning was possibly the best invention in the world. Hours outside in the sun and I was definitely needing a cool down. I finished the last of the water from the first bottle, and filled it again from the drinking fountain by the restrooms. Never knew when I'd get the chance again.

After using the restroom, I headed into the library proper. The librarian, a sweet-looking woman, smiled at me.

"Sorry, hun, you'll need to leave the backpack here."

"What? Oh, the backpack."

"No backpacks allowed inside the library. Too

many books getting up and walking out by themselves."

"Sure, I understand." I walked over and handed her the backpack.

"Full load, huh?" she asked as she hefted the bag back over the counter.

"Sleepover at a friend's house," I told her. "Just need to look up a few cheats for the game we're going to play," I lied. I was getting better at this, I thought. That probably wasn't a good thing. She smiled warmly.

"No problem. Computers are just behind the Self-help section."

"Appropriate," I said with a smile. She grinned at me, and I walked where she'd indicated.

I sat at the first terminal and moved the mouse. The screen popped up instantly. There wasn't much on it. A few icons for educational games, a library catalog, and the browser. I clicked the browser and ran a quick search for John and Vivian Daily.

It was harder than I thought, but eventually ended up on a virtual phone book site that gave me an address. I copied and pasted the address into a maps site, and got directions from the library. I looked around for a printer. There was an old one right between the two center computer terminals. I clicked print, expecting to hear the machine hum to life.

A popup sprang onto the screen, telling me I needed to see the librarian and pay a fee of a dime a page. I headed back to the counter.

"Hi," I said, getting her attention again. She smiled and waited. "I was just going to print something, and it says ten cents a page." I held up a twenty-dollar bill from my brother. "All I have is a twenty, can you break it?"

"Afraid not," she said, apologetically. "How many pages were you going to print?"

"Just one. Found the info I needed."

She looked around conspiratorially and leaned down. There were a few others in the library, but I suspected she was just being playful. It made me smile.

"You just go ahead and print your page, hun."

I thanked her, returning to the now-humming printer. It took longer than I thought it would to print, the machine really was an older model. When my directions and little map came out, I studied it for a long minute, then folded it and put it in my pocket.

Back at the counter, I smiled at the kind librarian.

"Ready to go?" she asked. I nodded, and she handed me my backpack. "Have fun with your friend. And if you're interested, we have a book fair going on next weekend. Lots of great stuff, you and your friend should come."

"I will, that sounds cool. Thank you," I said, and headed back out, pausing once more for a last drink from the fountain before climbing back onto the bike and heading back onto the road.

I couldn't help but think about Cody and Alan. I knew Alan was going to need medical care after the beating he was getting, and who knew what they'd done to Cody. I hoped they were both okay, all things considered. Both had sacrificed a lot to help me.

I'd have to find a way to get word to them once I'd rescued Hana. Although I was probably going to have to turn myself in once I'd done that. Couldn't stay on the run forever. Once I'd turned myself in, they'd throw me back into that place so fast the shockwave would probably kill me.

Twenty more minutes and I was in the right neighborhood. I was facing down a long road, lined with nice, comfortable homes and nearly to my destination, when I saw the police car round the corner, followed by a dark blue sedan.

I turned sharply into a yard and dropped behind the low, white fence. The cars came only about halfway down the block, stopping in front of what I believed to be the Daily house. Two officers got out of the police car, and to my surprise, Miss Moon got out of the blue sedan. How on earth had they tracked me this far?

They must have gotten a hold of the call with Thomas, or had pried the information out of him. I'd have to give him a hard time about that later, but I didn't really blame him at all. A guy could only take so much interrogation from trained professionals.

Leaving the bike, I crept closer as the three walked up to the door and rang the bell. I made it to the neighbor's yard without them spotting me, and dropped down behind a bush. Close enough to listen, but hidden from sight. The door opened and I peered around the bush.

"Yes? Can I help you?" asked a weary-looking woman.

There was a note of panic in her voice at the sight of the two cops and the social worker. She was probably torn between wild hope that they'd found her daughter, and terror that they'd found her daughter dead. My heart broke for her.

Don't worry lady, I thought, your daughter's alive, and I'm going to find her.

She was pretty and not very old, perhaps my

mother's age, but looked very tired. She looked like the world had been pressing down on her too hard, for too long. If this was Hana's mother, it probably had been.

"Mrs. Daily?" asked Miss Moon.

"Yes?" she asked again.

"My name is Darcy Moon, I'm with Social Services. I'd like to ask you a few quick questions, if I may."

"Of course," said the woman. "Would you like to come in?"

"No, thank you, we're in a bit of a rush. This won't take long."

Miss Moon reached into her satchel and pulled out a couple of papers and an envelope, all paper-clipped together. The envelope, which was on the back of the stack, was the only part I could see at all from where I hid, but I immediately recognized the symbol drawn on the side I could see. It was our football team's logo. Thomas drew them on everything. Badly, I constantly pointed out to him.

That was the letter Thomas must have sent me with the information on Hana. The institute had probably gotten it days ago, read it, and just hadn't given it to me for whatever reason. No wonder they made it out here so fast.

I cursed my own stupidity for having Thomas mail the material. I should have just had him tell me over the phone. Then only Dr. Tilton would have known anything about it, and may not have connected it to my escape. Miss Moon held up a photograph of me.

"Mrs. Daily, this is Jackson Holt. He's a troubled young man, and a patient at the Brookview Institute. Have you seen him?"

"No, no I haven't. I'm sorry, what does this have to

do with me?" Mrs. Daily asked.

"We're not sure where he heard about your daughter, but recently he's become fixated on her disappearance," Miss Moon told her, holding up the papers with the information Thomas had sent me. "He recently escaped from Brookview, and we have reason to believe he might come here to talk to you."

"Why would he be interested in my daughter's abduction?" Mrs. Daily asked.

"Disappearance," one of the officers corrected. Mrs. Daily's expression turned dark.

"Abduction, officer. My daughter would never have run away."

"Either way," Miss Moon interrupted forcefully, "this young man's fixation is not healthy, and his mental condition is unstable. It's very important that if he comes to talk to you that you report to us immediately. Please call me at this number the moment you hear anything." Miss Moon handed her a business card.

"Is he dangerous?" Mrs. Daily asked, looking concerned. Miss Moon hesitated.

"I don't believe so, no," she finally replied. I felt a surge of relief. Miss Moon still believed I wasn't dangerous. I appreciated that more than I could ever tell her. "He isn't well though, and without his medication he's prone to seizures that can harm him and anyone too close to him. He's not a bad kid, Mrs. Daily. He's only trying to help, but he is the one who truly needs our help right now."

"I understand. I'll call right away."

"Thank you. Have a nice evening, Mrs. Daily." Miss Moon said, turning to walk away. The two officers followed.

They wore blue, but I looked closely at them anyway, realizing that one of these might even be the kidnapper. Neither looked at all familiar, though I hadn't seen the man's face clearly in anything but the nightmare, and that memory was blurry. I had to try, though. Just one glimpse of the right man and all of my belief in the reality of what I had seen and heard would be confirmed. The doubt had slipped back in.

Finding a kidnapping victim named Hana could have been a coincidence. Or maybe I had heard about it three years ago, and it had slipped into my mind, to manifest as a schizophrenic hallucination years later.

No, I firmly reminded myself. Hana was real. That was her mother. She was still in trouble and only I believed it. Only I could help her. I waited until Miss Moon and the officers had left before I moved out from behind the bush. I heard a gasp behind me, from the direction of the Daily's house.

I spun around, and there stood Mrs. Daily, staring right at me. She hadn't gone in from the porch yet. We stared at each other a long moment. She looked more startled than anything else. I probably looked terrified.

Mrs. Daily looked at the card still clutched in her hand, and then back to me.

"I can help her," I said, praying that the hope in the woman's eyes would win out over her fear and concern. She hesitated another long moment, then pulled a phone out and began dialing.

I bolted the few more houses back down to the bike and hopped on, pedaling faster than I'd ever ridden before. One block, then two, then three.

The police car, followed by the sedan, whipped

sharply around the corner ahead of me. Spotting me, the police car's sirens and lights flared to life. Cursing, I fishtailed the back tire around and pedaled hard.

The sirens gained on me faster than I would have thought possible. A quick glance around showed me in the middle of a long stretch of houses. Another half block to the next intersection, and I knew that I didn't have that long. I stopped the bike and hopped off, racing for the nearest house's fence.

I jumped, hauled myself over, and dropped to the ground behind. The police car screeched to a halt on the other side of the fence. I ran straight across the yard and to the back fence. Jumping that one as well, I was momentarily disoriented, finding myself in the back lot of a small convenience store instead of another home's yard like I expected.

Racing around the front of the building, I saw a city bus pull up to the stop in front of the little store. Jumping onto the bus as soon as the doors opened, I quickly pushed a dollar into the ticket machine at the front of the bus. It spat out a ticket a moment later, with me watching frantically behind.

The bus pulled away from the curb. It was only two seconds after it had pulled back into traffic that the first of the officers came around from the back of the shop. I dropped into a seat and sat low, watching behind as inconspicuously as possible as the bus drove away.

The officer looked around frantically, the other officer appearing behind him. I saw the officer shout, probably curse, then run into the store. He obviously thought I might have ducked inside.

I took a deep breath and sank low in my seat. That

was close, I knew. I'd have to change buses soon, too. It wouldn't be long before they figured out where I'd gone. But for a few minutes, I thought, I could rest and figure out my next move as I gained a little distance.

Mrs. Daily wouldn't help me. I didn't blame her. Imagine being told a crazy person had escaped an asylum and was coming to your house, then you spot him moments later. I'd probably have called the cops too. It sure stunted my search efforts, though. I didn't have any more leads.

Leaning back, I closed my eyes.

"I'm coming, Hana," I said softly.

He's coming, the whisper came. I sat up sharply, thinking she might have heard me, but then I heard the crunch of tires of gravel echoing down the tunnel. Cursing, I pulled the stop button and jumped to my feet.

The bus stopped a few hundred yards later, and I hopped off, ignoring the driver wishing me a good day. My vision flickered, and I saw the dark figure come walking down the tunnel. I stumbled and shook my head to clear it. I was at another store. I went around back, fighting the vision out of my mind. Falling down behind a dumpster, I gave up fighting and the seizure took me.

The silver belt buckle with the rattlesnake glinted in the flickering yellow light as the sheriff removed it. I struggled, without my conscious efforts, to pull against the chains. I knew it was pointless, Hana knew it was pointless, but we had to try. My wrists burned in pain as the raw wounds on them were rubbed and pulled once more on the metal shackles. Pain shot through my broken arm at the pressure.

I kicked out, no, Hana kicked out, I reminded myself forcefully, and received a sharp, ringing slap for my troubles. The dark figure chuckled.

"You never stop fighting. One of these days I'll finish breaking you and you won't fight back. I think I like you best like this, though. Let's play."

Rough hands grabbed at me, and the real pain started. It was a long time before everything went dark again.

Chapter Twenty-Four

Lonely Mountain

I woke up behind the dumpster. It was dark out, but the lot was lit with a street light. I moved to sit up and gasped as pain shot through my hand. I looked down and saw the bruising already forming on the back of my left hand.

Glancing around, I realized my thrashing during my seizure had probably resulted in my slamming a hand against the dumpster I'd been hiding behind.

Standing carefully, I fought off the dizziness. Once stable, I headed back out toward the front of the store. I had no idea what time it was, but the lot was empty and the store was closed. So much for stocking up on food, I thought.

I started walking. It didn't matter which way I went. I still had no leads, and no idea where I was going.

"Hana, help me," I whispered as I walked the dark street.

Are you there? came the whisper.

She'd been saying that a lot lately, I realized. It didn't sound like she was calling it out, either. Maybe she couldn't hear me, but maybe when we connected like this, she could feel me. She didn't respond when I spoke to her, but she seemed to be trying to connect to something.

"I'm here, Hana. I'm here. I can't find you. Please, help me find you," I said, hearing my voice crack as tears threatened.

Is anyone there? she whispered.

She couldn't hear me. I felt my heart drop. I stopped, and slowly turned back the way I'd come. Something odd caught my attention.

There was an odd pulling sensation inside my head. It was incredibly subtle, but as I slowly turned back around again, I could feel it fade in, and then out again as I passed a certain point.

Looking that direction, there wasn't much. I'd made it near the edge of town, and beyond a handful of shops, and the small, lower class neighborhood I could just barely see beyond them, I didn't think there was anything else out that way.

Turning my gaze higher, I noticed a black absence of stars rising above the horizon. I didn't understand for a moment, as exhaustion, frustration, pain, and hope all serving to jumble my senses. It was a mountain, I realized.

I hadn't realized Harbor Glen was this close to the mountains. Turning back and forth again slowly, I was able to focus in on that incredibly faint pulling sensation.

She was in a tunnel, kind of like a cave, I realized. Of course she was in the mountains! This used to be a coal town, I remembered. Harbor Glen was a ridiculous name, since there wasn't a harbor within a hundred miles of here, but there it was.

Those mountains nearby were probably riddled with tunnels and caves. Hana was there, waiting for me.

She was real, she was in need, and I was coming.

I pulled out another peanut butter sandwich, and broke into a tired jog. I made it another couple of miles closer to the mountains before I realized I had to stop and sleep, or I'd never make it.

My body was on the verge of collapse, and without rest it would shut down before much longer. There was less and less out here the further I got. In the distance down a side road, I could see a small park. That would have to do, I decided.

I walked the rest of the way to the park, and found a small cluster of trees and bushes to one side. The sky was clear, so I wasn't afraid of rain. I simply took off my backpack, and pulled out the sleeping bag. It was adorned with a big Hello Kitty picture, and was pink. Not the best for camouflage, I thought wryly, but it was getting colder by the hour and I was glad I had it.

Pushing it and the backpack deeper into the bushes, I made myself a small, mostly-covered little nest. I tucked my legs into the sleeping bag. It only came up to the top of my stomach. Pulling out the emergency blanket, I covered the rest of myself with that, tucking half of it below me to insulate from the ground. Scouting for the win, I thought smugly.

It took only seconds for me to fall asleep. I slept dreamlessly and hard.

When I woke up, it was warm. It took a moment to orient myself again, and remember where I was. Oh, that's right, I thought. I'm sleeping on the cold, hard ground under a bush at the edge of Harbor Glen. Why? Because I'm crazy, that's why, I thought ruefully. I stretched out a few aches, and pulled myself and my things out from under the bush.

I suddenly realized the sound of children playing had been going on for some time. It stopped suddenly when I came out from the bush. I turned around. There were three kids playing on the small jungle gym of the tiny neighborhood park. All three had stopped and were staring at me. I quickly glanced around. There were no adults. Relieved, I smiled at the kids.

"Better than backyard camping," I said to them. The older boy smiled. The two girls frowned, until one of them spotted the Hello Kitty sleeping bag.

"I have the same bag!" she said excitedly. "Hello Kitty is my favorite!"

"Mine too!" I said, playing along. She laughed.

"Hello Kitty is for girls," said the boy.

"Nah, Hello Kitty is way too awesome to just be for girls," I told him as I rolled the sleeping bag up.

"See!" the little girl exclaimed. The youngest girl, maybe five years old, just watched, silently.

"You guys live close by?" I asked as I started working on folding the blanket up.

"Right there," said the boy, pointing at the house across the street. "And don't try anything funny, my dad can see us from here." Mentally I cursed. Great, he was probably watching us right now.

"Hey, I'm just a kid, like you," I told him as I walked to one side and refilled my water bottle at the drinking fountain, drinking my own fill as well. "I gotta go anyway. Have fun!"

"Bye!" called the older girl.

I turned slowly toward the mountains, feeling for that pull again. There it was. A surge of relief washed over me. The mountain was closer than I thought it was. I jogged that direction, pulling a sandwich out.

Four more, I counted. I needed to ration. I didn't know how long it was going to take to get to her.

Eating slowly as I ran, I headed for the road I knew would take me up into the mountains themselves. I kept hoping I'd find another store and could fill the remaining space in my bag with more food and water, but never saw another. It wouldn't be long before I really regretted not taking the time to find one, I knew.

It took two hours of running, mixed with a couple of breaks, to get to where I couldn't see houses anymore. The heavy trees and undergrowth blocked out anything but the road ahead and behind. At a steady climb, my thighs were burning far sooner than I would have liked.

Man, for a workout, this beat laps on a level field hands down, I thought to myself with a smile. Not only was it better exercise, but it was much prettier. The trees all around swayed in a gentle treetop breeze that I couldn't feel down here. The trees' leaves were just gaining the richness of green that came in the summertime, ready to display their vibrancy for the next several months until autumn set them afire.

The air was clean and fresh, the road quiet and peaceful, and the sounds of the woods all around was comforting. I felt the gentle pull of Hana's mind in the back of my own, and followed the road steadily toward her. For the first time in a month, I felt really good.

I was already sick of peanut butter sandwiches, but I was infinitely grateful to Lily for the gift. Smart girl, I thought. Good protein, easy to store, and easy to eat on the run. The only drawback was that they made me thirsty. I wouldn't have access to safe water up here, so if I was out here for more than two days, I'd be in trouble. The two small bottles she'd packed me wouldn't last long.

At the end of the first day in the mountains, I was beyond bored. I made a rough camp with the emergency blanket and para-cord, and had even built a small fire. I slept okay, though animal sounds kept waking me up nervously.

By the end of the second day, I was out of water and peanut butter sandwiches. I'd seen exactly six cars in two days, and I'd hidden in the underbrush every time. None of them was a sheriff's car, though.

Mid-day on the third day, I had almost given up and was considering flagging down the next car, whenever it appeared. I was hungry, thirsty, and very tired.

...forty-nine that time. Getting longer... came the whisper.

I paused and focused on it. I closed my eyes and reached for the voice. An image flickered into my mind. The flickering yellow bulb illuminated my vision. Hana was staring at it. She just stared. I waited for a few minutes, and it went out completely. Totally dark again, the only light from the distant entrance of the tunnel just around the far bend.

One, two, three, four... she counted. She was counting the length of time the bulb was out, I realized. I counted with her.

Forty-eight. Shorter than last time, I knew. My God, I thought. I had never in my life been that bored. Talk about another torture. She was counting the brown-outs in the flickering bulb that was her only real light source.

I heard a car and ducked down into the bushes on the side of the road. It was white, I thought, as I watched it come into view. Not a cop car, though. Looked like a small SUV. Probably a family heading up camping. Middle of the week though, I thought. Except it's probably summer break by now. Remembering that brought a flood of longing and loneliness. I should be out camping myself, maybe with Thomas.

I am camping, I reminded myself. This barely counts, I argued. Really? This is the most hardcore camping you've ever done. In fact, it's about time you went hunting for food and water. Real roughing it, champ! I laughed to myself as the SUV passed by.

As the end of the third day neared, I was so bored and hungry that I was making up rap lyrics to the rhythm of my stomach grumbles. The stomach pains were secondary, though. Thirst was having a bigger impact on my morale and energy than anything else.

In answer to an unspoken prayer, it rained that night. Using my emergency blanket as a rain-catcher, I was able to refill both my water bottles, and drink more than I should have of the clean, fresh water. I'd bought myself another two days, I knew. Now if I could find some food.

Tomorrow, I told myself, tonight I needed sleep. Sleep came hard that night, the heavy rain sounding on my emergency blanket tent making it difficult to rest. It didn't help that I was wet, and cold.

Not to mention a bit itchy in awkward places from my use of leaves as toilet paper. It wasn't poison oak or poison ivy or anything, I knew enough to recognize both, but even safe leaves weren't the most comfortable or efficient things to wipe with.

The next day, I was searching for food as much as I

was traveling. I did find a bush with some nice-looking purple berries on it, but the berries were viciously bitter, and totally inedible. Hunger was gnawing away at my energy and morale. I didn't know how long I still had to go. I could still feel the pull, and it felt stronger somehow, but I didn't know what that meant.

"Where are you, Hana?" I asked aloud, for the millionth time. She didn't answer.

It was around mid-day that I stopped for a break, and fell asleep by the side of the road. I don't know how long I slept for.

"Jackson," came a voice. I groaned and rolled over. I wasn't comfortable.

"Jackson," came the voice, louder this time. A hand shook me. I stirred slowly, groggily.

"What?" I grumbled, still not fully awake.

"Time to go home, Jackson." That got my attention.

"Wait, what?" I asked, forcing my eyes open. My vision was blurry, and the muted light from a gray, cloud-filled sky didn't help. I managed to focus. It was Miss Moon, standing over me.

"Come on, Jackson. Let's get you someplace safe and dry," she said.

"No," I protested weakly, "I have to find her. I'm close. I'm so close."

"Nothing is out here, Jackson. You're sick. Please let me get you back to where they can help you."

"Nobody can help. I have to help her." I began to struggle to my feet. I had more energy than I thought I would, considering I hadn't eaten in a couple of days. Miss Moon was stronger than she looked, though.

"There is no 'her', Jackson. Your symptoms are

back because you stopped taking your medication. Come back with me, Jackson. Let us help you." Thunder rolled in the distance. It would rain again soon, I knew.

"No!" I shouted, yanking my arm free and breaking into a run.

"Jackson!" she shouted as she ran after me.

She made good time, I thought as I ran. Even half-starved she couldn't keep up with me, but she'd come prepared, and wore pants and sneakers that day instead of the dress suits I'd always seen her in before.

I leaned into it and ran like I was running on a level field, ball in hand, and a clear pathway ahead of me. I was slowed some by the uneven ground, and the brush and logs in the way, but I climbed and jumped recklessly fast.

The pull was getting so strong. I followed it determinedly, the sounds of Miss Moon calling my name as she crashed through the woods behind me fading into the distance. It was getting stronger so quickly! I had to be so close. So close, just a few more yards, I told myself.

Without warning, I broke into a small clearing along the side of a sharp rock rise, almost a small cliff. Stumbling, I moved up against the rock face. Frantically, I looked for the tunnel entrance. I could feel her. She was right there, just a few yards ahead.

"Hana!" I screamed, my voice hoarse and dry. "Hana!" I pounded a fist against the unyielding rock as Miss Moon came up behind me. Thunder boomed, much closer than before.

"Jackson, stop it! It isn't real! There's no tunnel, there's no girl, there's nothing! You're sick, Jackson!

They have medicine that can help you!"

"No!" I shouted as she grabbed me from behind. I ran a little further along the stone, searching desperately for the opening.

"Jackson! This is out of control! You're going to kill yourself out here, and for what? There's nothing here, Jackson, you can see for yourself!" The clouds broke, and the water poured down on us in buckets.

"She's here! I can feel her! She has to be here!" I cried, my voice cracking.

"Nobody is out here but the two of us! Think of your mother and father! Think of your brother! Think what they're going through right now! Just stop and think about what you're doing to them. You have to come back and get help, Jackson!"

"I can't," I said, pleadingly. "I can't, she's right here. I know it!" Rain mixed with the tears I couldn't hold back anymore. Lightning flashed. I pounded again against the stone. "Hana! Where are you!" The thunder drowned out my cries.

"Jackson! Don't you want a normal life? All of this, this fantasy your mind has invented, it can all be fixed! We can make it go away, and you can go back to a normal life."

"No, it's all real! It's so real!" I cried, sliding down to my knees next to the wet stone. My knees squished into the mud.

"Schizophrenia can make things seem just as real as anything else," she said loudly, but gently, kneeling down beside me and putting a hand on my shoulder. "It's a terrible curse, and can make you believe so many things that just aren't real. You're not the only one, Jackson. Thousands of people have this condition. It's treatable, though. Just come back with me, and by the time school starts again, you can walk back in with all your friends and go back to a normal life. Isn't that what you want?"

I wept openly, head down in my hands, the mud soaking through my pants. More than just the rain chilled me to the bone. The doubts that had been growing for days came to the front of my thoughts. I could feel the pull. She was right there.

Except that she wasn't. She wasn't there. The rock face was solid. There was no sound except the rain, the thunder, and the sobs tearing from my chest. No cries for help from a trapped girl. No echoes from a hidden tunnel. There was nothing. We were alone.

I looked up at Miss Moon. Her hair was wet and plastered to her face, but her expression was one of tenderness and concern. This woman wasn't trying to mislead me. She was trying to help. They all had been trying to help, right from the beginning.

The medication had made the whisper go away. Maybe the dosage still needed adjusting, that's why I had that dream. If the medicine helped, didn't that mean it was a chemical problem?

Why was I the only one who could hear her? Why was I the only one who believed? That wasn't true, I corrected. Cody believed me. But Cody, as much as I hated to remind myself, was also at Brookview for mental instability. He wasn't exactly the most reliable witness.

"But the kidnapping. The Dailys," I protested weakly. "A girl named Hana…" I trailed off.

"You probably heard about it when it happened. Jackson, your mind created this whole thing from what you heard. Think about it. Why would a cop, of all people, kidnap a girl? How could he possibly keep her alive and captive in the mountains for three years with nobody noticing? How in the world could she be talking to you in your mind from miles away? Jackson, it's just not possible."

She was right, and I knew it. It wasn't possible. A chemical imbalance causing hallucinations was a far more plausible story. Besides, the last lynchpin of my belief, that pulling feeling leading me to this spot, had proven false. My biggest, most convincing evidence of her reality, had just been proven completely wrong.

Cold, wet, hungry, tired, and emotionally broken, I stood slowly with Miss Moon's help, and we made the long, rough walk back to the roadside, where her car was parked. We both climbed in, ignoring the clean, dry seats and our wet, muddy clothes. She didn't seem to care, and I was beyond caring about anything.

Everything made so much more sense now that I stopped arguing with my rational mind. It wasn't real. My disorder had created it. That's why the drugs helped. I needed the drugs. I'd never live a normal life without them.

My only chance at anything like a normal life was to go back, do my time and take my drugs. When I got out, in a few months from what Miss Moon was telling me, things could start getting back to normal.

I desperately wanted things to be back how they were. Going to school, playing football, kissing my girlfriend, hanging with Thomas, all the things I loved were still there, waiting for me. I just had to let go of the delusions.

I looked out the window as we drove, back toward

the place I felt the pull. There was nothing there. I turned front again, clenching my eyes shut tightly. There was nothing left for me here.

Chapter Twenty-Five
The Road to Recovery

I don't remember much from the next several weeks. Cody had gone when I got back. His insurance had run out, ironically, and they'd kicked him out the next day. Or rather, 'released him as his treatment plan was complete'.

Alan had been moved to a higher security facility after his assault on poor, innocent Frank at the choir performance. Even my efforts to bring Lily back in contact with her father were wasted. All of it had been wasted. All for a dumb delusion.

I fell into the deepest, darkest depression I'd ever experienced. The thick, black mess of my emotions dragged at my every step, my every thought. Nothing mattered. I didn't get visitors. I wasn't 'stable' enough for that, even if I'd had the points for it. I didn't care.

I took my drugs when they told me to, I ate my meals, I showered, I slept. None of it with any enthusiasm. The higher dosage medicine dulled my thoughts, food tasted like ash, and my sleep was hollow and empty.

My parents sent me a letter, but I didn't read it. It didn't matter. Things didn't turn again until creepy singing lady came to me one afternoon in the rec room, where I sat, staring absently at one of the TVs. I didn't even know what was on, and I'd been watching it for an hour.

"Did you help her?" she asked in that oddly melodic voice. It was weird that her creepy singing didn't use that voice, I thought dully.

"Help who?" I asked, slightly confused.

"Your girl," she said, as if it were an expected question. Slowly, I turned to look at her. I felt my anger building.

"There is no girl," I said darkly.

"You know, the girl who…"

"There is no girl," I said, more forcefully as I stood. "There is no girl! There is no girl! She's not real! Nothing is real!" My voice grew until I was shouting. Mrs. Morris appeared next to me.

"Jackson, calm down. Deep breaths, calm down," she said soothingly.

I glared furiously at the strange woman, who shook her head sadly and walked away. I dropped heavily down onto the couch, my head in my hands.

"Good control, good job. Keep breathing, nice and steady," Mrs. Morris said to me.

I don't know what it was about that encounter, but the anger I'd felt at that moment had pushed through the depression. It was the first thing in a month that had. After that, other emotions started pushing through.

The reality of my illness really hit me hard in those next few weeks. I really was sick. I suddenly had a profound sympathy for my fellow inmates, and most especially anyone suffering from delusions like I'd had. Schizophrenia was terrifying, overwhelming, and insidious.

I started reading more about it, borrowing books from the small library as I began earning points back. Reading about seemingly countless people who had suffered delusions like mine, believing anything from aliens transplanting their brain to the delusion that they were a resurrected god. Not all the stories were quite that outlandish, but in every case, the schizophrenic truly believed what they saw. They saw it, heard it, felt it, just like I had.

I'd have laughed at stories like that, just a few months ago. Now, I empathized. I'd been there. I knew how easy it was to fall into a trap like that. It made sense to me now. Everything we experienced in this world was interpreted by chemical and electrical signals in our brains. Everything we saw, smelled, touched, tasted, heard, everything. It was all transmitted to us by those little signals.

One little thing goes wrong in those signals, and suddenly you're riding a donkey and jousting with a windmill convinced you're a knight. It was such a scary thought, knowing how easy it was for our own brains to mislead us.

"Nothing is real," I said for weeks in my sessions, finding it hard to connect to anything real anymore, knowing that any of it could potentially be a hallucination.

A few weeks after yelling at the singing lady, I was in another in an endless stream of therapy sessions. Dr. Tilton had been transferred, and I'd had a new afternoon therapist for about a month. I couldn't pronounce her last name, so she just had me call her Georgia. I liked her much better than Dr. Tilton.

"I realized something today," I told her.

"What's that?" she asked, ready to take notes.

"There are real things," I said, trying to force more clarity through my drug-hazed mind.

"Oh?" she asked, encouraging me to explain.

"I mean, I see reality through all those little signals in my brain, but what's really there is really there, whether I sense it or not. So, even if I don't see something, like the rec room, I can't see that right now, it doesn't mean it isn't real. Just like my seeing something doesn't mean it is."

"So what does that mean to you?" she asked.

"It means that real reality, and my perception of reality, aren't the same thing." I'd read that in one of the books I'd been reading, and it really struck me.

"That's a good point".

"So the medicine isn't changing reality, it's just changing my perception of it. Fixing it, back to normal, right?"

"That's about right," she agreed. "So what is real, Jackson?"

"My parents are real. My brother is real."

"Good," she urged. I pushed my muddled brain to remember the things I'd been thinking about that were really real.

"My friend Thomas is real. School is real, this hospital is real. I'm real, you're real."

"That's right. And Hana?"

"Not real. People don't read minds."

"That's correct. What about the sheriff?"

"Not real. I mean, sheriffs are real, but not this one. Not the one with the snake belt."

I felt thick in the head, but was proud of my ability

to convey my message in spite of that. Pushing through the drug-induced haze was actually easier than pushing through the fog of depression. Now that that was gone, things had begun to get a little clearer.

"Very good. What else?"

"Football is real. My ex-girlfriend is real. That's it. My friends, my family, my life, those are all real."

"And so?" she prompted.

"So I need to work hard to get better, so I can go back out and live a real life, with real things. I miss my life."

"That's wonderful, Jackson! I'm so proud of you for making that decision!"

I like to think of that as my turning point, where I really started trying hard in therapy and group. I even joined in the occupational therapy, and did finger-painting and weaving pot-holders.

I didn't make any more friends, though. It took me a long while to realize that part of my mind wasn't entirely convinced when I met a new person that they were real.

I'd been back in for two months when I was able to visit with my family again. I wasn't at all sure how this was going to go. My father was uncomfortable with me because he thought I was crazy. My mother was going to be a total emotional wreck after two months. They hadn't even let her see me after Miss Moon had brought me back.

Miss Moon had visited a couple of times to check on my progress. The charges had all been dropped, and the judge had not, at Miss Moon's urging, imposed a minimum time for me to stay here.

She was always friendly, warmer than she'd been

before she'd rescued me from the woods. I think she could tell I had sort of a soft spot for her after that. She'd saved my life, in more ways than one.

I had asked how she found me out there, and she told me someone had heard about the Amber Alert, and had spotted me hiding in the bushes on the side of the road leading up into the mountains. They'd reported the sighting, a friend of hers on the force had notified her, and she'd headed straight out. I was forced to the disappointing realization that I was not as ninja as I thought I was.

Hesitantly, I stepped into the visitors' room. Like before, my parents were sitting on the far side of the table. I was surprised again that my brother was there. I'm not sure why that surprised me, after his sudden appearance during my escape.

He hadn't gotten busted for helping me. Even though someone had reported seeing me riding in a blue Honda, Brent had been able to produce six different witness all insisting he'd been hanging out with them at the Outlet Mall immediately before our mother called him home.

The Outlet Mall was completely the opposite direction from our house, so there was no way he could have been anywhere near Brookview at that time. I only knew all of this because of things my mother had said in her letter that I'd finally opened.

When I'd talked to her on the phone a week before the visit, she'd asked me about the blue Honda. I told her I didn't know, and that I'd hitchhiked with a couple of random guys. One of them might have been a blue Honda. Or the guy who reported it might have been hoping for a reward or something. She'd bought it.

I stepped forward as Mom rushed to hug me. She very nearly crushed the air from my lungs with her grip. I hugged her back as long as I could stand not breathing, then tapped out.

"Mom," I gasped.

She let me go, desperately trying to get her tears under control. My father stepped forward. He was still really awkward in how he approached me. He went straight for the handshake this time, though. I shook his hand firmly, trying to give him a clear-eyed gaze. I'm not sure how well it worked, but he seemed satisfied.

"Hello, Jackson."

"Hi, Dad."

As before, Brent pushed in and saved me, hugging me tightly.

"Hey, jailbird."

"Brent!" my mother scolded.

I laughed. It felt good to be talking to real people again. My family was real. I knew that for sure. We all sat, me on one side, my family on the other. I wondered idly what everyone would do if I pushed into a seat on that side of the table. Maybe I'd try that the next time, just to see.

"So what's new?" I asked them.

"Not much," Brent replied.

"Oh stop now, honey, tell him!"

"I made the Dean's List," he told me, making a face to show he knew I'd be a lot less impressed with that than Mom was.

"Nice! Always knew that big head had to be good for something."

"Jackson!" Mom scolded. I laughed again.

"Sorry, Mom. Seriously though, that's cool. Nice work."

"Thanks," he said.

"What about you two?" I asked my parents.

"Your father has transferred to a new division," Mom said.

"Oh, he doesn't want to hear about my boring work," he said uncomfortably. Mom gave him an annoyed look.

"And you?" I urged her. She smiled and shook her head.

"Nothing really new for me. I do have some news you'll appreciate, though."

"Oh yeah?" I asked, leaning forward.

"We've spoken with your doctors, and they feel that you will be ready to come home in another two weeks!" she said with a squeal. It took a second to sink in, and when it did, my reaction was tinged with resentment.

"When does the insurance run out?" I asked.

"Now Jackson…" Mom started. Dad interrupted her.

"Two weeks," he said. Something in his tone told me he'd been forced to the harsh revelation that insurance really was the driving force behind my stay.

"Now that has nothing to do with his release, and you know it. He's been exceptionally well behaved the whole time he's been back, and hasn't had a single recurrence," she said firmly.

He nodded dully, like they'd had this conversation more than once before. Dad was a sharp guy, though. He knew as well as I did that they were sending me home because of the insurance, now that he'd been forced to admit it, and it had wounded his pride in professional medicine.

He also didn't think I was really ready to come home, I knew. Not that he'd know one way or another, I thought with another surge of resentment. He hadn't spoken a single word to me on any of my phone calls the last few weeks, and hadn't written a single letter. I hadn't spoken a word with him since the day before my escape. He knew nothing about me, these days.

"So what's new in here? Any new girlfriends?" Brent asked with a grin.

"Oh, yeah. There's a new girl here who chews on her own shirt collar all the time. And you should see her finger-paint! Very sexy," I told him.

"Jackson!" Mom scolded again, but this time in a weary tone, knowing our banter was going to go the whole visit. He and I could go for hours making fun of each other, and she knew it.

"Two weeks, huh?" I asked, going back to Mom. She nodded excitedly. I smiled, the idea sounding very, very good to me. "That's awesome. I really miss home, and all of you," I told her. She started to cry again.

"This has been so hard on everyone. You've been a real trooper, though."

"It's okay Mom. It's almost over," I told her.

Saying it almost made it real to me, but it still felt a little like someone else's dream. I wondered if it was the schizophrenia making me feel a little disconnected from reality, or if it was the drugs. Either way, it was still hard to really focus in on anything. Soon though, I'd be home. That would help, I knew.

The time went by too quickly, as we gradually eased into a more casual conversation. It still felt a bit forced, but I appreciated the effort. It felt really good to just talk to someone again. Someone who wasn't a therapist, anyway.

Mom hugged me tightly as they prepared to leave. I got another awkward handshake from my father. I wondered if he and I would ever be right again. Brent hugged me again and whispered to me.

"You need anything?" I shook my head.

"I'm good, thanks." As he let go and stepped back, I added, "Hey, let's do a movie and pizza night when I come home. I haven't had pizza in forever, and the last movie I saw was 'Topper', thirty-one times in a row."

"Dude, you've missed some good ones," Brent said. "Don't worry though, I'll catch you up."

"Thanks, man. Bye, guys."

"I love you," Mom said.

"You too, Mom. See ya."

I walked out of the visitors' room and down the hall. Two weeks, I thought. Two more weeks and I'd be home.

I suddenly wasn't sure how I felt about that. I'd been working all this time to get back to normal, but I sure didn't feel normal. I didn't know if I knew how to be normal after what I'd been through.

Maybe there was no normal for me anymore.

Chapter Twenty-Six
Back to Normal

It took three weeks for my release, not two. I think my dad was arguing with the insurance company over my coverage, and held out an extra week in hopes they'd extend.

The day had finally come, and I stood just inside the metal-gated doorway that the choir had passed through what felt like an eternity ago. Over the past three weeks, they'd amped up the medication. Probably to get a few extra hundred bucks out of the insurance company before coverage capped, but for whatever reason, it had left me feeling really numbed.

I didn't like the feeling, but couldn't force myself to really get too upset about it. I stood calmly, waiting as my parents signed me out up front. They'd be back here in a few moments to pass me through the gate. Rip stood beside me.

"Going to be cool to be home, right?" he asked.

"Yeah, I guess," I answered, trying to think clearly.

"You're not excited?" I shrugged. "I'd be excited," he said.

"I just don't know how it's going to be. Nothing is the same anymore," I told him. He nodded, understanding.

"Life's like that though. Nothing ever stays the same for long. Everything changes, that's kind of the point."

"I just want things to be normal again."

"You'll find a new normal. Normal is fluid, and changes with everything else. Hey," he said to get me to look at him. I did. "You're a good kid. You take care of yourself and your family, and the rest of the world will fall into line. You got me?"

I nodded, and he held his hand out for a fist bump. I gave it with a little more force than was really necessary. He laughed.

"That's what I'm talking about," he said, shaking his hand. I knew it didn't hurt him, but I appreciated the gesture.

"Rip?" I asked him.

"Yeah, kid?"

"What if I end up back here?"

"Then I'll just have to keep looking out for you. As long as you don't steal my keys again."

I laughed at that, and watched my parents come up to the other side of the gate, showing ID to the guard on duty. I was pretty sure that guy was the only actual guard that worked at this place, despite the half a dozen guard stations I'd seen around. Low budget shack, I thought spitefully.

As cool as Rip was, and as nice as Mrs. Morris was, I would never feel anything but revulsion and loathing at the thought of this place. I hated this place even through the dull haze of over-medication.

I tried to be more charitable, knowing that despite their motivations, they had actually helped me with my problems. It didn't help. I hated this place and was not at all sad to be walking out those doors.

Maybe I could find Cody, I thought as the guard unlocked the gate. We hadn't ever exchanged contact information. I really hoped he was doing well. Maybe I could get him and Thomas together. They'd get along great, I thought.

"Hi, hun!" Mom said, running forward to hug me. I ignored my dad, avoiding another awkward handshake.

"Hi, Mom. Can we go?" I asked. She laughed.

"Eager to get back home, huh?"

"Yeah," I replied, though really I was more interested in leaving here than I was particularly excited about going home. I was still worried about how un-normal everything was going to feel.

She took my small bag from Rip, who gave me one last encouraging nod, and we walked out the doors. Nobody was chasing me this time. That made things more normal. Nobody was talking in my head. That made it more normal. I was with my family again. That was normal.

We went out into the parking lot and climbed into a car that was so familiar it was almost painful. I played with the scratch on the side of the seat belt casing. Brent had done that, throwing a matchbox car at me from the front seat. He had been grounded for that one. I smiled at the memory.

The drive home wasn't long, but it felt that way to me. Traveling more than a few hundred feet felt very odd. Mom was chattering with Dad. Every so often they'd try to rope me into the conversation, but my dull, one-word answers discouraged that pretty quickly.

I looked for things that were familiar. Once near our place, things got very familiar quickly, but everything had an oddly surreal quality about it. Again, I wasn't sure if that was the drugs, or if it was the schizophrenia.

It was autumn, I realized, as I watched the many trees with their red and gold leaves. It was beautiful, and I just sort of zoned out watching them pass for a while.

"...and you can start going back to school next week," she was saying. That caught my attention, and I tuned in a bit more.

"Next week?" I asked.

"That's right," my dad said with a smile. It was less forced than his handshakes had been. Maybe we'd be back to normal sooner than I realized.

"Can I go tomorrow?" I asked.

"I don't know, that might be a bit soon," Mom said.

"It could be good for him," Dad argued. "Getting him back to a normal routine as quickly as possible might just be the best thing for him."

"I agree," I added. "I'd like to get everything back to normal as soon as possible. Can I?"

"Well, I suppose," Mom said uncertainly. "Let's see how you do today."

The day went by in a haze, like most of my days did. It was oddly calm, unstructured, and relaxed. Very unlike Brookview. Mom might be right, I thought. I may need a few days to readjust.

Lying in bed, my own bed off the floor, felt strange too. My room felt soft, and sound was muted since it wasn't echoing off brick and linoleum all the time. I reached over and turned on the small mp3 player by my bedside, hooked into its little speaker dock.

Listening to my normal music felt odd too, which

was starting to feel normal. I closed my eyes and lay my head back against the pillow. I wanted to call Cody, or Thomas. Mom wouldn't let me have my phone yet, though. I didn't have the energy to argue it with her just yet. Maybe later.

The next morning, I felt a little better. My daily medication prescription was a lot lower than what they'd been giving me inside. I worried about whether the hallucinations would come back with the lower dosage, but at least I had Dr. Fitzpatrick's promise that one phone call if I was having any trouble with them and he'd call in a higher dosage for my prescription.

Of course, on the plus side, everything seemed a bit clearer when I woke up, with less of the drugs in my system. I immediately took my morning dose, already prepped in a little pill box that held my week's doses all neatly organized a dose at a time on the bedside table.

Standing, I started at the feel of carpet on my bare feet. Taking a moment to run my feet back and forth on the unfamiliar feeling of carpet, I was greeted by the smell of bacon. I couldn't get downstairs fast enough.

Mom was by the stove, frying up some fresh bacon and eggs, and humming a happy little tune. She'd taken the day off, I realized. I shouldn't have been surprised, but since I'd told her I wanted to go to school today, I expected her to be gone to work already.

"Bacon? Mom, have I told you lately that you rock?" I said, still a bit sleepily.

I glanced at the clock on the stove top. Just past nine thirty. Looked like I wasn't going to school after all. She turned and smiled at me. I saw the love and excitement in her eyes and decided not to bring it up. She was so psyched to have me home that it was the least I could do to spend the day with her. As soon as the thought came, I realized I really wanted to spend some time with her. Cody was right. These women-folk sure got into your mind.

We spent the day playing board games and chatting while the TV ran mom's favorite soaps in the background. She ignored them completely, but the background noise was nice.

The more we went through the day, the clearer things got. I was a bit nauseated, but I'd been warned that reducing my dosage like that would likely result in nausea for a few days, and dizziness if I exerted myself too much.

Mom had been right as usual, I thought, as I lay down to sleep in my own bed once more. I needed to readjust. I felt a lot better already. I had made my mom set an alarm for me. I was going to school in the morning.

When I awoke to my mother calling my name, I got up and got ready like I always used to. I styled my hair for the first time in months, and realized how long it had gotten. I'd have to have Mom trim it. Not short, of course, but back to where I liked it. No time now, though.

I picked out some of my favorite clothes, and went downstairs. The whole experience was surreal. The very normalness of it all seemed very abnormal.

I was halfway through the bowl of cereal when Mom came in and froze, staring at me.

"What?" I asked, mouth half full.

"You hate cereal," she said. I paused and thought about it. She was right, I did. I looked down at the bowl, and chewed a bit more. Finally, I shrugged.

"It's not that bad," I told her. She shook her head, but looked concerned. I'd changed, and we both knew it. A change in taste was an unexpected one though, I thought. I wondered if that was a side effect of the medications, too.

Cody had told me once that the anti-depressant they'd first put him on when he got put inside made everything taste like sawdust for two weeks before his system had adjusted. Probably just adjusting, I thought.

Mom drove me to school, and as we parked, she reached into her bag and handed me a cell phone.

"Now Jackson, I don't give one whit what the rules are about cell phone use in this school. If you have any problems, any problems at all, or even just feel like coming home, you call me and I'll be here in less than fifteen minutes."

"Whose phone is this?" I asked, looking over the unfamiliar device.

"It's yours, silly," she said. Then she realized and added, "Oh, but this is your new one. Yours broke right before you went into the hospital. Your dad got you this one after that, and I think you only had it a day. They've immigrated all your old settings and contacts and everything."

"Imported," I corrected her. She smiled.

"Whatever. Now go, have a little fun at school. They haven't been back from summer that long, so you won't be far behind."

"Okay, Mom. Thanks."

I let her kiss my cheek. We were far enough from the front of the school that I wasn't in easy visibility of most of the kids. Besides, the poor lady had a rough couple of months. She needed a little slack.

Rubbing at my cheek to clear any errant lipstick, I climbed out of the car, slung my backpack over my shoulder, and headed for school.

Thomas was waiting by the doors. I wondered if my mom had given him a heads up that I was coming.

"Jacks!" he called, jogging up to me. He slapped my hand and we bro-hugged it out.

"Hey, man," I said casually.

"It's awesome that you're back," he said. "This school sucks without you."

"Sucks with me, too," I said. Thomas grinned.

"Come on, we've got Trig together."

"Oh, joy," I said unenthusiastically. He clapped me on the shoulder and off we went.

We'd made it less than ten feet into the school when the whispering started. Not in my head, I had to clarify to myself after a moment of panic. The other students. There were points, giggles, whispers, and lots of faces being made my direction. Mostly faces of mock fear as I walked past.

Words like 'psycho', 'schizo', 'freak', and other, less pleasant ones, were tossed around liberally. None directly to my face, though. That would probably take a day or two, I thought. These cowards would need a few days to build up the nerve to get in my face, knowing I'd been supposedly put away for assaulting someone during a psychotic episode.

This was going to do unpleasant things to my rep, I knew. Already had, I corrected as I glanced around.

"Amber," I said in surprise as she rounded the corner in front of me. I felt a twinge of heartache, though not as much as I'd expected.

She was with another guy, holding his hand. I knew

him, a little. Kolby was on the basketball team. We were both jocks, but hung with a very different crowd. She looked down at their clasped hands and back up to me. She got uncomfortable almost instantly.

"Jackson… hi. Umm… you remember Kolby?"

"Yeah," I said to her, and, "Hey," to him. His mumbled response was just as uncomfortable as Amber seemed to be.

"I've got class," I said, moving to go around them. "Later."

"See you later," Amber said.

"You believe that girl?" I hissed sharply to Thomas. "I get sick, and she goes for the first available jock she can find."

"Second," Thomas corrected.

"What?"

"Second. She was with Curt from the track team the first week of school."

"Unbelievable," I muttered.

We made it to class, where I endured and ignored another barrage of whispered comments and not-so-subtle pointing. As the teacher came in, one I didn't recognize, I took a deep breath.

You can do this, I told myself. It's just school, you can handle school. The first bell rang and I jumped, causing a few giggles behind me.

I can do this, I thought again to myself. I hope.

Chapter Twenty-Seven
Reality

Making it through school was the hardest thing I'd done in a very long time. The whispered jokes, the pointing, the constant negative attention, it was all very overwhelming. Despite that, I did it again the next day, and the next, and the next. Sheer willpower, I told myself.

I actually realized that there was only one major difference between the people in Brookview and the ones here at school. That difference was very simple. The people in Brookview knew they were crazy.

I kept trying to find the normal I remembered, but it seemed to have vanished. I was seeing people differently. I was noticing the little bits of shallow ugliness that they casually slipped into normal, friendly conversation. Comments about someone's hair, someone's clothes, someone's skin, whatever. It was constant, superficial, and caustic.

None of these conversations seemed new or unusual, that was the really scary part. It was like I suddenly was just being made painfully aware of them. This place wasn't a school, I thought, it was a contest to see who could insult the most people without them realizing it.

If this is what school had been like before and I hadn't noticed, I had been blinder than I'd ever known, I thought to myself.

"Thomas!" I called as I spotted my friend coming out of his last class.

"Hey, man," he said. "How'd it go?" We only had one class together on Fridays, at second hour.

"I survived the week," I told him.

"Nicely done, bro," he said. "So you're hanging in okay?"

"Yeah," I said as we started walking toward the front doors to go home. I'd been doing the school thing for four days, and it had sapped more out of me than a week of therapy sessions ever had.

I kept waiting for normal to kick back in, but it never did. My only consolation was that everyone was still a little nervous around me, so nobody was making fun of me to my face. I thought about Cody.

If I'd been a chess club kid, it would have been different, I was sure. But I was a jock, a member of what had suddenly become obvious to me was a sort of protected class. I wondered if that would hold true if I never got back to football. Not that my dropping football for good was at all an option, I just wondered. Awareness was a strange, perspective-changing thing.

"So, I texted your mom," Thomas opened with.

"If you follow that with a joke, I might hit you," I said with a smile. He grinned.

"No joke. I asked her if I could walk you home today."

"Aw, thanks! Does this mean we're going steady?" I teased. He laughed.

"Come on, man. Your mom won't let you go

anywhere without direct supervision these days. I feel like she already thinks I'm babysitting you for her at school. I'm not, but she seems to think so. Anyway, I thought you needed a little something for your efforts, making it through your first week back. Thought we'd go by the convenience store around the corner and grab a slushee or something. Maybe check out the cheerleaders that always pass by on the way to the fields. You down?"

"Let's do it. Thanks, man." I told him.

He nodded and we headed that way. I'd been getting clearer-headed all week. The lower dosage was good. No return of the hallucinations, either, so all was as well as could be expected. I did consider more than once that week asking my mom to have me transferred to a new school, though.

We chatted as we walked, about casual things. He updated me on the latest game releases, some of the movies I'd missed, and the latest app for my phone that everyone had and I apparently needed, too.

"So, I have to ask," Thomas said, once we were sitting on the curb with our slushees. No cheerleaders, yet.

"What?" I asked.

"The hallucinations…" He hesitated. "Did they cure you, I mean?" he asked. I shrugged.

"Sort of. They've got me on medications that seem to have gotten rid of them. If I stop taking them, they'll probably come back. Dr. Fitzpatrick says they might come back anyway over time, as my body builds resistances, but it could be years, and they have other medications they can try when it does."

"So you're not going back to that place?" he asked.

"Not if I can help it," I told him earnestly.

"That bad?"

"Dude, if I had the choice between spending a week in that place, and spending a week in Deloy's locker, I'd take the locker."

"My God!" he exclaimed in mock horror. "The stench alone could kill you! Never mind the fungus!"

"Still better," I argued. He got more serious.

"I'm sorry, man. That sucks. You made it through, though. More proof you're hard core."

"I guess. You don't really win in there, though. You just sort of survive it."

"I call that a win," he said.

I thought about that, and nodded after a time. I remembered the lady who'd lost her husband, trying to kill herself in the cafeteria. I also remembered an incident, though only vaguely, while in my depression where someone had nearly beat an orderly to death with a chair because he'd taken her pudding cup. In a place like that, survival was definitely a win.

"Yeah, that's true."

The first little flock of cheerleaders passed. They were chattering and giggling, exactly as expected. Thomas raised his slushee in salute as they glanced our way. We'd done this a thousand times before, and we'd always gotten smiles, waves, even a few winks when we did this.

Not this time. Immediately the whispers and pointing started. I sighed.

"I'm sorry. I'm killing your groove."

"Don't say that, wingman! Don't worry, the novelty will wear off soon, and we'll be right back to normal."

"I don't think I'll ever be back to normal," I

admitted, my first real confession to him since I'd gotten back. He looked at me for a long moment.

"Hang in there, Jacks. It'll get better, I promise."

"I hope so. If it doesn't, I don't..." My words trailed off as a black and white car pulled into the parking lot.

"You don't what?" Thomas urged, then looked where I was now staring.

"Tell me what you see," I begged him, my voice shaking badly.

"A sheriff's cruiser. Why?" he asked, confused. I closed my eyes and took a deep breath. I let it out slowly and tried to calm myself.

"Just making sure."

"You okay?"

"Yeah, I'm good. Sorry."

"It's cool," he assured me.

I opened my eyes, but kept them down. That had scared me. I suspected I'd be jumpy around police cars for quite a while. Not a comforting thought.

The sheriff's cruiser pulled into a spot near our curb, and the door opened. The sheriff got out and walked past us to go into the convenience store. I only half glanced up, and my eyes locked onto one thing. I couldn't have looked away if I tried. I stared, eyes following the sheriff until he went into the store and out of sight.

"Jacks!" Thomas called. I realized he'd said it more than once.

"Thomas, tell me what you saw."

"A county sheriff, dude. Come on, you're freaking me out."

"Anything unusual about him?"

"No, man. Just a county sheriff. Let's get you home, I think you've been through a lot this week. Rest is probably a good idea."

"Don't patronize me, Thomas," I warned. "Nothing unusual at all?"

"No, Jackson. He was your average, ordinary, run-of-the-mill sheriff. Can we go now?" I inhaled deeply, letting it out again so slowly I thought my lungs would burst.

"Yeah. Let's go."

We stood and started walking out of the parking lot.

"Bad-ass snake belt, though. You see that thing?"

My blood ran ice cold, goosebumps racing across my skin. I cursed, sharply, but under my breath. Thomas had seen it, too.

"What?" he asked, his voice showing his concern. I didn't answer for a moment as I thought hard.

"Thomas, I need you to do two things for me."

"Sure, man. Anything," he said. His eyes were filled with worry.

"First, I need you to call social services and ask for Darcy Moon. Darcy Moon, got that?" I waited for his nod. "Tell her where I've gone."

"And where have you gone, Jackson?" he asked, slowly, carefully.

"Tell her I found the cop, and I'm following him into the mountains."

"What? Jackson, come on man," Thomas started, his voice showing his rising panic.

"Second," I interrupted, "I need you to check and tell me if that sheriff is still in the store."

"Jackson," he started.

"Please, Thomas. Please." I whispered.

He stared at me for a moment, then cursed deeply himself. He took a few steps to one side so he could see into the store.

"Yeah, he's there. He's in line, there are three people ahead of him. Jackson, come on. Let me take you home. This is crazy."

I grabbed him by the front of his shirt and pulled him in close.

"You don't understand, Thomas," I said, my intensity scaring even me. "That man in there is proof. Proof that I'm not crazy. I'm not crazy!"

I let him go and ran to the sheriff's cruiser.

"Jacks, what the hell are you doing?" he called.

"Call her, Thomas! Darcy Moon! Tell her!" I shouted back.

I reached through the open window of the cruiser and hit the trunk release. Running to the back, I opened the trunk and jumped in.

"Jackson!" Thomas called, running around behind the cruiser. "Are you frickin' kidding me right now?" he almost shouted.

"Get lost, you'll make him suspicious!" I hissed.

I pushed one corner of my backpack under the latch of the trunk and pulled it down. It made a metallic thunk as it hit the corner of my bag.

That was odd, I thought. I opened the small, zippered pocket on that corner, one that I never kept anything in, and pulled out Brent's pocketknife. I grinned.

My brother would have wet himself laughing too hard if he knew I'd taken it to school all week without realizing it. Right now though, I thought, it actually might be really handy. I pocketed it, and put the corner back under the latch. Pulling the trunk back down, I held onto it tightly to keep it from bouncing back up, even though it wasn't locked down.

"Jackson!" Thomas called. "Come on, man! This is so not okay!" I ignored him. "Ja…" he abruptly cut off. I heard him a few moments later, several feet further away. "Good afternoon, officer. Nice day for a slushee, wouldn't you say?"

"Hey, kid," the sheriff replied. "Sure is. Stay out of trouble, you hear?"

"Always do, officer, always do." His voice faded as he walked away. Good old Thomas, I thought with a smile.

The engine, which the officer had left running, purred as he pulled out of his spot and moved back onto the road. It was harder than I'd thought to keep the trunk held down while the car kept trying to bounce it up as we hit what had to be every pothole in the tri-state area.

What if he wasn't going to the mountains? I thought suddenly. He has to be, I thought. It's not Thursday, he only misses Thursdays. But what if he went this morning, my brain pointed out. No, evenings. It was almost always evenings, I told myself.

I was shaking again. He was real. The scary, psycho, evil cop was real, and he was going to the mountains where he kept Hana. I wouldn't have believed my own senses, but Thomas's? That rattlesnake belt buckle was very distinctive. This was the cop.

My mind wouldn't let it rest. I'd spent months teaching myself to question all of my senses. What if it's a coincidence, and he just happens to have the same belt? Maybe you saw that belt sometime a long time ago, and he just bought it from the same store?

Can't be, I argued with myself. I've never seen a belt like that. It looks custom. I'd never have had the chance to see it before, so how could I have hallucinated it so perfectly?

Maybe you just don't remember, my mind replied. Wow, I thought. I'm arguing with myself. I really am crazy. But not about this, I thought firmly. This is the guy, and he's taking me where he's keeping Hana.

Bouncing and jostling along, I kept changing positions to be able to maintain my downward pressure on the trunk lid. My arms were falling asleep. The sounds of traffic had long since died away.

I'd been holding nearly as long as I felt I possibly could and was trying to figure out what I'd do if it popped open, when I heard a familiar, terrifying sound; the crunching of tires on gravel.

The only thing worse than being crazy, I decided in that moment, was being both crazy and right.

Chapter Twenty-Eight
Busted

I lay as still as I could, covering my mouth with my free hand to mask the sound of my anxious, heavy breathing. I couldn't make it stop. I heard the engine shut off, and the car door open.

Boots on gravel crunched, circling slowly around the car. I held the trunk down as tight as I could, praying the layers of fabric keeping it from latching weren't also holding it up high enough to be noticeable.

The footsteps stopped not far from the trunk, and my heart leapt to a mile a minute. I held my breath completely and didn't move a muscle.

It felt like an eternity before I heard the boots crunching through the gravel, and moving away from the car. I waited for a full count of sixty once they had faded out completely before I opened the trunk.

I eased it up a fraction of an inch at a time until I could peer out. I could see the woods, leaves red and gold and rustling in a gentle breeze. The sun was still high, but it was definitely lower in the sky than it had been when I'd climbed in. We'd probably been driving at least an hour. I didn't see him anywhere.

Slowly, I opened the trunk the rest of the way, and climbed out. Easing the trunk back down, I pushed it firmly, but carefully, until I felt it click. I looked down at the gravel. Walking on this would be too loud, I knew.

I slipped off my shoes, and held them in my hand. The gravel was sharp, but it was much quieter walking this way. The graveled area was a semi-circle, wrapping around the front of a mineshaft leading into the stone.

The opening was boarded, but only by a few boards with a sign saying "Keep Out". There was plenty of room for a grown man to work his way through there without too much trouble.

I moved out beyond the gravel, circling wide to one side of the tunnel once I'd made it to the dirt. I slipped my shoes back on, as they wouldn't make nearly as much noise on the soft earth, and I might need to run hard and fast at any moment.

Keeping a close eye on the entrance, I saw nothing. I crouched down low behind a tree, and listened carefully. It was quiet for several moments, then I heard a girl cry out.

Cursing under my breath, I almost wished I really had been crazy. Now what was I going to do? Good job thinking ahead, I chastised myself. What did I think was going to happen when he got here?

I couldn't just sit here and listen to her being assaulted and wait for him to leave. Maybe I could spook him away. I hunted around until I found a dry, fallen branch. Picking it up, I bent it hard until it snapped.

The sound went off like a gunshot, much louder than I had expected. Dropping the broken branch, I sprinted around the semicircle a hundred feet or so and ducked behind some heavy brush. A fraction of a second later, the sheriff came out of the opening, stepping over the low board. He had his gun out.

I was abruptly reminded that I'd been spotted the last time I tried to go stealth mode in the woods. I forced my breathing to go as slowly and steadily as I could, and tried to keep from shaking.

His eyes scanned the forest around the graveled area carefully, gun ready. I picked up another stick, and waiting until his eyes were as far away from me as possible, tossed it a hundred feet toward the other side.

It made a rustling sound as it went through a bush, and the sheriff spun, gun leveled, facing that direction. He held still for a long time, listening. Walking slowly further out from the tunnel, his eyes scanned the brush again. He was walking straight toward me. I held my breath and eased even lower in the brush.

"Car 146, please respond."

Both the sheriff and I jumped at the unexpected voice. It took me a moment to recognize that the sound had come from the CB radio in his cruiser. The sheriff looked angry. He also didn't lower the gun as he side-stepped to the car and reached in through the window to grab the mic.

"This is Car 146, over," he said. I took the opportunity to study the man.

He was well built, and looked pretty strong. I'd seen cops that looked like lifting donuts was their only exercise, but this was not one of those guys. The thing that really struck me though was that he looked totally normal.

Like completely and totally, kiss the wife, hug the kids, sing them lullabies, and walk the dog normal. It was disconcerting. I had expected him to look… I don't know, creepy, I guess. He really didn't, though. I could have passed a guy like this a thousand times on the street and never looked twice.

"Car 146, report to 3rd and Lincoln in Harbor Glen right away."

"Dispatch, I'm officially off duty and am almost home."

"It's an emergency, Car 146. Captain's orders. Possible hostage situation. All units are called in, off duty or on."

"You've got to be kidding me," he muttered to himself, before pressing down the button on the mic again. "Car 146 en route, eta twenty minutes."

Slamming the mic back on its hook in the car, he cursed loudly and angrily as he holstered his revolver and climbed back into his cruiser.

Revving the engine, he spun out, flinging gravel everywhere as he raced onto the narrow dirt road leading away from the abandoned mine and toward the main road.

I waited a full minute after I no longer heard the car before sprinting on the gravel to the mine, and climbing the lower board to step inside.

There was a pair of car batteries just inside the entrance, connected to a pair of wires looped over hooks drilled into the stone wall of the tunnel. The wires ran down deeper into the tunnel.

I was a lot further in than I expected when I saw the little yellow light, flickering as it always did. Something about actually being there, knowing it was all real, was almost scarier than thinking I'd gone insane. This was it, I knew. I had to get to her, and get her out of here.

After that, we had to figure out how to get help. Hopefully, Thomas had called Miss Moon, and she was bringing the posse out to help rescue us. It was us, I realized, that needed rescuing now. I'd made it all the way out here, but it would take days to walk back. Much longer, since I probably would have to carry Hana most, maybe all of the way.

We'd deal with that once I had her out, I decided. From the light, it was several more feet to where I knew she'd be. I couldn't see anything, though. My eyes hadn't adjusted yet to the darkness of the tunnel. I stopped for a moment, trying to focus on her. There was a shifting sound and I saw movement.

"Hana?" I called, softly.

The movement stopped dead. It was silent a long moment before there was a response. The voice that greeted me was broken and raw, and barely sounded human, let alone like a girl my own age.

"Hel… hello?" the voice asked. It was shaky and cracked, but held something I recognized deeply within myself. Her voice held hope.

"Hana, I'm here to help," I said as I moved forward and into the yellow light.

"It's you," the voice croaked.

I froze. She knew me. I didn't have any idea how that was possible, but somehow she knew me.

"Hana, we have to get you out of here. We need to cover as much ground as possible before he comes back."

"I knew you'd come for me," she said, and I heard the sob hitch in her throat.

"I know, I'm here now."

It wasn't the time to ask her how she knew me, or

why she thought I would come for her. She wasn't wrong, after all. I had come for her. I moved quickly to her now, knowing she wasn't going to be afraid of me. When I got close enough to really see, I fought back a surge of nausea.

The girl in front of me barely looked alive. She was starved and wasted away until she looked like all skin and bones. Her naked skin was caked in filth and grime, and her hair had been roughly hacked semi-short. What was there was probably once blonde, but now was so matted and crusted with dirt and grime that it would probably have to be totally shaved.

She was chained to the wall about mid-way up, leaving her enough chain to stand, or lie down if she chose, though I doubted this girl had stood in a long time. Her sunken cheeks were streaked with clean lines as her tears washed little channels in the dirt.

Just at the edge of her hands' reach was a small trickle of water running out of the wall. That's what I'd heard before, during my seizures. It was close enough for her to reach, but probably only with her fingertips. I doubted she could get enough gathered at once to wash with, and probably only barely enough sucked off her fingers to keep alive.

The water ran into a small pool that reeked like an outhouse. She'd been using it as one, I instantly knew, the water slowly overflowing and running down away into the mine. It wasn't a fast flush though, and while not totally overpowering, was probably a constant stench she'd lived with for years. I swallowed hard and knelt down beside her.

"Hana, can you walk?" I asked. I already knew the answer before she shook her head. "Okay, that's okay.

Hold on, let me figure this out."

I gently took her hands. They were shaking, though I didn't know whether with cold, with fear, or with relief. She made a small cry in the back of her throat when I touched her hands, and with a quick glance at her arm I remembered the break. That arm looked straight, but was badly swollen, and the bruising covering her forearm was almost black.

Taking another slow breath, I gently looked over the shackles. The lock looked ancient. For all I knew, these had been here since the mine closed down.

The good news was that it meant I might be able to get it open. The bad news was that my getting it open probably hinged on the entire mechanism not being totally rusted shut.

I gave them a simple tug, and she winced as the metal rubbed her raw, bleeding wrists. Those wrists were probably scar tissue on top of scar tissue on top of scar tissue, I knew.

"Sorry," I said softly. She just nodded.

I pulled hard on the chain attached to the wall, but it didn't budge. Cursing softly, I looked at the keyhole in the shackles. Suddenly, I had an idea. Reaching into my pocket, I pulled out Brent's pocketknife.

The knife blades were both too big, I saw immediately. The nail file might work, but I didn't know for sure. Nothing else looked even close. Nail file it is, I decided.

"So what's a nice girl like you doing in a place like this?" I asked casually, as I inserted the file into the keyhole on one shackle. She laughed.

It was an odd sound, at once rough and raw, and somehow beautiful. It was a sound I didn't think she'd made in a very long time, and one she probably thought she'd never make again. I smiled at her, as I worked at the lock.

"What's your name?" she croaked out.

"Jackson."

"Thank you, Jackson." I paused and looked at her.

Her eyes were absolutely stunning. Her body may have been severely damaged by the man's evil, but her eyes shone with hope, relief, and gratitude. I'd never seen anything so beautiful in my entire life. I swallowed back hard on my tears as I began to choke up. I nodded and went back to the lock.

"Don't thank me yet," I cautioned. "We're not out of the woods. Literally or figuratively," I smiled. She returned the smile.

With a sudden grind, I felt something inside the lock shift.

"Wait, I think I've got something."

I kept working at it, and the mechanism with a lot of resistance slowly turned. Sharply, the shackle popped open. We both stared at each other, stunned. Suddenly, I grinned and turned to the other shackle.

She slowly rotated the wrist around, moving it side to side in a fluid, testing motion, eyes full of awe and wonder. I tried not to think that it was the first time she'd had a free hand in over three years.

I focused on the other lock. This one went faster, for some reason. It took only a couple of minutes before I felt the mechanism shift. I had to push a lot harder to get this one to complete its turn though, and when it gave right at the end, the nail file snapped, and the broken end went straight into my other hand.

I cried out and dropped the knife as her other hand

came free. I cursed, loudly, and started sucking on the wound.

"Are you okay?" she asked, softly.

"Yeah, I'm fine. It's wide, but not too deep. Gonna bleed a lot, though. Come on, let's get you ready." I reached out and took two handfuls of water from the tiny, trickling waterfall, and rubbed at her face. Several layers of grime came off with a few more handfuls, but she'd need a real shower, maybe five or six real showers, before she'd be really clean again.

I stripped my shirt off and helped her put it on. It was long enough to cover her, though only barely. I leaned over and drank as much of the water trickling down as possible, trying not to think about the fact that the other end of that stream was a pool of this girl's waste. The water tasted surprisingly clean, so it wasn't too hard to ignore its destination.

"Drink as much as you can. I don't know when we'll get clean water again."

She nodded and leaned over. I helped her shift closer so she took what was probably her first long, full drink of water in three years as well.

"Okay, are you ready?" I asked. She nodded.

I scooped her up and was stunned at how little she weighed. The poor girl was so thin and frail I was half afraid she'd break if I weren't extra careful holding her. She winced as we gently adjusted her broken arm into her lap. I ran awkwardly with her to the entryway, and made it through the boards without too much trouble.

She gasped as the late afternoon light hit her eyes, squinting them shut against the unaccustomed brightness. I watched her for a moment. It was like watching someone seeing a forest for the first time.

Hana probably felt like it was her first time seeing the outside of that tunnel. After three years of what she'd been through, all of the memories of her old life probably seemed like fantasies.

Looking around, I wasn't sure which way to go. Spotting the dirt trail, I headed that way. If we could flag down a car, we could be on easy street back to town. Nobody would refuse a lift to a hospital for a girl that looked like that.

I winced as I shifted my grip with my wounded hand. She noticed, eyes full of concern, but to my relief she didn't say anything.

We had taken only five steps when the sound of a car coming down the dirt trail hit me. We exchanged a quick, panicked look, and I bolted to the side, running back along the rock face around the slow curve and into the wooded area.

I ran as quickly as I could, carrying her and trying to stay quiet, but couldn't resist a look back. The sheriff's car pulled into the gravel quickly, sliding a bit as the sheriff hit the brakes. He immediately drew his gun and charged to the tunnel entrance. He was holding my backpack, I realized with horror.

I had no idea how he'd found it. Maybe the trunk hadn't latched all the way when I'd closed it, and he'd jarred it loose and got out to close it again. Maybe he'd stopped to pull out his gear for the possible hostage situation.

Either way, I thought, this was probably about to turn into a murder situation, so I needed to focus on getting gone as fast as possible.

I looked forward again and leaned into my dangerous run. I was moving fast, despite carrying the girl and having to navigate the underbrush, but it was louder than I'd hoped. We had gone plenty far enough to not see the tunnel anymore, so I slowed slightly to reduce the amount of noise we were making.

"Shh, stay quiet," I whispered to her. She just nodded, and held on as tightly as her weakened body would allow.

We both heard the roar of outrage from the man as he clearly discovered his pet had disappeared. Exchanging a glance, we grit our teeth and I kept running.

The crashing of someone who cares a lot more about speed than stealth rang from behind. Branches snapped, leaves were torn free, the noise was impressive. And coming this way. I didn't know how he knew we'd gone this way, but we were in a lot of trouble.

I took some comfort in the fact that the noise we were making was probably easily masked by the ruckus he was making. I sped up, hoping his crashing would drown out mine.

We turned a sharper bend in the rock face, and I froze. The length of rock face I was staring at was the same face I'd been pounding against when Miss Moon had caught up with me.

With a quick mental replay of our run, I realized that the spot where Hana had been chained in the tunnel was probably less than ten or twenty feet straight through the rock here. Right where I'd felt the pull. I'd been right all along. About everything.

It was jarring, thinking about how close I'd come to rescuing her, three months earlier. Miss Moon had been there too. We'd have been back in town and getting help in less than an hour.

The crashing got closer, and I started running again. Still following the rock face, I got to the place where Miss Moon and I had gone straight back out to reach her car and the road. The road must loop around this curve I realized. So if we headed straight that way…

"Freeze" commanded a deep, and very angry voice. I looked back, and he was there, far closer than I thought, gun aimed straight at us.

"I'm sorry," I said to Hana, as my eyes welled up with tears. "I tried."

Chapter Twenty-Nine
The Day I Died

Hana looked at me with nothing but gratitude. There was no sorrow, no anger, no resentment that I had completely failed and now we were both going to die. Just gratitude. I could read it in her eyes.

She was grateful I had come, grateful that I had tried. She was grateful that I'd broken her chains, and that I'd given her the gift of seeing the sky one last time. The gift of laughing, and seeing a smiling face one last time. She was ready to die.

I was not.

I turned my glare on the sheriff as I slowly turned to completely face him. He seemed a little surprised by my expression, but was clearly amused by it.

"You forgot this," he said, tossing my blue backpack at my feet.

"They know where I am," I snarled.

"Who does?" he asked, unconcerned.

"Everyone, by now. My friend called my social worker." I realized how dumb that sounded as soon as I said it. He laughed.

"Well I'd better just run for the hills then!" he mocked. "Listen, kid, you get points for bravery, but you lose them all for stupidity. I have to know though, how did you find me?"

"Hana called me," I told him. She gave me a smile.

"Try again," he said.

"What do you care?" I asked. "You're going to kill us anyway."

"Well sure," he responded, "but I have to know how you found out about me so I can make sure nobody else does."

"I told you, she called me," I told him. It felt good to say it out loud and know it was the truth.

"Kid, I'm going to ask you one last time."

"You're going to kill us," I reminded him.

"If you don't tell me, I'll make sure to do it real slow," he snarled.

"Even if you kill us before the cavalry gets here, they're going to come up here. They're going to search for us."

"They've been looking for her for years," he said, dismissively. "Nobody's ever come close to finding her."

"I did," I pointed out. "Besides, I was right here in this exact spot with my caseworker the last time I came up here trying to find her. She knows this place, and the cops will be all over this part of the mountain looking for me."

"I am the cops, kid."

"No, you're one cop. A dirty, twisted, jacked up cop who's going down, whether you kill us or not."

"Might as well just kill you then. I was getting bored with her, anyway. Maybe I'll play with you for a while first though, kid. You seem like you could use a little humbling. Bye, darlin', it's been fun," he said to Hana and aimed the gun.

"Jackson?" called a voice.

It was Miss Moon. I prayed she'd brought the cavalry, because otherwise this guy was going to kill all three of us.

"Miss Moon!" I shouted.

"Shut up!" the sheriff snapped.

"Jackson!" she called. She'd heard me.

The sheriff growled. The moment Miss Moon was in view, he leveled the gun. She started talking the moment she saw me. She didn't notice the sheriff for another few seconds.

"Jackson! Are you kidding me? I thought we'd been through thi…" It was at this moment that she really took in my condition and noticed Hana. "What in the world…" Then she noticed the sheriff, and then his gun, pointed straight at her.

"Well this is just turning into a real party," he snarled. Get over there," he ordered, gesturing with the gun toward me and Hana.

Miss Moon moved slowly over to me, watching the gun carefully. When she got close, she looked at me, then at Hana.

"My God…" she said in hushed, awed tones, "you were right all along…"

"Listen, lady," the sheriff interrupted, "This is real sweet and all, but I have three bodies to bury now, and I ain't got all night."

"Please tell me you brought the cops," I told her. She looked sheepish. "Seriously?" I asked her incredulously. She hadn't believed me. I once again felt betrayed by someone I'd confided in.

"I'm sorry," she said.

"Okay," the sheriff said, stepping wide to one side,

"follow the rock wall back to the tunnel. It'll be a lot easier to ditch your bodies back there."

"Why on earth would we make it easier for you to hide us?" I asked in amazement.

The sound of the gunshot reached me just slightly after the bullet did. It ripped into my right shoulder with an oddly dull feeling. It took almost a full second for the pain to hit me. Miss Moon was already screaming by this point.

I stumbled to the side, almost dropping Hana. Miss Moon caught her, and gently took her from me, trying to support my weight as she did so. I was too stunned to scream as the pain tore the air right out of my lungs. I gasped uselessly for several seconds.

To my great pride, I did not fall. Thanks to Miss Moon, of course. I leaned heavily on her, and her small frame struggled under the weight of both Hana's frail body, and the partial weight of my much larger one.

"Let's try this again, shall we?" asked the sheriff cheerfully. "Go back to the tunnel. Am I clear?"

Miss Moon nodded and shuffled forward, careful to let me keep using her for support. I almost fell again, willing myself to move. I staggered along, the pain surging with each step, each step taking more and more will to keep going.

My bare chest and stomach was covered in my own blood, and it felt like it was positively gushing out of the hole in my shoulder. I had broken into a cold sweat, and was having trouble breathing steadily.

"Hold on, Jackson," she whispered as we worked our way slowly back to the tunnel.

"For what?" I gasped out, angrily. "For the cavalry that isn't coming?"

"I'm sorry, Jackson, I…"

"Shut up!" yelled the sheriff.

We trudged in silence. Each step seemed to take an enormous effort, slowly getting harder and harder. The edges of my vision were blurring slightly. We made it to the gravel area, and the three of us stumbled toward the tunnel entrance.

As we reached it, I stopped, and turned.

"No," I said.

"I'm sorry?" asked the sheriff, looking like he wasn't sure he'd just heard what he thought he'd heard.

"No," I repeated, letting go of Miss Moon and using all my strength to stand tall and defiant. "You can kill me if you want, but I'm dying right here, under the open sky. You won't kill me in some dark tunnel like a rat."

"Oh, I'll definitely kill you in the tunnel," he said coldly, "in a couple of weeks when I get bored of skinning you slowly alive, but I'm killing them first." He swung the gun to the side where Miss Moon stood, holding Hana.

I didn't even have time to shout. I turned and lunged, shoving the pair of them away with my own body. This time, the bullet tore into my back, tearing in at an angle toward the middle of my chest.

The sound of rapid gunfire rang in the clearing as I fell, and I was sure the sheriff had just killed all three of us. I landed hard in the gravel, and I felt the sharp rocks cutting into my bare skin. It was trivial, relatively, so I didn't pay much attention.

Miss Moon and Hana fell as well, and I watched their fall almost in slow motion. Miss Moon turned Hana slightly as they fell, so the girl landed on top of

Miss Moon. Their fall was much gentler than mine, I noticed in a detached sort of way. Almost controlled.

My gaze flicked down to the sheriff as I felt my life's blood spilling away. I couldn't breathe, but that somehow didn't seem important.

He was falling, too. I was confused for a long moment, until the four officers in blue burst into view, guns leveled and smoking. They were all shouting as they converged on the fallen sheriff.

I looked back to Miss Moon and Hana. Their eyes were open and panicked, but neither looked hurt. They hadn't been hurt, I realized with a huge swell of relief.

The sheriff had shot me, and then… the other officers… I lost the trail of thought as my thinking became fuzzy. A pair of paramedics carrying a portable stretcher ran in behind the four officers.

Now how did they get here, I wondered absently. The edges of my vision darkened, and began to draw closer together.

Distantly, I could hear Hana and Miss Moon shouting at me as my case worker rolled me over, calling my name. I looked at Hana. Now she wept again, plainly and with fear. Not fear for herself, but fear for me. I smiled gently at her as the paramedics reached me.

They say that when you die, your life flashes before your eyes. For me, that was only partly true. As my vision faded, and sounds grew slower and further away, I saw the visions of my life.

But it was only the happy moments, the exciting moments. The moments where I laughed, the moments where I had joy. Even the moments that thrilled me, like my first ride on a roller coaster, and my first kiss.

In the end, when my life left me, my heart was filled with peace and joy. As the last of my visions flashed past, I expected it all to go cold and black. Instead, my world flooded with warmth, light, and stillness.

And then there was a whisper.

Epilogue
Awake

Seven and a half minutes. That's how long I was clinically dead. Reviving me had taken the work of the two exceptional paramedics with a defibrillator who had come along behind the Harbor Glen police department. That wasn't what really brought me back, though.

I was in a coma for some time after extensive surgery to repair the damage of the two bullets. Nobody was sure if I would ever wake up. I felt as though I'd simply fallen asleep, and I think I could have slept forever if it hadn't been for her.

Are you there? came the whisper, reaching to my mind in that place that to this day I can't remember. I heard her voice, and it called to me. The whisper wasn't speaking to the emptiness. She was speaking to me. She called to me, and I came.

When my eyes opened, they were flooded with a sharp, piercing light. Not the warm, comfortable light I had just come from, but the cold, emotionless light of the hospital fluorescents. I winced and took a moment to gather myself.

I was disoriented and confused. Last I knew I had been lying on the gravel, looking into the face of the girl who whispered in my mind. Hana, that was her name. Slowly, things were coming back to me. She had been crying, and her face was full of fear.

The face I now looked into was also crying, but not out of fear or worry, but out of relief and joy. The face smiled down at me as it tried to control the sobs threatening to take over. Tears flowed freely down a face I knew.

"Hi, Mom," I said, my voice dry and cracking.

"You came back," she said, unable to keep her own voice from breaking. She covered her mouth with her hand, as though the physical barrier could contain the emotion that overwhelmed her.

"I'm here," was all I could get out.

She leaned down and hugged me tightly. I let her cry on me for a few minutes. She seemed to need it. That, and it gave me the chance to sort myself out.

I was in a hospital, with air tubes and IV's and other cables and hoses I couldn't identify attached all over me. I didn't hurt right at that moment, which surprised me since my last clear memory before things got a bit fuzzy was taking the second bullet in the back.

I'd thought Miss Moon and Hana had been shot as well, but remembered they looked fine, though upset, and that the four other cops had just arrived. The sheriff had been shot as well. I didn't know how anyone was doing.

"Mom?" I croaked. She finally pulled back, wiping at her face with her sleeve.

"Yes, hun?" she asked, visibly trying to regain her composure.

"How are they?"

"Who?" she asked, momentarily confused.

"Hana… and Miss Moon…" I closed my eyes again for a moment. The light was so bright and my eyes felt dry. My mother was already nodding enthusiastically.

"They're just fine, baby. Miss Moon is great and will come visit you sometime soon. Hana is… she was in pretty bad shape when you got to her."

My eyes snapped open and I looked at her with concern. I instantly regretted the quick movement as my head swam. My mother shook her head quickly.

"No, no, I just meant that she was in rough shape. She's fine too, they're still nursing her back to health," she clarified. I felt the relief rush over me. "She's just down the hall. Maybe she can come visit you later, too."

She paused, and looked like there was more she had to say. I stayed quiet and waited for her to be ready to say it. It took a while, and when she spoke it came out in a mournful rush, guilt dripping from her voice.

"Oh honey, I'm so sorry! We didn't believe you, and you saved that girl! You saved her! That poor girl, and we didn't believe you…" She broke into sobs again and leaned back over me, head in her hands.

"Mom," I said, trying to soothe her. "It's okay. I didn't believe myself for a while. I wouldn't have believed me either if it had been someone else. It's okay, Mom. Reall…" my voice broke again and I coughed.

My mother almost frantically scrambled for the water mug beside the bed. She pressed the straw to my lips and I took a long drink. I nodded, and she pulled the mug away.

"Are you okay? Let me call the nurse,"

"No, Mom, I'm fine. Don't call the nurse yet. I just

want to lie here for a minute without them poking at me."

"All right, but we'll call the nurse in a few minutes, the doctor will need to know you're awake."

"Okay. Where's Dad and Brent?"

"Hun," she hesitated a long moment before continuing. "Jackson, you've been asleep for a long time."

"Like what, ten years? Do I have a beard?" I asked, smiling at her. She laughed shakily.

"No, just three weeks." I had joked about the ten years, but my relief to hear it had only been three weeks was tremendous. "But your father had to go back to work. He'll be here soon, though. I'll text him and tell him you're awake. He'll come."

"It's okay if he doesn't," I said. "I know he's disappointed in me."

"Oh, hun, why would you ever think that?"

"Because he thought I was crazy. Everyone thought I was crazy. Except Cody. He believed me."

"Oh, your friend from Brookview," she said, nodding. I frowned.

"How do you know about Cody?" I didn't recall ever saying anything about him to them. Maybe Dr. Fitzpatrick had told them about him.

"He's been here at least once a day for two weeks," she told me. "So has Thomas. Those two have sure become fast friends. They'll probably be by later this afternoon to see you. Want me to tell them you're awake?"

I smiled at that. I had no idea how Cody had found me, but I knew he and Thomas would get along great. I was glad they'd met and become friends as well. Cody needed a few more of those, and Thomas was as good a friend as they came.

"No, if they're coming anyway it'll be fun to surprise them," I said. My mother smiled and nodded.

"So Hana is okay?" I asked, a little reluctant to bring her up again.

"Oh, she's doing great! The doctors are going to let her go home next week. She's a lovely girl, Jackson. The things she's been through…" Mom shuddered. "She's fine now though, thanks to you. Her parents will probably be all over you once they hear you're awake, too. You brought their baby back home to them. I can't imagine… If I'd lost you…" she tapered off, ready to cry again.

"It's okay Mom," I consoled her, "I'm here, I'm alive, and I am going to be fine. Doctor says I'm going to be fine, right?" I asked, suddenly realizing I hadn't yet taken a full stock assessment of my own condition.

I wiggled my fingers and toes. Everything seemed to work, though I felt a twinge in my shoulder.

"Yes, you're going to be fine. It's just that…"

"Just that what?" I asked when she stopped.

"Your shoulder was severely damaged. They had to do some pretty major surgery. You'll have almost full use of your arm and right hand, but you'll probably never throw a football again."

I closed my eyes and took a moment to process that. Football almost felt like part of an old life, it had been so long. I missed it, a lot. But that, like my old, normal life, was now lost to me. I nodded slowly.

"Jacks!" I heard the call from the doorway.

"Thomas!" I tried to shout. My voice cracked again and my mother grabbed the water for me. He came in,

Cody right behind him. "Cody!" I called.

The pair came and stood by my bedside, and suddenly everything felt normal again, like my new reality had suddenly clicked into place.

"What's up, guys?" I asked.

"You tell me," Cody said.

"Oh, not much here. Just hanging out," I said casually.

"What was it like?" Thomas asked, straight to the point as usual.

"What?" I asked.

"Being dead."

"A lot like being alive, only less painful," I told him, making a dramatically pained face. "Seriously though, I don't really remember. Got shot, had a flashback of every birthday party I've ever had, then woke up here. You know, the usual."

"No afterlife stories? Hey, does this mean you're a zombie?" Cody asked. I thought about it. I truly couldn't remember anything beyond my own memory replay. I shook my head.

"Sorry, no afterlife stories. I might be a zombie though. I'll let you know if I ever have a craving for brains. I mean, you're safe, but someone's got to warn Thomas." They both laughed. "How did you even find me?" I asked Cody, unable to shake the question from my mind.

"Dude, are you kidding? Your face has been plastered all over every news station in the country. I couldn't change a channel without seeing that ugly mug for a full two weeks. And now that you're awake, it's going to start all over again." He shook his head disgustedly and I laughed.

"Thanks," I told him.

"For what?"

"Helping me get out. Coming to see me here all the time, even though I wasn't awake. Being my friend. Believing me."

"Easy bro, your mom's here. Don't want to give up any of my man chips by getting all emotional."

"Don't worry, you've got plenty to spare," I told him. He smiled.

We chatted for hours, just catching up. My mother stayed right at hand, but let us boys just hang out.

Thomas had a new girlfriend, Cody had transferred to a new school where nobody knew he was trans, and he'd never been more comfortable. His parents were finally coming around.

Turned out he was actually going to my school now, and we even had a few classes together. He'd told Thomas, who had been cool with it, but aside from the two of us, to the whole school he was just Cody Lewis. No more, no less.

Thomas, it turned out, was responsible for my unexpected rescue at the hands of the police and paramedics. After calling Miss Moon and realizing she didn't believe me, he had called the police and told them Miss Moon had just abducted me, and he thought she might have stabbed me. He told them she was racing up into the woods, maybe to hide my body. They'd sent two cars and a paramedic. They had found her car on the side of the road and come quickly at the sound of a gunshot.

I owed him my life. I owed both of them my life. Thomas owed Miss Moon an apology. She'd spent six hours in handcuffs as everything got cleared up.

Both of them were blown away by my tale of the rescue. I might have embellished a little, but neither of them called me on it, even though they'd probably heard every tiny detail on the news already.

They told me I was a hero, and everyone at school was talking about how awesome it was that I'd been shot by a cop, totally missing the entire point, as usual.

I wasn't a hero, though. Hana was. Years of agonizing torture, never knowing which day would be her last, or if she'd ever see anyone but that monster again, and she never lost hope. Every day she called out for help. Every day she found ways to keep sane, to keep focused, to make attempts to escape like she had when she'd tried to rip her hands free of the shackles.

That was the day I'd had the seizure in Dr. Garner's office and been put away in Brookview, I learned.

It was that hope that had finally reached me, I was certain. Her hope was so strong that it had bridged the gap between her mind and mine. Why mine, I still didn't know. Maybe because I was receptive. Maybe because we were already connected somehow.

It didn't matter. In the darkest pits of a hellish nightmare, she was still reaching out toward the light. That was beautiful in a way I'd never understood before.

I felt her there, a moment before I heard the whisper.

Are you there? came the whisper. I turned and saw her in the doorway. I smiled as I saw her. She looked so much better she was unrecognizable, except for those eyes. I'd know those eyes anywhere. She smiled back and walked over to my bedside. Cody and Thomas made room between them.

Something in her eyes warmed me as much as any light in the afterlife ever could. Gently, silently, she reached for my hand. Reaching out, my hand slipped comfortably into hers, like it truly belonged there.

I'm here, my thoughts whispered to her. The spark in her eyes told me that she'd heard me.

As I looked at the three by my bedside, the thought occurred to me that even though I knew I'd die again eventually, I didn't want to do it anytime soon. I didn't fear death anymore. I'd already done it once, after all.

But I had some living to do first.

About the Author

Christopher Bailey lives in Washington with his amazing wife with their first child, anxiously anticipating the arrival of their second. Working professionally with families for more than twelve years has given him a unique outsider's perspective on many of the personal struggles individuals of all demographics go through in our society.

Inspired by his frustrations with a society so full of fear and labeling, his fifth novel 'Whisper' was written with the dream that someone out there will read it and find in themselves what this book is all about; hope and friendship.

If you know someone struggling with depression, anxiety, or other destructive emotional obstacles, please find a way to let them know that someone cares, and that they're never truly alone if they can only open up enough to let someone else be there for them.

Coming Soon

SUB-HEROES

Tales of a Fourth Grade Super Hero

By

Christopher Bailey